Award-winning, best-selling novelist Gianrico Carofiglio was born in Bari in 1961 and worked for many years as a prosecutor specializing in organized crime. He was appointed advisor of the anti-Mafia committee in the Italian parliament in 2007 and served as a senator from 2008 to 2013. Carofiglio is best known for the Guido Guerrieri crime series: *Involuntary Witness, A Walk in the Dark, Reasonable Doubts, Temporary Perfections, A Fine Line* and *The Measure of Time*, all six published by Bitter Lemon Press. His other novels include *The Silence of the Wave* and *The Cold Summer*. Carofiglio's books have sold more than six million copies and have been translated all over the world.

THE
MEASURE
OF TIME

Gianrico Carofiglio

Translated by Howard Curtis

BITTER LEMON PRESS
LONDON

BITTER LEMON PRESS

First published in the United Kingdom in 2021 by
Bitter Lemon Press, 47 Wilmington Square, London WC1X 0ET

www.bitterlemonpress.com

First published in Italian as *La misura del tempo* by Giulio Einaudi editore, 2019
© Gianrico Carofiglio, 2019

English translation © Howard Curtis, 2021

This edition published by arrangement with
Rosaria Carpinelli Consulenze Editoriali srl.

A CIP record for this book is available from the British Library

ISBN 978-1-913394-48-6
eBook USC ISBN: 978-1-913394-49-3
eBook ROW ISBN: 978-1-913394-50-9

Typeset by Tetragon, London
Printed and bound by CPI Group (UK) Ltd, Croydon CR0 4YY

1

"What do we have today, Pasquale?" I asked as I walked into the office, thinking as I did so, for the umpteenth time, that this was a ritual I was tired of.

"Let's see… The Colella woman should finally be coming to pay. Then there's the expert witness in the Moretti trial, the public contracts case – he's coming to pick up the papers, but says he wants to talk to you for five minutes. And at seven there's a new client, a woman."

"Who is she?"

With his usual slight aloofness, Pasquale leafed through the spiral notepad he always carries with him. Each one of us has something that identifies us and with which, assuming we're aware of it, we identify. For Pasquale it's his notepad. He buys them himself, without putting them on the practice's stationery expenses, and he always gets the same ones, an old-fashioned kind to be found only in a dusty and rather heart-warming old stationer's in the Libertà district. They have rough black covers with slightly red edges, like the ones my grandfather used.

"Her name's Delle Foglie. She phoned yesterday afternoon and asked for an appointment as soon as possible. She said it's about something serious concerning her son."

"Just Delle Foglie?"

"How do you mean, Avvocato?"

"Did she only give her surname?"

"Just the surname, yes."

For a few months, so many years earlier that I preferred not to count them, I'd known a girl named Delle Foglie. It was a period very distant in time and extremely distant in my memory. A period I hadn't thought about since it had happened and then melted away. While Pasquale spoke, vague, unreal memories came back into my mind, almost as if they concerned someone else, events I thought I knew about because somebody had told me about them, not because they'd really happened to me.

"She'll be here at seven. But if you have other commitments," Pasquale added, maybe noticing something strange in my expression, "I can call her back."

"No, no. Seven's fine."

Pasquale went back to his post in the waiting room. I thought for a few minutes about this new client and decided she wasn't the Delle Foglie I'd known before. There was no reason it should be her, I told myself, somewhat irrationally, and dismissed the matter from my mind.

At this point I should have devoted myself to studying the case files for the following day's hearings. I didn't feel like it. Nothing new about that: for some years now legal papers had been filling me with a sense of nausea, and the syndrome was getting slowly but inexorably worse.

Somebody once wrote that we should be capable of dying young. Not in the sense of really dying, but in the sense of stopping what we're doing when we realize we've exhausted our desire to do it, or our strength, or when we realize we've reached the limit of our talent, if we have any. Everything that comes after that limit is repetition. We should be capable of dying young in order to stay alive, but that almost never happens. I'd often thought that thanks to what I'd earned in my profession, of which I'd only spent a small part, I could quit, sell the practice and devote myself to something else. Travel, studying, reading. Maybe trying to write. Anything just to escape the grip of time. Time that kept passing, never changing. Nearly motionless in its daily repetition, yet fading fast.

Time accelerates with age, they say. The thought wasn't a new one, but that day it had been bouncing around unpleasantly in my head.

At the appeal court that morning, I'd run into a colleague of mine, almost a friend. A civil lawyer named Enrico Garibaldi – "No relation to the general," he would say like a child whenever he was introduced to someone.

A pleasant guy – you could have a good laugh with him. A really nice person and a good professional too. We'd occasionally hung out together.

"Everything all right, Enrico?" I'd asked him with a smile as I shook his hand. It wasn't a real question, just something you say. Everything all right? Yes, everything's fine, and you? Everything's fine, we really should get together one of these evenings, bye, see you soon.

"Not too good, to be honest," he replied. And after a brief pause, but before I could ask him anything or even just prepare myself (face, tone of voice, all the essentials), he continued: "My mother died two days ago."

The air went out of me for a moment, as if I'd been punched in the stomach.

"Oh God, I'm sorry, Enrico, I didn't know. I'm so sorry, forgive me…"

"Don't worry, Guido. Obviously you weren't to know. And anyway, I'm ashamed to say this, but it was a liberation. A year of illness had taken away all her dignity. Not just hers, poor thing. Ours, too."

7

He paused. His eyes became watery. I remained silent, basically because I didn't know what to say. He hesitated, then decided he needed to talk. Maybe he'd been waiting to meet me – well, not specifically me, he'd been waiting to meet somebody and I'd happened to show up – to get things off his chest, at least a little.

"You know, you realize you're losing your dignity when you become intolerant and irritable, when you actually *tell off* a person humiliated by old age and illness. A person who doesn't understand why her children are treating her so harshly." He couldn't continue. "Oh shit," was all he added, his voice breaking. Then his lips quivered and he started crying. I overcame the impulse to look around me to check if anybody was watching us and wondering what was happening. My usual problem with other people's judgement.

"How about a coffee?"

He stared at me in surprise. Then he sniffed and nodded, a flash of gratitude in his eyes. So we left the courthouse and as we walked he began to tell me about it.

"You know what the worst thing was, Guido? That before she died, she didn't sleep for ten days. I mean, when she realized she was going to die. Eighty-eight years old and yet, like everyone else, she was scared of dying. The psychologist who helped us, me and my brother, explained it to me. She was scared of going to sleep and not waking up again. That's why she couldn't sleep. It's something I can't come to terms with, something I find disturbing. When you get to that age you should be resigned, I always thought."

"Maybe we're never resigned…"

"No, we're never resigned."

"There's something Marcello Mastroianni said in an interview when he was already old. It was more or less: 'I like having dinner with my friends. So why do I have to die?'"

Enrico smiled, nodding as if sharing the sentiment. On the surface, the words were bitter. But perhaps they made him feel less alone with his sadness.

We sat down in a cafe near the courthouse. A fairly awful place which, for that very reason, could almost always guarantee you a free table where you wouldn't be disturbed.

"Have you ever noticed, Guido, how life seems to accelerate with age?"

"I notice it almost every day."

"Before her situation got worse, Mamma often said it. 'I have the thoughts of a young girl and the body of an old woman. Why?'"

I remembered my parents. They had passed away when they were still young, not quite sixty, a few months apart. Almost like Philemon and Baucis, a myth my mother loved. I hadn't had time to have a proper talk with them. I knew very little about my father and mother. For example, I'd never known if before they met and got engaged, then married, either of them had had someone else. A desperate relationship that had ended tragically, lots of brief affairs, whatever. When I was small I found it completely unimaginable that my father could have touched a woman other than my mother, and more than unimaginable that my mother had touched a man other than my father. On some subjects they were both very bashful. When I was eight and had no idea about matters of sex and reproduction, my father gave me a lecture. It so happened that I'd asked something about eggs. Why in some cases they were normal eggs, the kind we ate – which I liked a lot – whereas in other cases they had chicks in them which emerged after a while, as clearly shown in schoolbooks and in comic strips and cartoons. My father explained to me that the presence of the chick depended on whether or not the hen had gone and taken a *walk* with the rooster. "If the hen takes a walk with the rooster," he said, "chicks are born. Otherwise, we can eat the eggs."

The explanation raised many more problems than it solved. While my father went back to whatever he'd been doing, clearly considering his educational duty fulfilled, I was asking myself – and would continue to ask myself for years – nagging questions, like: When exactly did the chick appear inside the egg? Was there a specific itinerary for the *walk* that would produce this mind-blowing outcome? What happened if the rooster and the hen were shut up in a chicken coop and not allowed to take walks?

With time, I started to have less confused ideas about certain matters, and sometimes I thought of asking my father what had induced him to tell me such a surreal story.

But I didn't.

I sometimes make an inventory of what my parents left me. Mostly good, even crucial things. For example, a deliberately simple notion of honesty, a concept about which there shouldn't be subtle distinctions. Respect for others. A love of ideas.

Other things they passed down to me are more ambiguous, and may be positive or negative depending on how they insert themselves in the structure of a personality. Among these is the conviction, as radical as a moral imperative, that you should always get by on your own. I think the precept has a long history, that it comes from an old, almost ancestral, fear of being in debt.

I reflected on this many years later, when examining my great difficulty in accepting help. Being able to get by on your own is good. Thinking you *always* must get by on your own, without *ever* asking for help, is a weakness disguised as a strength. If you don't know how to ask for help, it generally means you don't know what to do when it's offered to you willingly and when it would be moral to accept it (and immoral to refuse it).

"A few months before she died, when she was still lucid," Enrico went on, "Mamma said something that shocked me."

"Do you feel like telling me?"

"Yes. She said it was hard for her to imagine the world without her. 'When you're young and you think of a world and a time when you didn't exist, it doesn't bother you, because history seems to have an implicit direction of travel that leads inevitably to the moment when you burst on the scene. The world without us before we're here is a long period of preparation. The world without us after we've gone, on the other hand, is simply the world without us. As long as it seems a distant thing, we manage to alleviate the dread of that thought. But I know that in a few weeks, a few months at most, I won't be here any more and the world will still go on, without even a ripple. Without even a tremor. You'll mourn me, then you'll have to deal with practical matters and you'll stop mourning. And anyway you'll be relieved that all the pain is over. You'll be able to look away and get on with living. Which is only right. And that'll be the end of it.'"

I took a deep breath and let the air out. "What was your mother's name?"

"Agnese. For forty-two years she taught Italian and Latin. Her students loved her. Even now I meet people who remember her and say that the reason they've learned to love books and reading and so many other things is because of her."

We stayed in that cafe a while longer. By the time we left, his eyes were no longer red from weeping.

I somehow managed to prepare for the next day's cases and get through my other afternoon chores.

At exactly seven, I heard the doorbell in the distance – my office is the furthest one from the main door – and half a minute later Pasquale popped his head in, asked if he could show in Signora Delle Foglie, I said yes, and he opened the door wide and admitted a woman.

She was tall and quite slim, with short grey hair, and was wearing a leather jacket that was a little big and shapeless on her.

She came towards the desk and I stood up. She saw the surprise in my eyes.

"Hello, Guido. Don't you recognize me? Lorenza."

It was her. If I'd passed her in the street I wouldn't have recognized her.

There she was in front of me. At this point I knew perfectly well who she was, but equally I didn't have the faintest idea. It was a feeling I'd never before experienced so intensely, not even when I'd occasionally met old school friends I hadn't seen for decades who'd turned into fat, bald gentlemen.

Since I didn't know who she was, I also didn't know how to greet her. I came round to the front of the desk. She, too, didn't know how to behave and so we embraced awkwardly, both aware of how forced and unspontaneous the gesture was. There was the smell of a recently smoked cigarette about her, as well as the denser, more unpleasant smell of many other cigarettes, smoked one after the other, which had impregnated her clothes and hair and stained her hands and nails with nicotine.

I motioned her to sit down and sat down myself.

"You're just the same, Guido. It's almost weird, looking at you. Apart from a few grey hairs, you're just the same."

I smiled, embarrassed. I was looking for a way to return the compliment, but couldn't find one. I thought I'd offend her if I told her too big a lie, like: You haven't changed either.

When we'd first met, she was almost thirty and I was almost twenty-five. Now she was fifty-seven, she looked older than that, and she was in my office to talk to me about a serious, urgent matter concerning her son.

2

"Before coming here I did my sums. It's been twenty-seven years."

"Oh yes," I replied almost simultaneously, congratulating myself on my effort at originality.

"I've often been tempted to drop by and say hello, have a chat. Especially when I read about you in the papers in connection with some trial or other. I've even caught sight of you in the street, but I've never had the guts to call out to you."

I'd never noticed her in the street. The last time I'd seen her was September 1987, then she'd vanished from my life. I hadn't seen her again and hadn't heard anything about her.

I had assumed – for as long as I'd thought about it – that she'd left Bari, which was something she'd always said she wanted to do. With a slight sense of dizziness, I realized I'd never told anyone about her, or about those months when our paths had crossed. Maybe that was why my memory of her had faded until it had become intangible. As time passes, a memory untold becomes less and less real and gets mixed up with the even more intangible material in our minds: dreams, fantasies, private legends.

I didn't say any of this.

"What … what do you do for a living?"

"I teach. I do other things too, but basically I'm a schoolteacher."

"Even back then you did a whole lot of things…"

"Not quite the same kinds of things... But anyway, that doesn't matter, I'm not here to talk about me." Her voice had hardened, as if to protect a vulnerable area.

I shrugged, tried to smile and gave her a questioning look. Her jaw muscles tightened.

"I'm here to see you for a professional reason. Meaning your profession, obviously."

"What's happened?"

She hesitated, then her hand went to a pocket of her jacket in an automatic gesture, as if searching for a packet of cigarettes.

"I don't know how to begin."

"Going to see a criminal lawyer is almost always an unpleasant experience. A person's unlikely to feel at ease, but we're in no hurry. My colleague Pasquale has already told me it's something to do with your son."

"My son, yes."

"How old is he?"

"Iacopo has just turned twenty-five. He's old enough to have already had quite serious problems with the law – and not just the law." Before continuing, she breathed in and cleared her throat. "Right now he's in prison. He's been there for more than two years. He was found guilty of murder."

She told me what had happened, and there was nothing good about her story.

Iacopo had always been a problem child – maybe because he'd never really had a father, but who can say? She didn't go into detail about that and I didn't ask any questions, just did a rapid mental calculation: he couldn't have been my son.

In any case, Lorenza continued, ever since he was in high school he'd never stopped getting in trouble. Petty incidents with drugs, fights, stealing from supermarkets, two exam failures, beating up the new boyfriend of a girl who'd dumped him. One way or another, she'd managed to help him graduate from school, and he'd even enrolled at university – law, just to be original – but hadn't done any exams. Instead, he'd been involved in a robbery for which he had been arrested. At that point he didn't have an actual criminal record and had got away with a suspended sentence. But he hadn't learned his lesson: Lorenza was sure he sold drugs in discos, and for a long time she'd wondered how to keep him away from bad company.

All this was the introduction. She hadn't yet got on to the reason she was now sitting in front of me, in my office.

Less than three years previously, Iacopo had been arrested and charged with having killed a guy, in all likelihood his usual narcotics supplier.

There had been a trial in the high court and, in May of the previous year, he had been sentenced to twenty-four years' imprisonment, plus costs. This, in very broad terms, was the gist of the case.

"Before going into details," I said, "I have to ask you a question. If Iacopo has already been tried, that means he had a lawyer. We have ethical obligations towards our colleagues and —"

"He died." I thought I caught a hint of impatience in her voice. "He died a few weeks ago. So I don't think there are any ethical problems."

"Who was he?"

He was – had been – Michele Costamagna, an excellent professional, until disease had eaten his brain. Apart from being competent, he had always been able, at least in the days when he'd been at the top of his game, to pull the right strings whenever possible. In the last few years, even before the disease, he'd lost some of his appeal because many of his friends – judges, prosecutors, high-ranking officials, senior civil servants – had started to retire and the new ones, especially the judges, were less malleable and not so likely to be members of the city's exclusive clubs. But in the years when I was a young lawyer, Costamagna was one of the people you had to go to if a case was particularly serious. In most cases, he could patch things up. I'd never heard about anything definitely illegal, but all in all, Costamagna was like The Wolf in *Pulp Fiction*: he solved problems. And that was why he'd always made sure he was well paid. Beyond the limits of greed, according to some.

A couple of years earlier he had fallen ill, and his decline, which had already started, had grown rapid and increasingly obvious. He would lose the thread during closing arguments, would get confused in cross-examinations and in general throughout hearings; he would sometimes forget the name of his client or that of the judge. In his final weeks, he hadn't even managed to get to court. He had died just after Christmas, and it was now the beginning of February.

In short, it could be assumed that, at least in his final year, Costamagna's client hadn't received – to put it euphemistically – adequate representation. Of course there was the whole apparatus of his practice, the trainees, his daughter, but a murder trial in the high court was the old man's exclusive prerogative.

So if Iacopo had been represented in the high court by Avvocato Costamagna – by the shadow of what Avvocato Costamagna had been, for good or ill – he certainly hadn't had the best possible defence.

All this was easy to assume, and it was basically what Lorenza told me. They had gone to Costamagna due to his old reputation and on the advice of a relative. He had asked for a whole lot of money, but the defence had been weak, if not actually non-existent, both during the preliminary investigation and in court. After the sentence, he had assured them that things would go differently at appeal. As they always did, he'd added with a flash of his old arrogance. And he had asked for a further advance payment. Costamagna – or more likely one of the colleagues in his practice – had written a motion of appeal a few pages long. Lorenza was no expert, but it had struck her as really weak.

"Then his condition got worse. A couple of appointments were cancelled, and he was admitted to hospital and died."

"Has the date for the appeal hearing already been set?"

"The first one's in two weeks."

"What?" I was aware of a high pitch in my voice that I hadn't managed to moderate. "Two weeks?"

"Yes. A few days ago I went to Costamagna's office. I spoke to one of his colleagues, who struck me as an idiot. He asked me for another advance payment. I told him I'd already paid a lot of money and he said that was for the original trial and the drafting of the appeal motion. Now they needed to prepare for the hearing, to evaluate new evidence and decide on what requests to make. He used technical expressions I couldn't repeat to you. I didn't understand, and I think he was using them specifically to make sure I didn't understand."

"That's not uncommon."

"I lost my cool. I told him that after what I'd paid the practice, a lot of it under the table, he couldn't tell me it still wasn't enough, and at such a difficult time, when the appeal was about to start."

"Do you remember who he was?"

She said a name. A person for whom the definition of idiot was needlessly charitable. I wouldn't even have given him the role of a lawyer in a school play. I avoided sharing this judgement of mine, just nodded and asked her to continue.

"He told me if we weren't satisfied with the service provided by the Costamagna practice, we could go elsewhere. Then I really raised my voice. I screamed at him, let out everything I felt. He turned red, and said that if that was the case it was best to suspend our professional relationship and he suggested I leave. Over the next few days I started wondering if it hadn't been stupid on my part to react in that way. I didn't know what to do or where to go. Then I thought of you."

An unpleasant thought wormed its way into my mind. She hadn't come to me because she thought I was a good lawyer. She'd come to me because she didn't know which way to turn. She was broke and obviously assumed, considering our shared past, that I would work on credit or, even better, for free. That annoyed me, and I decided to make things clear: I'd already worked as a lawyer for charity too many times.

Dear madam (you'll excuse the formal tone, which may seem strange to you given that we've been naked together in the same bed, but in view of the situation I prefer a certain degree of formality), I will gladly accept the task of examining the case file relating to the legal proceedings against your son. First, however, I would ask you to go to the office outside and pay the deposit indicated by my colleagues. The fact that many years ago we were … intimate for a few months is, unfortunately, irrelevant when it comes to work. Demanding work, I should add: a case that's already quite compromised and that relates to a rather serious matter. In other words, a task that, were I to accept it, would require a great deal of time and effort.

As I was making these rapid, unpleasant observations in my head, it struck me that we hadn't talked even for a second about the substance of the proceedings. About what the boy was actually accused of, and if he was innocent or guilty.

So I dropped the deposit – and my dignity, and my offended self-esteem – and asked her to sum up the facts of the trial. Basically, what was the charge? And above all, what was the evidence that had led to the conviction?

She told me. And I didn't like what I heard, didn't like it at all. From what I understood of her account, which was quite thorough even though she wasn't an expert, her son was in a bad position. The evidence against him may have been circumstantial, but it was also – in legal jargon – serious, specific and concordant.

"Guido, I've come to you because I didn't know who to turn to. Going to Costamagna was a mistake, I realize that now. But everyone told me he was good, and also well connected. You must know how it feels when you find yourself involved in something like that. It's like suddenly discovering you have a serious illness. You start to panic, you look for help, you ask around about who might be the best choice and…"

"I know, it's not easy to see things clearly. And in fact Costamagna was a good lawyer. Maybe even an excellent lawyer. Unfortunately, in his last years, the disease compromised his abilities. What I mean," I continued, "is that you mustn't blame yourself for going to him. Quite simply, things deteriorated."

She nodded, as if to thank me for taking a weight off her shoulders: the feeling that she had made the wrong choice and was somehow partly responsible for the way things had turned out. Then she resumed.

"I want to make it clear I'm not expecting you to work for free. It's just that I don't have any money right now. To draw up the appeal motion, Costamagna stripped me of my savings, and I've even got into debt. I'm only a substitute teacher, and I also make do with other jobs, but it isn't easy. I promise, though, I'll pay you what I owe you, I just need some breathing space."

Strange how our minds work. I'd been annoyed at the idea that she'd come to me because she was broke. And now that she'd said it explicitly, my annoyance had vanished. Once freed from the semi-darkness of my susceptible ego, the whole thing became quite normal, with nothing offensive about it at all.

So, in total contradiction to what I'd been thinking just a little while earlier, I made a gesture with my hand as if to clear the air between us.

"Don't worry about the money. We can talk about that later. Right now there are a couple of things we need to clarify: one urgent and important, the other very important although less urgent. The urgent one concerns the first appeal hearing. Do you remember the exact date?"

It was only sixteen days away. The legal limit for adding new grounds to the appeal motion and for formulating requests for the submission of new evidence not submitted at the original trial is fifteen days, so there was no time to prepare. Among other things, new counsel still had to be formally appointed, for which the person concerned would have to make a request directly to the prison administration. All we could do was ask for an extension. In certain situations, you can ask the judge not to insist on a time limit that has been missed and to assign a new one. But then you need to show that unforeseen circumstances have made it impossible to observe the time limit previously established. In this case, we would have to show that the death of Avvocato Costamagna was the *force majeure* on which to base our request. It couldn't be taken for granted that we'd get our extension. Which meant we had an uphill struggle right from the start. I was just in the middle of these thoughts when Lorenza resumed speaking.

"Guido, Iacopo's innocent. He's got into a lot of trouble, he's a difficult boy, some of which may be my fault, but he didn't commit that murder."

They all say that, the parents or friends or lovers. My child, my colleague, my lover can't have done anything like that. Trust me, I know him. If we always believed the nearest and dearest, the crime of homicide (and many others, to be honest) would vanish from the statistics.

I nodded without commenting. Commenting on certain subjects is inadvisable – especially to the lovers, friends and mothers of defendants. But she must have read my thoughts.

"I'm not saying that because I'm his mother. I'm saying it because when the murder was committed Iacopo was with me, at home. You'll see it in the file: what I said in my testimony is the truth, even though the judges didn't believe me."

Okay, this was a little different from the usual statements, like "My son's a good boy, he wouldn't hurt a fly." It remained for me to find out if it was the truth.

A lot of those who are suspected of murder are guilty; many of those who are tried for murder are guilty; very many – the vast majority – of those who are convicted of murder are guilty. That doesn't mean there aren't innocent people who are suspected, tried and even convicted. But I can assure you there aren't many of these, not many at all, irrespective of the fact that in many cases they're acquitted. They're acquitted because of flaws in the investigations, because of procedural irregularities, even because the defence counsel has been really good. Only in a small number of cases because they're innocent.

So if Lorenza's son had been convicted of murder, he was probably guilty.

These were not reflections to share with the mother of an accused man.

"All right," I said. "I'll need copies of the papers as soon as possible, tomorrow even. And your son will have to appoint me as his counsel and revoke any previous appointment. Before doing anything I'll have to call Costamagna's practice and inform them that I've been entrusted with the case."

"Why?"

"Professional courtesy. That way we pretend to respect each other. Then I'll go straight to the head of the appeal court and discuss the need to extend the time limit. It isn't an easy situation, it's only right you should know that. If the judge won't bend, we're in real trouble. Is there anything you'd like to ask me?"

"No thanks," was all she said.

I shrugged. "Then I'd say that's all for now."

3

The next morning I went to court with my colleague, Consuelo Favia. She was born in Peru and was adopted by a friend of mine, a civil lawyer, when she was four. Her features – olive complexion, very mobile dark eyes, plump cheeks with high cheekbones – clearly show she's from the Andes, but in every other respect she's unmistakably a citizen of Bari, and that includes her accent, typical of the downtown area, and her ability to speak in impeccable dialect when necessary. She came to work with me when she was a girl and had just passed her professional exams. Now she's the senior lawyer in the practice. Every time I think about that – to me she's still a girl – I feel an unease that I have to dismiss in order to avoid other thoughts flooding in.

As we walked to the courthouse, I told her about my meeting with Lorenza. I omitted telling her that we'd known each other before, I'm not quite sure why.

"What was your impression?"

"Of her or her story?"

"Both."

I didn't reply immediately. In reality I wasn't sure what my impression had been, either of her or of what she'd told me.

Usually in such cases – and in this more than in others – I have two conflicting feelings. One derives from my natural, naive tendency to believe people: the reason why, as a young boy, it was easy for people to get me to drink. The other, mistrust, is an intellectual fact, and derives from my knowledge of how things usually are.

"I don't know," I replied at last. "She says that when the murder was committed the boy was with her at home. If it's true…"

"Obviously she testified to that, and obviously the judges didn't believe her."

"Yes. We'll need to examine everything very carefully. When the papers arrive I'll have copies made of the ruling so that you, Tancredi and Annapaola can read it immediately. Then we'll meet and decide what to do."

"You'll have to ask Judge Marinelli for an extension, otherwise there won't be much to assess."

We parted at the entrance to the courthouse. I went off to handle a couple of exciting trials for fraudulent bankruptcy and she to bring a civil action against a stalker. Consuelo is a defence lawyer, but she has the soul of a prosecutor. It's a lot of effort for her to defend people of whose innocence she isn't convinced. So we share the tasks in a fairly natural way: I mostly defend accused people, she defends mostly victims, in particular victims of crimes like sexual violence, stalking and abuse. No defendant and no defence counsel is ever pleased to have her on the plaintiff's side.

When I got back to the office early in the afternoon, a complete copy of the file relating to the case of Lorenza's son was waiting for me on my desk. Iacopo Cardace, the young man was called. The surname didn't mean anything to me, so the father probably wasn't somebody I'd known when the mother and I had been going out together – *going out together*? What a banal expression, I thought.

There was also an envelope with a handwritten note.

This is the case file. Today I went to see Iacopo and told him to appoint you and revoke all previous appointments. You should get the message from the prison as soon as possible.

Thank you.

L.

The handwriting was sharp-edged, elegant, slightly hard to read.

I went out to have a bite to eat in the health food store with canteen attached near the office, resisting the impulse to also have a glass of wine. Then I paid a brief visit to the Feltrinelli bookshop, which was also close by. I wandered between the shelves, which for me is a kind of sedative, nodded to a few people who were often in the shop in the early afternoon, and bought a volume of Kafka's aphorisms and fragments after reading some of them. Number thirty-eight said: "A man was amazed at how easily he went along the road to eternity; the fact was, he was rushing along it downhill."

I went back to the office and drew up a plan of action. I'm very good at drawing up plans in order to buy time and put off the moment when I have to really get down to work.

I would get through the dull afternoon chores – mostly appointments, because it was Friday and there were no court hearings the next day – then phone Costamagna's practice and inform them of developments. I was sure they wouldn't tear their hair out: a very weak case, and a client unable to make further exorbitant down payments, which were completely unjustified anyway now that the old man was no longer around.

Then I would take the file home with me and take a look at the case. Annapaola had gone to London with two friends.

She would be back the following Monday. I had no desire to call other people to go out with and I had no desire to go out on my own. It was an ideal evening for starting to figure out what I was getting into.

When I called the Costamagna practice I asked for his daughter, who'd inherited it. She resembled her father only in appearance, which wasn't a compliment – he'd always been on the large side.

I informed her of the fact that their client Cardace had probably appointed me that morning, even though the message from the prison hadn't arrived yet.

"I hope everything's sorted with the payments," I said, more than anything to see how she reacted.

"I didn't deal with it. It was Dad and Pinelli" – the man Lorenza had rightly described as an idiot – "but I'm familiar with the paperwork."

Paperwork. A man who'd been in prison for quite some time and who in all probability would be there for a long time to come. *Paperwork.* Vocabulary reveals a lot about people, I thought. Then I thought that maybe my reflections were banal. It often happens, I can't help myself. Mariella Costamagna continued speaking.

"I think there's still some money pending, but don't worry. Considering the circumstances, we won't insist."

I had to hold back a few rude remarks. If Lorenza had told me the truth about the fees she'd been charged – and I didn't have many doubts about that, knowing Costamagna – it was a lie to state that there was money pending. Even worse, it was actually obscene. More or less like the use of the word paperwork.

"Anyway, I don't envy you," she went on. "It's an open-and-shut case, Dad said. The kid's guilty, there's not much you can do. At most try to limit the damage. Maybe, if he confesses, you could get a slightly reduced sentence."

We hung up and the nasty feeling left by these last words remained with me the whole afternoon, like an unpleasant taste in my mouth. I was seized with a kind of urgency to read the case file and find out how things stood.

I asked Pasquale to make three copies of the ruling. One for Consuelo, one for Annapaola, one for Tancredi.

Annapaola is a private investigator who used to be a crime reporter, and even before that all kinds of other things, not all of them as clear as day. It's thanks to her that I overcame my entrenched scepticism towards her profession. Until I entrusted her with an investigation and saw the results, I was convinced that private investigators were basically good at three things: finding evidence of marital infidelity, in all its varied and often imaginative forms (they're almost all good at that); getting defence lawyers in trouble, so that they end up on trial for aiding and abetting; and earning large sums of money without producing any results other than verbose and pointless reports.

Annapaola also deals with investigations into marital infidelity – she has to make a living – but whenever she gets to investigate more serious (sometimes very serious) matters, she's capable of making the most unexpected discoveries, of getting the most unlikely people to talk. Whether she's working for the accused or – which, like Consuelo, she prefers – for the victim.

Incidentally, she's also my girlfriend. More or less. The jury's still out on the definition. A few months earlier we happened to talk about it one evening at my place, after dinner.

"But do you tell other people I'm your girlfriend, Guerrieri?"

"I thought you'd forbidden me. So: no."

"Oh yes. You're right. Good. I like it when you obey me." She paused then continued: "But it also bothers me a bit."

"What does?"

"I thought that if you'd replied yes I'd have been upset. Now that you tell me no I'm more upset. Am I consistent?"

"You're consistency personified. That's why you're my girlfriend but also my non-girlfriend. Scott Fitzgerald said the ability to hold two opposing ideas in the mind at the same time is the test of a first-rate intelligence."

"Have I ever told you your quotations are a bit tiresome?"

"I think you have."

"Anyway, getting back to the whole girlfriend thing. I'd like you to say it and not say it. It's not so complicated. You're a lawyer, it's your job to say one thing and mean the opposite. Find a way."

"This conversation reminds me of the joke about the Jewish mother who gives her son two ties for his birthday."

"I know I won't be able to stop you telling me it."

"No, you won't. So, there's this Jewish mother who gives her son two ties. The next day he puts one of them on and goes to see her. She looks at him sadly. 'I knew it – you don't like the other one.'"

"I thought it'd be worse," she commented, and after a few seconds, as if all at once she'd had a brilliant idea, added: "Of course, if I'm not your girlfriend, it becomes more interesting. You know what I think? We could indulge in steamy clandestine sex."

"We could," I admitted.

Carmelo Tancredi had been a policeman. I might even say he was the best cop I'd ever known, except, maybe, for an old marshal of carabinieri in Turin. He'd worked for more than thirty years in the Flying Squad, had retired with the rank of deputy chief inspector and had recently graduated with a degree in psychology.

But then it had struck him that he wasn't tired of working (especially not *that* work: talking to people, making people talk, discovering what happened, how it happened and who it was) and had no desire to go fishing every day in his dinghy, even though he loves that boat more than if it were a Labrador puppy. Fishing a couple of times a month is wonderful, he told me once; fishing a couple of times a week starts to seem like a nightmare.

So when Annapaola, after a dinner the three of us had had, suggested to him that they join forces and set up a real detective agency, he'd taken just five minutes to accept. Since then they had worked together – often for my practice, sometimes for other people. Apart from anything else, I think they have a lot of fun.

I got home, stooping under the weight of my rucksack, which was filled with the two folders Lorenza had left for me. The ruling, documents relating to the investigation, trial transcripts.

"Hi, Mr Punchbag," I said, addressing the punchbag hanging by a chain from a beam in the middle of the living room. He gave an imperceptible nod. He's a taciturn fellow, who doesn't much like to move unless it's absolutely necessary. Which naturally happens when we both do a bit of boxing. He takes the punches very calmly. He never reacts. He takes and I give, but he always wins in the end. There's a metaphor in there somewhere, I guess. One of these days I'll find out what it is.

We're friends, Mr Punchbag and I. He isn't demonstrative, that's for sure, but it's also sure that he conceals delicate feelings behind that impassive leather mask of his.

We went through a difficult time, the day of my fiftieth birthday. The kids (I include Pasquale among the kids, even though he's in his seventies) had bought me a lovely, shiny new punchbag, the kind you see in the glossy videos showing world champions like Floyd Mayweather Jr pretending to train. (A great boxer, by the way, but too much of a pin-up for my taste.)

The idea was that I should finally replace that old object that had taken too many punches and was full of cracks and patched up with duct tape. You could even say there was something undignified about it.

After the surprise party organized by Annapaola (I was inclined to think there was nothing to celebrate, but I realize that's rather an obvious position) we'd been left alone, he and I. Or rather, we weren't alone. There, hanging on a wall, calm and self-assured, almost mocking, was the new one.

I sat down on the sofa facing Mr Punchbag. One of the cracks on his surface, a result of the thousands of punches so politely taken, gave him a very melancholy expression. Like that of a dog that's about to be abandoned at the side of the road by a thoughtless master. Or better still: by a total arsehole.

"Are you sad, friend?" I'd asked in embarrassment. He, in his dignified way, had not replied, conscious that the life of things, like that of people, has a childhood, an adulthood and an ending.

Like an idiot, I felt moved. What was I doing with that beautiful new shiny brown leather bag with its gold lettering? How did I know if it was able to listen – and therefore to talk – like Mr Punchbag? I spent about ten psychiatrically significant minutes sitting on the sofa, balanced precariously between two somewhat incompatible lines of thought.

The first said: It's fine to play, it's fine to indulge in the notion of talking to this old *inanimate* object, but every whim must have a limit. Things are things, we can project our needs and fantasies onto them, and up to a point that's fine. Confusing them with living beings, however, is deranged, a sign of immaturity, something like believing you can read fortunes in coffee dregs. Don't be a child, hang this beautiful new leather punchbag and get rid of the other one. Take it down to the street, put it in a dustbin, and have done with it.

The second said: Are you that kind of person? What about all the evenings you've spent together, all the things you've confided in him, all the times he's listened to you, all the advice he's given you – don't they mean anything to you?

I can't guarantee those were the exact words, but I swear this was the tone of the inner dialogue (to tell the truth, I'm not even sure that it was only inner and that I hadn't got carried away and actually started speaking out loud).

It lasted half an hour.

Then I made up my mind. The new bag would go in the office, in the conference room. Completely useless, but it was so beautiful and elegant – *a piece of decoration*, a bathroom salesman would have said – that it could happily hang in an office as a designer item. My colleagues wouldn't be offended, thinking that I hadn't appreciated their gift, and I wouldn't commit an act so horrible as that of betraying an old friend.

I took some duct tape, stuck it over Mr Punchbag in the places where the cracks were most noticeable and gave him a little punch, just an amicable little punch. Partly because without gloves, friend or no friend, it hurts. He looked at me with gratitude, and the crisis was over.

All right, I've digressed.

So: I had a rucksack full of transcripts and a specific schedule.

First of all I went a few rounds and chatted a little with Mr Punchbag.

After the punches, a few press-ups and some work on the horizontal bar. The horizontal bar was a novelty. Months earlier, on the fitness trail at the San Francesco pine grove, I'd had a bet with Annapaola about which of us could do the most pull-ups. I'd lost, eleven to her fourteen. Now, eleven wouldn't be all that bad for a man over fifty – the problem is that mechanisms as irrational as they are difficult to control are triggered whenever you're in physical competition with a woman. Even if she *is* more than ten years younger, used to be a semi-professional athlete and has the biceps of a good middleweight. Anyway, to cut a long story short, I'd had a horizontal bar installed in the entrance, made by a manufacturer who was somewhat surprised by the order, and now I exercised in secret every other day, hoping I would get my revenge for the humiliation sooner or later.

Having finished my exercises, I took a quick shower and, following the schedule I'd drawn up, made myself *spaghetti all'assassina*.

It's a typical Bari recipe, deceptively easy to prepare.

I got the instructions, handwritten in an exercise book, from an old lady in Bari, and as usual I followed them strictly.

Pour a few spoonfuls of oil into a large pan and add some finely chopped garlic and chilli peppers. When the garlic is golden, add passata, some small tomatoes, washed and cut in half, and a pinch of salt. Cook for ten minutes on a low heat while you boil salted water.

Cook the spaghetti in the water for just three minutes, drain it and add it to the sauce, having first removed the garlic. Finish cooking the spaghetti in the sauce until it has absorbed it. Increase the heat until you've got rid of the moisture and the spaghetti is seared and crunchy.

It's a dish that, for reasons I can't explain, cheers me up. Maybe, as somebody once said, it reminds me of something I can't remember.

In any case, I opened a bottle of Cacc'e mmitte di Lucera, a gift from a satisfied client (it does happen sometimes) and had dinner. I was actually in a good mood.

Then I washed up, poured myself another glass of wine, regretted for the millionth time that I'd quit smoking and sat down at the table, with the case file in front of me.

4

The ruling was of average quality. Written in the usual jargon of legal documents, a little long-winded but thorough and, at first sight, technically sound.

It began with a summary of the investigation. On the day of the murder, the accused and the victim had spoken twice on the phone. Both the conversations had been intercepted and recorded because the telephone of the victim – Cosimo Gaglione, known as Mino – was being tapped within the context of an investigation by the Narcotics section of the Flying Squad. From these telephone calls, which were quite short, it could be inferred, according to the prosecution and the judges, that there was an unspecified bone of contention between the two men. During the second call, the accused said very clearly that they needed to discuss the matter face to face. The tone of these words was aggressive and suggested a great deal of anger on Cardace's part and the intention to call the other man to account for what apparently seemed to him an unfair or disrespectful act.

In the afternoon Cardace was seen by a witness in the vicinity of Gaglione's apartment, not long before the murder took place.

At 7.47 p.m. Gaglione called 118 from his own mobile phone (the one being tapped by Narcotics) asking for urgent help. Speaking in a laboured manner, he said that he was at home, that somebody had shot him and that he was losing a lot of blood. A few minutes later, almost simultaneously, an ambulance and two Flying Squad cars arrived at his building. The police officers, having intercepted the call, had heard his request for help.

Once on the scene, neither group was able to do anything other than observe that Gaglione was dead. As would later be ascertained by the forensics team and the pathologist, he had been shot three times with a .38 calibre revolver (no cartridges had been found at the scene of the crime): one had hit him glancingly in the side and two more in the right leg, severing the femoral artery and causing him to bleed to death. In the course of the search, a large amount of MDMA had been found. The men from the Flying Squad had set off in search of Cardace. They had tracked him down outside a bar about a couple of hours later, in the company of friends. He had twelve Ecstasy pills on him, of the same kind as those found in Gaglione's apartment. Cardace had been arrested for possession of narcotics and once at Headquarters had undergone a gunshot residue test.

Within a few days the technicians of the Forensics department's central laboratory had communicated their findings: the jacket worn that evening by Cardace was contaminated with particles of lead, barium and antimony derived from the shooting of a firearm. A warrant had then been requested and issued for Cardace's arrest on the charges of premeditated murder and unauthorized carrying of firearms.

After this summary of the preliminary investigation, the judge who had written the ruling launched into a long and somewhat pedantic summary of the criteria fixed by law for the evaluation of evidence. At the end of this rather superfluous digression, he moved on to an analytical examination of the individual items of evidence.

First of all, it is necessary to read and interpret the transcripts of the two telephone calls between the accused and the victim on the day of the murder. In this regard, it is important to make it clear that it was the telephone of the victim, Cosimo Gaglione, which had been under surveillance for about two weeks. These intercepts had been authorized within the context of a wide-ranging investigation relating to the traffic in narcotics of a synthetic type (Ecstasy and methamphetamine). There had already been calls in the previous few days between Gaglione's telephone and that of the accused. From these calls there emerged elements that led the officers to suspect the involvement of Cardace in this illegal traffic.

On 13 October at 1.26 p.m., there is a first call from Cardace's telephone. The substance of the brief conversation is cryptic, but the tone is obviously angry. Cardace seems very upset by events that happened the day before, although the nature of these events is not made clear. The conversation ends abruptly because Gaglione receives another call on another telephone (the ringing can be heard on the recording and this fact is also indicated in the transcript). Gaglione hangs up, saying he will call back.

The second call is at 4.18 p.m., once again from the telephone of Cardace, who first of all complains very excitedly that he has not been called back. Gaglione's answer is very sharp and aggressive ("I'm doing my own stuff, if I want to call I will, if I don't I won't, so stop pissing me off" – a translation of the dialect used). Cardace raises his voice and replies that Gaglione should not treat him like this, otherwise he will "smash his face in" and it will not take him long to find a replacement (in all likelihood another supplier of narcotics). At this point, Gaglione becomes worried that the contents of the conversation may be incriminating if it should so happen that their phones are being tapped. He therefore says: "If you want to talk, forget about the phone, I'm at home."

Cardace cuts short the conversation, saying in a tone of barely controlled anger: "I'm coming now."

What emerges from these two telephone conversations is a situation of serious personal conflict between two individuals involved in an illegal business, in particular a demand that Cardace has to make of Gaglione. The way in which the second call is cut off does not in any way suggest that a reconciliation is imminent and Cardace's laconic conclusion – "I'm coming now" – points rather to a continuation of the quarrel without the mediation of a telephone call.

The second item of evidence consists of the statement of the witness Antonia Sassanelli, who works in a cafe in the immediate vicinity of the victim's residence. She (like many other potential witnesses) was questioned by the police in the immediate aftermath of the crime. She was shown a specially prepared photograph album, which included a photograph of Cardace. The woman stated that she knew him from having seen him on several occasions in the cafe, often in the company of Gaglione, who was well known to her because he lived in the vicinity and was a frequent customer of the cafe. After a first phase of (almost instinctive) reticence towards the police, Sassanelli stated that she had seen Cardace in the cafe that afternoon together with another person she had never seen before. She was not in a position to indicate the exact time but did state that it had happened not very long before the arrival of the police and of "all that kerfuffle", to quote the witness verbatim. Such statements were reiterated in the course of her testimony in court.

The witness is reliable and her initial reticence strengthens rather than weakens her credibility. She had been familiar with Cardace for some time (even if only by sight), and provided a sufficiently exact idea as to help pinpoint the time when she saw the accused in the cafe that afternoon.

It is therefore possible to establish the presence of Cardace – in the company of another individual it has not been possible to identify – in the immediate vicinity of the victim's residence shortly before the murder. In this respect it is important to specify that Gaglione's residence is about two miles from Cardace's residence. It can be ruled out with a reasonable degree of certainty that Cardace left home and went more than two miles simply to have coffee in a cafe on the outskirts of the city.

The ruling then went on to examine the results of the forensics investigation.

The test carried out on Cardace, the results of which were provided by the central laboratories of the police Forensics department within a very short period of time, made it possible to ascertain that particles of lead, barium and antimony were present on the fibres of his jacket. Such particles do not exist in nature and derive exclusively from the phenomenon of the shooting of a firearm. It is therefore possible to state that Cardace used a firearm or at least was very close to a firearm being used.

This fact, already quite significant in itself, gains a crucial weight if seen within the overall inclusive framework of the evidence.

The defence has tried to counter this fundamental piece of evidence.

During the preliminary phase of the investigation, the accused consistently availed himself of the right to remain silent. At the trial Cardace opted of his own free will to make a statement in which he basically tried to present an alternative explanation to that of the prosecution of the results of the forensic investigation. He stated that a few days prior to the murder, wearing the same jacket as mentioned above, he had gone to a quarry in the province to practise target shooting with a friend. He specified that he did not wish to indicate the particulars of the above-mentioned friend in order not to expose him to legal consequences, given that he was the unauthorized possessor of the firearm used on that occasion. He concluded by denying that he was responsible for the murder and suggesting that the contamination on his jacket, as ascertained by the forensics team of the State Police, was to be linked to the use of a firearm in the days immediately preceding the murder.

Needless to say, such a vague, entirely unconfirmed suggestion, made of his own free will by the accused in the course of his statement (thus avoiding the scrutiny of examination in court), is totally unfit to establish a case of reasonable doubt.

At this point the ruling lingered over the one piece of counter-evidence put forward by the defence, that is, the testimony of the defendant's mother, which the judges had not believed.

Lorenza had stated that from 7.30 to 8.20 p.m. (the murder of Gaglione had been committed just before 7.47, the time of the telephone call to 118) Iacopo was at home with her. The assistant prosecutor had subjected her to an aggressive cross-examination, making her contradict herself and eventually bringing up the fact that she had a criminal record, having been charged with aiding and abetting and with resisting an officer of the law, which had definitely put her in a bad light with the judges and jury. In short, the ruling described the witness as unreliable, "firstly because as mother of the accused she has an interest in his acquittal, and secondly because she has a previous conviction for offences against the administration of justice".

My eyes were starting to smart and I told myself that maybe it was time to go to bed. Partly because that first reading had spoiled the good mood I'd been in at dinner and I didn't want the situation to get worse. It looked as if Costamagna's daughter was right, and I can't say if I was upset more by this observation – that she was right, regardless of the matter in hand – or the rather uncertain nature of the case I had just taken on.

Of course the work was only just starting, in fact it hadn't even started yet; of course I also had to read the transcripts; of course it was necessary to check for possible flaws in the investigation or procedural irregularities, if there were any. But for the moment I had in front of me a straightforward ruling that provided a perfectly adequate explanation for what appeared to be a completely justified sentence.

It was this, more or less, that I told myself, speaking out loud – speaking out loud when I'm on my own is an old habit of mine that has got worse with age.

I told Mr Punchbag that I was going to bed and that we'd see each other the next morning if he was still around. He looked at me the way you look at someone who's made an unfunny joke. I took out the mobile phone I'd left in my rucksack and noticed there were a few messages. A couple were from annoying colleagues to whom I would reply the following Monday, maybe. A third was an invitation from a film club.

The fourth was from Annapaola. It said: *Hi Guerrieri, everything here objectively boring, but let's not tell the girls. Actually, the fact that I leave feeling happy and free and after a day I miss you is getting tiresome. Are you having fun without me? Have you picked up one of those crazy women lawyers who go all starry-eyed every time they see you in court?*

The message was from more than an hour earlier. Once I'd removed the idiotic smile that had leapt to my lips, I replied. With two messages.

The first was this: *Hi kid, sorry to delay answering but I'm having a party with these gorgeous Cuban dancers. Let's talk when we have more time.*

The second, immediately afterwards, was: *I miss you too. Please come back soon.*

5

I opened my eyes exactly six hours after switching off the light. I got up immediately, had a quick shower, made my usual black coffee, ate a few pieces of shortbread from the bakery near my building, then, to silence my health-freak conscience (which was a little fragile, to tell the truth), told myself I would have a fruit juice later in the morning and went back to the table and the case file. More specifically, to the transcript of Lorenza's testimony.

I skimmed quickly through the preliminaries and moved on to the main part.

AVVOCATO COSTAMAGNA: Signora Delle Foglie, do you remember the day the police came to your home? The day you later learned that a murder had been committed and that your son was suspected of the crime?

WITNESS: Yes, of course.

AVVOCATO COSTAMAGNA: Does your son Iacopo live with you?

WITNESS: Yes, I mean, up until then, when he was arrested.

AVVOCATO COSTAMAGNA: Of course. Do you remember what you had been doing that afternoon?

WITNESS: I'd been working.

AVVOCATO COSTAMAGNA: Can you tell us what work you do?

WITNESS: Actually, I have more than one job. I'm a self-employed teacher, I do substitute teaching, sometimes for long periods, sometimes for a whole year. But I also do other things to make ends meet: I give private lessons and sometimes I keep elderly ladies company.

AVVOCATO COSTAMAGNA: Like a carer?

WITNESS: Not exactly. I don't provide what I'd call material care. I keep them company when they're alone. These are old people who are completely self-sufficient. Sometimes I read to them, we talk…

AVVOCATO COSTAMAGNA: That afternoon, what had you done?

WITNESS: I'd gone to see one of these old ladies.

AVVOCATO COSTAMAGNA: I see. Do you remember what time you got home?

WITNESS: I can't say the exact time, but my shift at that lady's was from three to seven, from her home to mine is more or less twenty minutes on foot, so I'd say I got home roughly around 7.15.

AVVOCATO COSTAMAGNA: Was your son Iacopo at home?

WITNESS: No, but he came in soon after me.

AVVOCATO COSTAMAGNA: Can you tell us how soon after?

WITNESS: Ten minutes, maybe a little more.

AVVOCATO COSTAMAGNA: So is it correct to say that at 7.47 your son —

ASSISTANT PROSECUTOR: Objection, Your Honour, defence is drawing conclusions, which he obviously can't do at this point.

PRESIDING JUDGE: Avvocato, stick to questions. You can draw any conclusions you wish in your closing statement.

AVVOCATO COSTAMAGNA: I'm sorry, Your Honour, but you can't stop me, I need to —

PRESIDING JUDGE: Avvocato, please don't argue with my decisions. If you have other questions ask them. The question to which the prosecution objected is not admissible.

AVVOCATO COSTAMAGNA: So you got home at 7.15 and your son ten minutes later. After coming home, did he go out again?

WITNESS: Yes.

AVVOCATO COSTAMAGNA: How soon afterwards?

WITNESS: I couldn't say exactly. Not immediately. An hour later, slightly more.

AVVOCATO COSTAMAGNA: Are you sure?

WITNESS: I'm certain.

AVVOCATO COSTAMAGNA: Thank you, I have no other questions.

PRESIDING JUDGE: Does the prosecution wish to cross-examine?

ASSISTANT PROSECUTOR: Yes, Your Honour, thank you. Good morning, signora, as you know I'm the assistant prosecutor and I'm going to ask you some questions to get a clearer idea of what you've just told us. Is that all right?

WITNESS: Yes.

ASSISTANT PROSECUTOR: You told us that your son got home … at what time, did you say?

WITNESS: About 7.30 or just before.

ASSISTANT PROSECUTOR: And then he went out again?

WITNESS: About an hour later.

ASSISTANT PROSECUTOR: Then the police came to your home?

WITNESS: Yes.

ASSISTANT PROSECUTOR: At what time did the police arrive?

WITNESS: I couldn't say exactly.

ASSISTANT PROSECUTOR: Had you already gone to bed?

WITNESS: No, I was watching television. It might have been about eleven, maybe a little earlier. My son had been gone for some time by then.

ASSISTANT PROSECUTOR: Would you be surprised if I told you that the police came to your home at about 9.30?

WITNESS: As I said, I can't remember exactly what time the police came to my home.

ASSISTANT PROSECUTOR: But it seems you remember very well the time your son came home.

WITNESS: But that's because —

ASSISTANT PROSECUTOR: Please don't interrupt, I haven't yet asked my question. So, if I've understood correctly, you worked as a substitute teacher but also had other jobs. Is that correct?

WITNESS: Yes, that's correct.

ASSISTANT PROSECUTOR: Still?

WITNESS: I'm sorry?

ASSISTANT PROSECUTOR: I asked you if you still do various jobs, including this assistance to elderly people, this keeping them company.

WITNESS: Yes.

ASSISTANT PROSECUTOR: And in particular, do you still work with the lady you were with that afternoon?

WITNESS: Yes.

ASSISTANT PROSECUTOR: How old is this lady? What's her name?

WITNESS: She's eighty-seven now. Her name is Rosa Bonomo.

ASSISTANT PROSECUTOR: Do you do the same shift you did then?

WITNESS: I always go there in the afternoon.

ASSISTANT PROSECUTOR: Yes, but do you do exactly the same shift you did then?

WITNESS: No, not exactly. Let's say the schedule is more flexible now, it depends on requirements.

ASSISTANT PROSECUTOR: Is that a recent change?

WITNESS: No.

ASSISTANT PROSECUTOR: How long ago did your schedule with this lady change?

WITNESS: Do you want the exact date?

ASSISTANT PROSECUTOR: You needn't get upset, signora. I just want you to tell us what you remember. If you can't remember, you only have to say so.

WITNESS: I'm sorry. I don't know exactly. More than a year, anyway.

ASSISTANT PROSECUTOR: For what reason did you go from a fixed schedule to a flexible schedule?

WITNESS: She's an old lady, but she's completely self-sufficient. To be on the safe side, though, her children found a permanent carer, a woman from Moldova. But she – the woman from Moldova, I mean – also has another job, so when she's not there, or when her children aren't taking turns to keep their mother company, I go. Actually, it's almost every day.

ASSISTANT PROSECUTOR: Do you know this woman from Moldova?

WITNESS: I meet her when I arrive or when I leave.

ASSISTANT PROSECUTOR: When did you first meet?

WITNESS: When she started working for Signora Bonomo.

ASSISTANT PROSECUTOR: And when exactly was that?

WITNESS: I couldn't say exactly.

ASSISTANT PROSECUTOR: Then let me ask you a different question. When the events that are the subject of this trial occurred, did you already know this woman from Moldova?

WITNESS: …

ASSISTANT PROSECUTOR: Your Honour, can it be entered in the record that the witness is hesitating to answer?

47

PRESIDING JUDGE: So entered. Signora, please answer the question. When these events occurred, did you already know this woman from Moldova?

WITNESS: Maybe… I don't know, maybe yes… I'm not sure.

ASSISTANT PROSECUTOR: We can easily check, but I'd like to hear it from you.

WITNESS: Maybe I already knew her.

ASSISTANT PROSECUTOR: Does that mean she had already taken up service with the lady at whose house you worked? Or did you first meet before this woman from Moldova started working —

WITNESS: No, no.

ASSISTANT PROSECUTOR: No, what?

WITNESS: I didn't know her before —

ASSISTANT PROSECUTOR: So you met her when she took up service?

WITNESS: I assume so.

ASSISTANT PROSECUTOR: You assume so?

WITNESS: She'd already taken up service. I remember now.

ASSISTANT PROSECUTOR: So you'd already started the flexible schedule you told us about?

WITNESS: No, I definitely had the shift from three to seven.

ASSISTANT PROSECUTOR: But you told us it was when the woman from Moldova arrived that you started a flexible schedule.

WITNESS: I wasn't accurate.

ASSISTANT PROSECUTOR: At what time did you get back home that afternoon or evening?

WITNESS: About 7.15, I already said.

ASSISTANT PROSECUTOR: How can you be so precise about the time? You told us that you could state with certainty that you left the home of the elderly lady you worked for at seven basically because that was the schedule you were on before the woman from Moldova arrived.

WITNESS: I see, yes, you're right, I wasn't accurate, I got confused. I mean that for a while, even after the woman from Moldova arrived, I continued doing that fixed schedule. It wasn't until later that the situation changed in the way I said, after a trial period, I think. I got confused about that, but I'm sure I got home no later than 7.20 and that my son arrived soon afterwards.

ASSISTANT PROSECUTOR: Which, as it happens, would allow you to give your son an alibi. Don't you think it strange that on all the other questions of time you say you can't be accurate and yet —

AVVOCATO COSTAMAGNA: Objection, Your Honour, prosecution is arguing with the witness, badgering her, and even asking her for an opinion, which is obviously inadmissible.

PRESIDING JUDGE: Let's drop the word "badgering", Avvocato. That seems to me an exaggeration. That said, Assistant Prosecutor, the witness has answered. Any evaluation of the evidence can be left until the time is right, in other words, when we come to closing statements. If you have other questions, please proceed.

ASSISTANT PROSECUTOR: Very well, Your Honour. Signora, I still have a few questions. Do you have a criminal record?

WITNESS: No.

ASSISTANT PROSECUTOR: You've never been subject to legal proceedings?

WITNESS: No.

ASSISTANT PROSECUTOR: Would you be surprised if I told you that I have here a judgement concerning you, relating to a charge of resisting an officer of the law and aiding and abetting?

WITNESS: I've never been convicted of anything. I don't know what you're talking about.

ASSISTANT PROSECUTOR: Actually, I asked you if you had ever been subject to legal proceedings. This in fact is a ruling not to proceed because of an amnesty. May I approach, Your Honour? I would like to show the witness the document.

AVVOCATO COSTAMAGNA: Your Honour, I object to the assistant prosecutor's methods. We don't know what this document is, it wasn't produced during the discovery phase and is now suddenly brought up in contempt of all the rules of discovery and of correct consultation between the parties. I object most strongly.

PRESIDING JUDGE: Assistant Prosecutor, before showing the document to the witness, please put it at the disposal of the defence. Avvocato Costamagna, do you need time to examine the document?

AVVOCATO COSTAMAGNA: Your Honour, while reiterating my objection to any inopportune production of documents, I ask you only for a few minutes, long enough to understand what it's about and if it's even slightly pertinent to the object of this trial, which I doubt.

At 10.25 the hearing is suspended and the witness is taken by the bailiff into the witness room. At 10.40 the hearing resumes.

PRESIDING JUDGE: We may resume. Does the defence have any observations to make?

AVVOCATO COSTAMAGNA: The document is completely

irrelevant to the object of this trial. A ruling not to proceed because of an amnesty, regarding events that supposedly happened almost thirty years ago. I object to any request to produce this document and to any use being made of it at this trial, and I repeat my objection to this method of suddenly bringing out documents when there is a specific phase of proceedings when such requests may be made.

ASSISTANT PROSECUTOR: Your Honour, I fear that this impassioned reaction on the part of the defence is the result of a misunderstanding. I haven't asked to produce this ruling, although naturally I reserve the right to do so should the need arise. I simply wanted to show it to the witness in order to jog her memory. She has denied ever being subject to legal proceedings, whereas this ruling demonstrates the opposite.

PRESIDING JUDGE: Show the witness the ruling, Assistant Prosecutor.

At this point the assistant prosecutor shows the document to the witness.

ASSISTANT PROSECUTOR: So, signora, do you remember being subject to legal proceedings for the charges of aiding and abetting and resisting an officer of the law?

WITNESS: I was never put on trial.

ASSISTANT PROSECUTOR: It says here that you struggled with officers of the Treasury Police to prevent them from arresting a drug dealer. It also says that there is no evidence for an acquittal, but that since there has been an amnesty – the last amnesty, Your Honour, the one in 1990 – the charge, or rather, the charges are to

51

be declared null and void. Don't you remember being involved in anything like that? Weren't you ever taken to a Treasury Police station in relation to the arrest of a drug dealer who was a friend of yours?

WITNESS: Many years ago there was something like that. But it was all a mistake. He wasn't a drug dealer, he was a young man who had a few small pieces of hashish and the officers —

ASSISTANT PROSECUTOR: So now you're starting to remember. To be precise, they were officers of the Treasury Police.

WITNESS: All right, I don't even remember what they were. The Treasury officers, or whatever they were, didn't say that's what they were, they didn't identify themselves.

ASSISTANT PROSECUTOR: Were you taken to a station and charged with aiding and abetting and with resisting an officer of the law?

WITNESS: We went to a station, they took some statements, I have no idea what it was all about, I mean, I don't remember, we're talking about twenty-five years ago. I never heard any more about it. I didn't even know this ruling you've shown me existed.

ASSISTANT PROSECUTOR: Before this ruling was issued you were informed. You could have forgone the amnesty, asked for a trial and hoped for acquittal. Why didn't you do so?

WITNESS: I have no idea what you're talking about.

ASSISTANT PROSECUTOR: I fear this is a problem of yours. Anyway, thank you, I have no further questions. I place the document at the disposal of the court.

PRESIDING JUDGE: The court orders that it be admitted as evidence. Does the defence wish to re-examine the witness?

AVVOCATO COSTAMAGNA: No, thank you, Your Honour. We reserve the right to examine the document at a later time and to ascertain whether or not to make a further request for evidence regarding it.

Assistant Prosecutor Cotturri had been good, although Costamagna hadn't been entirely wrong in objecting to that ruling being displayed. According to the code of criminal procedure, the submission of documentary evidence should be requested during the introductory phase of the trial. This is a non-mandatory rule, and one interpreted with a certain flexibility, but its aim is to avoid evidence being suddenly sprung on the court, to safeguard the integrity of the proceedings, and to avoid one or other party having to deal with unexpected evidence for which they have not been able to prepare.

The assistant prosecutor had overcome the problem in the proper way: he had asked Lorenza if she had ever been subject to legal proceedings, and it was only after receiving a negative answer that he had brought up that old case that had ended with the implementation of the amnesty. The ruling, therefore, didn't directly prove anything, but once a certain testimony had been obtained, it helped indirectly to cast doubts on the reliability of the witness. As it had indeed done.

I leafed through the papers in search of a copy of that ruling, even though I already knew I wouldn't find much that was useful. A ruling that implements the declaring of a charge to be null and void, as in an amnesty, simply says that although there is no evidence for acquittal, the charge should be declared null and void anyway. Apart from amnesties, other reasons for this might be the statute of limitations, the withdrawal of the action, or the death of the offender.

The only interesting thing, apart from the ritual formulas, was the charge. Lorenza had been charged "as under articles 81, 337 and 278 of the penal code, with violating several provisions of the law by struggling with Sergeant Gattuso and Officer Scarano as they were attempting to arrest Nicola Damiani for the offence of possession of narcotics of the hashish type for the purposes of dealing, thus helping the above-mentioned Damiani to escape or otherwise evade investigation. Offence committed in Torre Canne, Fasano, 5 July 1987."

It struck me that the Lorenza I had known so many years before – the memories were starting to come back to the surface – was definitely the kind of person to struggle with Treasury officers in order to help a friend "escape or otherwise evade investigation".

It had seemed, at the time, that she wasn't afraid of anything, and that she hated the police for deeply rooted ideological reasons.

Then I looked again at the date beneath the charge.

5 July 1987.

In other words, when we were still seeing each other. We had met in the spring of that same year.

Lorenza

The only things I remember clearly are the beginning and the end.

The rest of it, in my memory, is as disjointed and haphazard as a painting by Braque. I don't know which episodes happened first and which later. Not with any accuracy, at least.

The beginning is when I met Lorenza, one evening in March 1987.

I had graduated the previous year and was a trainee in a legal practice. Becoming a defence lawyer wasn't my dream, but it should be said that I'd never had clear ideas about what my dream was. Anyway, I was a trainee while waiting to clarify my ideas. Sooner or later.

It was the mid-eighties. The moral decline of that period is represented with almost metaphorical effectiveness by padded shoulders. When we wore jackets or coats we all of us, male or female, looked like mannequins. You just have to look at the photos.

It was a time when the soundscape of our lives was starting to change irreversibly. A period still full of noises and sounds that no longer exist today.

For example, the noise of a token or a coin inserted in a public telephone, and the noise, similar and yet very different, of the click when a token or its equivalent value in lire was used up.

The noise as you turned the dial of a home telephone – a strange grey object, pot-bellied and reassuring. The different sounds of a typewriter. The sound of the keys – rhythmical or tentative depending on how good the typist was – which was also, and above all, produced by the heads of the keys, with the letters on them, beating on the paper. The sound of the platen, which you turned with grainy black knobs. The sound of the little lever that took you back to the beginning. The sound of the paper bail that hit the sheet as if to inflict a wound on it and render it powerless.

The click of the tape recorder when you started and stopped it; the urgent, slightly dizzying noise of the tape winding back.

The almost frenetic tapping of the calculator as it printed the result on a roll of paper.

It was an analogue world still made up (not for much longer, though we didn't know that then) of wheels, gears and switches.

I had recently broken up, not altogether amicably, with my girlfriend Rossana. We'd been together, through ups and downs, for most of our time at university. When we said goodbye, she told me a series of things about me, none of them pleasant, as far as I recall: I had a tendency to rationalize everything out of a fear of intimacy; I used irony to avoid responsibility for my feelings; I was incapable of true commitment and, in spite of appearances, I was someone who led a passive existence. Things like that.

That afternoon in March 1987, having been unattached for a couple of weeks, I was dawdling on my way to the office. In Via Sparano I bumped into a guy named Saverio, otherwise known as Verio (yes, whoever had thought of the nickname hadn't made much of an effort), who I'd occasionally hung out with. He was a year older than me, was studying medicine, lived in Poggiofranco, was gay (there weren't a lot of people in those days who declared it openly), had a certain tendency to talk too much and when very young had been a champion horse rider, a sport he had abandoned for unknown reasons.

We hugged and he gave me two big kisses on my cheeks, the kind that make a smacking sound.

"Guido Guerrieri, great to see you, it's been a while. Going anywhere nice?"

"To work," I replied, in a tone that implied that if I didn't have to earn a living, I'd certainly know how to spend my afternoons.

"Work," he repeated. The word seemed to make an impression. "You're becoming a lawyer, is that right?"

"I don't know. I'm trying it, but I'm not sure it's right for me. How about you? How long before you graduate?"

"A year, more or less. Then I don't know. Maybe I'd like to go abroad to specialize."

"Great," I said, just to say something.

"Are you still with that blonde girl? What's her name?"

"Rossana. No, not any more."

"Sorry to hear that. She had blue, almost violet eyes, really special. Like Elizabeth Taylor."

The subject made me uncomfortable. So I uttered a series of things about relationships that end after a while, that's life, and other banalities that I fortunately don't remember.

"What are you doing this evening?" he asked me.

"I don't have any plans," I replied, a touch cautiously.

"Why don't you come to a party? It's at the home of a friend of mine, there'll be loads of people. Maybe you'll meet somebody, seeing as how you're a free man now."

My first thought was that I had no particular desire to go to a gay party, but he hadn't actually said it was a gay party, he was only trying to be nice. I felt ashamed of my reactionary mistrust, and I told myself it was a good idea to start seeing new people. In short, at the end of these few seconds of reflection, I replied thank you, I'd be happy to come. Fantastic, he said. He'd pick me up from my place around 9.30. He asked me to remind him of my address – which he'd never known, as far as I recalled – and said goodbye.

6

On Tuesday – after a very quick trip to Rome to present an appeal at the Supreme Court – Consuelo, Annapaola and Tancredi met with me in the office. All three of them had read the ruling and it was clear after a few minutes that all three were convinced Lorenza's son was guilty. The worst of it was that I was inclined to think the same.

"The kid's a lowlife," Tancredi said when I asked him for his opinion.

"Why?"

"Have you seen his record?"

"Yes, he was put on probation as a minor, for armed robbery. In the end, the case was declared null and void."

"My colleagues dealt with it – my former colleagues at the Squad. I dropped by and they were kind enough to give me copies of the arrest transcript and the statements of the victim, a lady who'd made a withdrawal at the post office."

"And what emerges from that?"

"What emerges is that, like I said, your new client is a lowlife. Or at least he was when he was a minor. He and someone else who wasn't caught, whose name he didn't give up – which suggests he was already a fully formed criminal before he was eighteen – were apparently in the post office watching out for people who were making cash transactions or collecting their pensions. They saw this lady who'd withdrawn a substantial sum, followed her home, grabbed her at the front door of her building and stuck a knife to her throat. What particularly marks them down as two nasty pieces of work is what they said to her."

"What was that?"

"'Keep your eyes down, bitch, and don't look us in the face. If you look us in the face you're dead.' Something along those lines."

"Nice. How much did they take from her?"

"Eight hundred euros."

"And then what happened?"

"They were unlucky. Or at least, he was unlucky, because the other guy managed to get away. Two guys from the street crimes team were passing on motorbikes. They heard screams, saw two kids running and followed them. One they caught, and that was our client. Or rather, your client."

"What happened to the money?"

"He had it, so the woman got it all back. The kid was put on probation, he behaved well – or *pretended* to behave well – and in the end the case was declared null and void. But it was a nasty robbery and the modus operandi suggests they'd done it before."

I took a deep breath. I wondered if it had been a good idea to take on this assignment.

"All right, let's not let ourselves be influenced by that." I hadn't even finished the sentence before it struck me as being as fake as a brass sovereign.

The situation didn't improve with Annapaola's contribution.

"I also read the ruling. Last night. The long and the short of it is, I think the guy's guilty. The investigation was clean and the verdict is perfectly justified."

I turned to Consuelo, though I wasn't sure I could expect any help from her.

"I agree. I also think he's guilty. It was a nasty murder, and I don't understand why you took on the case. There, I've said it."

I felt the surge of irritation that goes through me every time I discuss these subjects with Consuelo and have to confront her prosecutorial intransigence. If it was up to her, we would only deal with plaintiffs in civil cases or with defendants who were unequivocally innocent. There's no doubt she should have been a prosecutor or a judge rather than a counsel for the defence.

I waited a few seconds until the wave of irritation faded, otherwise I'd have started at a total disadvantage and would have been beaten in the debate that was about to start.

"I also know he's probably guilty. Or rather: I get the impression he's guilty."

"Then why have you agreed to defend him?" Consuelo asked. "We've talked about this so often. As a practice, we don't handle organized crime."

"First of all, this has nothing to with organized crime. Worst-case scenario, if Cardace really is guilty, we're dealing with a settling of scores between low-level dealers. And anyway, I have news for you: if we had to make a living agreeing only to defend those who were guaranteed innocent, we might as well go and work in the fields."

"Working in the fields isn't bad," Annapaola said, in that typical tone of hers, where you can't tell if she's serious or if she's pulling your leg.

"Have you read the court transcripts?" I asked.

I knew that wasn't possible, given that I hadn't had copies made for them. My question was only there to gain a little breathing space in the ongoing debate. They replied no, obviously.

"I have. The defence was practically non-existent."

"Wasn't Costamagna his lawyer?" Annapaola asked. The implication being: Costamagna was good.

"He was already ill, and a few weeks ago he died. In his last months he wasn't the same any more. He may just have been worn out, but that's not the basic point. The basic point is that, to all intents and purposes, Cardace didn't get proper representation. There was practically no evidence presented in his defence, apart from his mother's testimony, and there was no cross-examination. Guilty or not guilty, the kid has a right to a decent defence."

Nobody said a word. They seemed less sure of themselves now.

"We'd need to ask for new evidence to be admitted, if we found any," Consuelo said, in a more conciliatory tone than before. "Except that the time limit's already up. The hearing's in ten days."

As almost always happened after an initial argumentative phase, she was starting to think like a lawyer and not like an inquisitor.

"We'll have to ask for an extension. I'm going to see Judge Marinelli tomorrow to let him know."

"As long as he's prepared to compromise," she said.

"I'll tell him clearly what the problem is, assuming he doesn't already know. I think he and Costamagna were friends, or at any rate knew each other well. I imagine he knows what the situation was like in the man's last months."

"You haven't met the kid yet, have you?" Annapaola asked.

"I'm going there today for an initial interview. We'll see what kind of person he is."

"What do you want us to do?" Tancredi asked.

"First of all I'd read the phone intercepts carefully to get an idea of the context and see if those two conversations between Cardace and Gaglione just before the murder really are so unambiguous. Then I think we should look at the question of the forensics test. It's an indisputable fact that they found powder residue on his jacket, but in statements he made the kid said he'd been shooting a few days earlier, wearing the same jacket, and that would explain it. We need to establish if that's at all possible."

"Theoretically, yes," Tancredi said. "Gunshot residue can stay on fabric for up to a few days. That said, the story he told can't be used. The judges were right not to take it into account. It'd be interesting to know a little more about this phantom shooting session. If there's any truth to it or if it was just something his lawyer dreamed up to create a bit of doubt."

"I'll talk about it to the kid. I also think we should look at the area around the victim's apartment, just to get a better idea. And I repeat, let's study the intercepts. If we have any doubts about the way they were transcribed, let's get hold of the recordings. Apart from anything else, they were admitted in evidence under article 270 even though they related to another case, the one against Gaglione for dealing, and we have to decide if there's any point in requesting the ones that weren't admitted."

"Why, do you think there were problems with the way the intercepts were allowed in evidence?" Consuelo asked.

"It wasn't flawless, but frankly I don't see any grounds for claiming they're unusable. But let's look at them anyway, and maybe we'll talk about it again. Apart from the request for an extension, let's try to figure out if we need to add further grounds to the appeal, though at first sight I don't think so: the appeal is succinct, but it contains what we need."

Tancredi shifted on his chair. "I think I'll go and talk to a few more of my former colleagues in the Squad, to see if there are any alternative avenues they didn't follow up on. I want to get a better idea of who the dead man was, how they got on to him in the first place, what circles he moved in, if there were people who didn't like him. I also want to see what they know about Cardace, apart from what's written in the file."

"I'll check out the area around Gaglione's place, plus the cafe where he was seen," Annapaola said. "In the ruling, there's no mention of any security footage being admitted in evidence. Is it in any of the other documents?"

"I don't think so. To tell the truth, I hadn't even thought of it."

"When I'm over there, then, I'll see if there are any security cameras. Though of course the footage won't still be around after two years. But that's a good reason for you to ask: why didn't you get hold of it? It'd suggest a shortcoming in the investigation."

"Provided that *is* what happened," Tancredi said, automatically defending his former colleagues. "Maybe they did get hold of it, maybe they viewed it and didn't find anything important. In the meantime, significant evidence emerged about Cardace, so they dropped the footage and didn't even mention it in the reports."

"Let's check. If there are cameras, and nothing was done about the footage, it might be worth bringing it up."

I looked around. Nobody added anything else, and we brought the meeting to a close.

Once again, I didn't say that I knew the defendant's mother. That I'd known her (or thought I'd known her) many, many years earlier.

7

In my early years in the profession I liked going into prisons. Around the age of thirty, it gave me the feeling I was someone who was dealing with serious things. Someone on whose work serious things *depended*. Which, to an extent, was true.

But what interested me was the vain, even narcissistic aspect of the matter, even though I wouldn't admit it even to myself. So I spoke about going into prisons, *having* to go there, as if it were an unpleasant duty. But actually, going through those gates that opened and closed behind me gave me an unhealthy sense of gratification. I could access that mysterious, forbidden place whenever I wanted, meet the creatures who were kept there, and *leave* whenever I wanted.

With the passing of the years, the gratification gradually faded and turned into routine. That opening and closing and more opening and closing of gates, that creaking of hinges and noise of bolts, those measured steps of men and women in uniform became components of a larger rhythm, regular and repetitive, along with the mornings at the courthouse, filled with hearings and bureaucracy, and the afternoons in the office, filled with clients and case files.

Finally I went beyond the monotony of routine, and going into a prison became increasingly unbearable. Because of the prison population. I'm not making a theoretical observation, or being what they call a bleeding-heart liberal. I simply find it harder to bear the idea of people confined behind bars. It's unavoidable, in many cases, but knowing that doesn't help.

The name of the sergeant who walked me to the lawyers' room was Smaldino. He was a kind man, kind to the prisoners, too. He was from a village somewhere inland, and I knew that his hobby was breeding and training dogs. We hadn't seen each other in a while.

"How long have you and I known each other, Avvocato Guerrieri?"

"At least twenty years, I'm sorry to say. Maybe a bit more."

"I arrived in Bari twenty-three years ago. I came here from Rebibbia and before that I was in Sardinia. You were one of the first lawyers I met. You were a boy then. So we've known each other for twenty-three years."

"Not long till your pension now."

"Two more years and I'll be able to devote myself to my dogs full-time."

We were walking side by side, the rhythm of our footsteps alternating, and looking ahead of us as we talked. That's why I didn't immediately see the grimace that had just passed across Smaldino's face, but I sensed it from an imperceptible change of tone.

"Do you remember D'Ippolito?"

"The inspector with the moustache? Of course I remember him."

"He retired last year. And three weeks later he had a stroke. Luckily they didn't manage to save him, he would have been a vegetable. Ever since it happened, I've been scared it could happen to me too. You wait so long for that time of life, you think you'll be young enough to devote yourself to the things you like. Instead, you die."

"Damn, I'm sorry about poor D'Ippolito." I really was sorry. He was another of those prison officers I'd got on well with. Even the prisoners had spoken well of him. No abuse, no violence.

"Right. Life's really absurd."

We got to the lawyers' room.

"I'll send you your client now. I'm sorry if I told you a story that's made you sad."

"One day I'd like to come and see your dogs," I said by way of goodbye.

His face lit up. "It would be an honour."

Sitting down at the desk, I opened my bag, took out the ruling, the trial transcripts and a notepad and laid out everything in front of me.

It was another five or six minutes before a young officer opened the door and admitted my client: Iacopo Cardace.

He was of medium height, and solidly built. He was wearing jeans and a grey sweatshirt beneath which you could sense the muscles. He had light brown, almost blond hair, and his face was marked with acne scars. His expression was evasive, his eyes half-closed as if he'd only just woken up. Overall, he aroused an immediate antipathy in me.

It sometimes happens with clients, but with this young man the phenomenon was particularly intense, and it took an effort to suppress the feeling.

"Good morning, Signor Cardace. As you already know, I'm Avvocato Guerrieri. I think your mother told you I'd be coming to see you."

"Are you replacing Costamagna?"

"Not exactly. I'm here because you appointed me, on the advice of your mother. My practice has no connection with that of Avvocato Costamagna."

I became aware that my tone was a little resentful. It was a result of the hostility the boy aroused in me and of the annoyance I felt at being somehow equated to Costamagna.

He nodded apathetically and sniffed.

"Right," I resumed. "Let's see where we stand at the moment. If anything I say to you isn't clear, just ask me to explain. Okay?"

"Okay."

"So, on the day of the hearing we'll request a brief extension. We'll do this because you didn't appoint me until after the time limit for presenting new requests for evidence and possible new grounds for appeal had already passed. So that we can formulate these requests for evidence, and generally plan an effective strategy for your defence, we're going to need your help. So now I'm going to ask you a few questions."

I stopped there. When I have clients charged with serious crimes that involve the use of violence, and in particular when I have clients charged with homicide, I never ask them to tell me the truth.

I prefer them to decide. Knowing the whole truth can be a double-edged sword.

Knowing exactly what happened (and therefore also if the client is guilty) helps you get a clearer picture of the territory in which you will have to move. It helps you avoid dangerous topics, arguments that could suddenly be turned against you; it allows you to concentrate on the weak points of the prosecution case without unwittingly turning them into strong, decisive points – as happens when the defence is badly thought out and the defence counsel isn't very good.

Knowing exactly what happened does, however, have some not insignificant disadvantages from a psychological point of view. If the defendant is guilty and tells you so, this complicates how acceptable (to yourself) your choices as a defender are. For some, doing your best – even if respecting the rules – to obtain the acquittal of a defendant who has committed a brutal murder, a nasty armed robbery, an act of extortion, a rape, is the source of more than a slight sense of unease, which may backfire on you and have an impact on the efficacy of the defence.

Fortunately, in the majority of cases, clients spare you the bother of confronting this ethical dilemma. Usually they lie, even to their lawyers, perhaps because they're conscious of the risks that might derive from an excess of truth. In this way, they simplify things and make our lives less complicated from a moral point of view. For those of us who have morals.

"I didn't kill Gaglione. The whole thing's ridiculous, and I want you to know that I didn't kill him. And I don't want you to answer me like the other lawyer."

"What did the other lawyer say?"

"The thing is, I only talked to him twice. Which I think is odd, if someone's supposed to be defending you on a murder charge."

Yes, it was odd. More than odd – downright wrong. But it accorded with Costamagna's professional style, with the ideology that shone through his way of working and which he flaunted like a manifesto. What he felt for his clients (regardless of how good he'd been at defending them) was the contempt typical of many good lawyers. The clients, especially those guilty of serious crimes and coming from the underclass, were mainly opportunities for personal gain and, at the same time, opportunities to satisfy his own ego.

I'm defending you because I want to show that I'm the best. Let's be quite clear about this: I couldn't care less what happens to you.

"He said it didn't matter if I was guilty or innocent," he went on. "The problem was that it looked as if I was guilty. Trials aren't about innocence or guilt, he kept saying. They're about who wins and who loses."

Precisely. I felt as if I could hear this refrain of Costamagna's. Innocence doesn't interest us, and the same is true of guilt. A phrase that could also be understood in a technical sense: that what counts in trials is the algebra of the evidence. If it's right, there's a guilty verdict; if it's wrong, there's an acquittal. Except that for Costamagna, the phrase summed up a conception of our profession and, more generally, of the world. Moral categories and dilemmas don't interest us. What matters is winning.

"Okay. You didn't kill Gaglione. Without sharing the opinion of your previous counsel, I do have to tell you that the evidence produced at the trial is very serious. The ruling is quite persuasive and we'll have to find something concrete to propose to the appeal court as an alternative. I want you to tell me about the nature of your relationship with Gaglione and then, in detail, how you spent the day of the murder."

He nodded, and his eyes grew a little less empty, came back to life. He started speaking and continued for half an hour.

The two of them had met in a gym. Both practised mixed martial arts and Brazilian jiu-jitsu, violent disciplines that are now mostly seen on television and in tournaments. Gaglione had started supplying Cardace with synthetic drugs, which he pushed in discos around the province, and banned body-building substances, sold in gyms to stupid kids who wanted to see their muscles grow in a few weeks.

Cardace had never known who Gaglione got his supplies from. That isn't the kind of question you ask in that world. You know what the other person decides to tell you, he said in the vaguely sententious tone of someone who wants to show he follows a system of adult rules.

In the days preceding the murder, there had been a problem with some substances sold to bodybuilders by Cardace (who had got them from Gaglione). The owner of a gym had complained, claiming that he'd had the substances analysed and had ascertained that their composition didn't correspond to what he'd paid for. So he'd asked for his money back. That morning Cardace had called Gaglione to complain in his turn and find out what had happened.

Yes, it was true, the telephone calls had been a little animated because of that problem. Yes, it was true that he'd gone to Gaglione's place to sort things out in person, because there are some things it's best not to deal with over the phone. The two had talked things over and had made peace, and Gaglione, as a sign of reconciliation, had gifted Cardace about fifteen pills of a new version of Ecstasy that he himself had received only a few days earlier. They had parted amicably. As he went on his way, Cardace had run into an acquaintance named Sabino – he didn't know his surname – and they had gone for a coffee together.

Then he had returned home and soon afterwards had gone out again. The policeman had tracked him down outside a bar where he'd been hanging out with some friends (maybe customers, I thought) and had taken him to Headquarters. There they had given him a gunshot residue test and had arrested him for the Ecstasy pills they'd found on him. The same ones that Gaglione had given him. Since then he had been in prison.

"Why did you go to Gaglione's apartment? Why didn't you meet him outside?"

"He was paranoid at the time. He was scared of going out."

"Why?"

"Among the various things Mino did was security. For discos, nightclubs, concerts. A few days before – maybe about ten days, I don't know exactly – he'd worked at a disco called Chilometro Zero. Do you know it?"

I nodded vaguely. I knew there was a place of that name, but nothing else.

"Anyway, there was a fight. Two drunk guys had been pestering some girls and when one of the guys who was with these girls stood in their way they beat him up. That caused the usual ruckus and security intervened, including Mino. The two drunks were thrown out, but one of them wouldn't calm down. He kept screaming, challenging everyone. Mino went up to him and told him to stop and get out, and the guy tried to headbutt him. That pissed Mino off and he gave him a good beating, leaving him on the ground. In the following days it turned out that the guy belonged to a major family. The kind you don't want to mess with. Apparently the father of the boy was a very dangerous man."

"And so Gaglione was worried about possible reprisals?"

"Yes, he was very worried. He went out only if it was absolutely necessary, and was even thinking of leaving Bari for a while. Maybe he'd even tried to get in touch with those people, to apologize and get the matter closed."

"Who was the guy he beat up? What family did he belong to?"

"I don't know. Gaglione didn't tell me."

It struck me that although Cardace looked like a petty criminal (which is what he was), he was well spoken. He even had a beautiful voice, a detail I hadn't noticed at first. If I'd talked to him on the phone, I would have imagined him looking completely different.

As he spoke I kept looking for some resemblance to his mother. The colouring was his father's, whoever that was. Lorenza's hair was dark, or rather, it had been – now it was an opaque grey. There: opaque was the adjective that described her, in general. She was opaque, like the characters in a fantasy novel, beings who have lost their consistency and gradually become more and more evanescent. In other words, the exact opposite of the girl I'd known all those years ago. The creature of the past had been a luminous entity, who had seemed to glitter with her own almost tangible light.

Cardace's mouth was similar to his mother's. The ears, too, a little larger than average. And as I listened to him speak, there was every now and again an inflection that seemed to have landed from a different place and a distant past.

"You didn't mention these things in your statements. Why?"

"Avvocato Costamagna told me not to. He said it was all too vague, that the judges wouldn't believe me, that they'd think it was an attempt to muddy the waters. They'd consider it completely irrelevant. And on the other hand, if a Mafia family really was involved, it was best not to alarm them with a statement that wouldn't be of any use to me in court anyway."

Costamagna's advice sounded terrible, but in itself wasn't devoid of sense. Alluding to a possible connection with organized crime in order to suggest a narrative different from that of the prosecution, as followed in the ruling, was worthless from a procedural point of view. It would have been too easy, in order to instil the idea of reasonable doubt, to maintain in general terms – without giving any more specific indication about people and context – that a murder victim feared reprisals from organized crime. Putting forward alternative hypotheses without any basis in fact, without any indication of individuals who might have been involved – both of which are indispensable if such hypotheses are to be considered by the judges – is pointless, if not counterproductive.

And Costamagna was right on the second point, too. Assuming Gaglione really had aroused the avenging fury of some Mafia boss, and assuming that the murder was the result of that, there was a real risk that the mafiosi in question would feel threatened by the mention of a possible alternative lead that involved them.

"Now we have to talk about the most important thing. The powder residue that was found on your jacket. I've read your statements. You maintained that you went shooting a few days earlier, wearing that jacket. You said you were in a quarry, with a friend, doing target practice. I'd like to know a bit more about that."

Cardace massaged his shoulder, as if his muscles were aching. It struck me he probably kept up his training, even in prison. His strong, muscular form was in strange contrast to the weakness of his expression. He shifted on his chair and crossed his legs. Tancredi had taught me that this might be a symptom of lying, or of reluctance to speak. I made a note of it. Making notes almost always makes me feel a little ridiculous, as if I were striking a pose, trying to live up to a certain image. But I've often reread my notes and got some good ideas from them that hadn't even occurred to me as I was listening to somebody or reading something.

"Yes. I'd gone shooting with a friend in a quarry. A few days earlier, I don't know how many days."

"That's what you said in court. Nobody was able to question you because these were statements and you weren't examined. But if we want to make use of this fact at the appeal hearing we need something more. The ruling says there's absolutely no possibility of confirming this information, so it's completely irrelevant. They're not wrong."

"I don't know what else I could say."

"Well, for example, you could tell me right now who you went shooting with, who the gun belonged to, what kind of gun it was, where this quarry is, and then we'll decide what use to make of the information."

"The quarry is near Trani. The gun was a 7.65 calibre and it wasn't mine."

I took a deep breath to overcome my irritation. "Who did you go shooting with?"

He looked away, massaged his shoulder again and shook his head. "I don't want to say. He's a friend of mine. If I say who he is I'll get him in trouble."

"Look, Cardace, let's clarify a few simple concepts. I'm not the kind of lawyer who wants to know everything about his client's life. In fact, as far as I'm concerned, the less I know the better. Some things, though, are useful to know if a defence has any chance at all of succeeding. If things stay as they were at the original trial, if we don't bring in some new evidence that allows us to call seriously into question the narrative that's at the basis of the ruling, you can be sure they'll confirm that original verdict. Did you read the ruling?"

"Yes."

"Well, since you strike me as a bright young man" – *a bright young man?* Why the hell are you talking like that, Guerrieri? I thought in a flash – "you'll have realized that it's well thought out and persuasive. To attempt to attack a ruling like that we need something concrete, not vague tales without any indication of places, people or circumstances."

He was looking at me, again with the obtuse expression he'd had at the beginning of the interview. He shook his head in silence.

It occurred to me that this expression had been studied and practised at length, however unconsciously, just to make whoever he was speaking to feel nervous. Even when it wasn't a good idea to make the person he was speaking to feel nervous. The silence lasted a couple of minutes. Then I told myself that, for many reasons, now was not the time to insist. I'd be talking just to satisfy my bruised ego. Which made it a very bad idea. It's always a bad idea to satisfy your ego, and very bad when you have to convince somebody, especially if serious consequences may follow from whether or not you convince them. Knowing when to keep quiet is an essential talent. Few things so wrong-foot a person who's trying to provoke you as a neutral and therefore indecipherable silence. This type of silence sends a very clear message that the provocation hasn't succeeded.

Leaving at that moment was the most appropriate thing to do, even though keeping quiet cost me quite a bit of effort.

"It's up to you. In that case, we're done for today. We'll meet again in a few days, at the hearing."

As I imagined, he looked disoriented. "But what happens at the hearing? Does the trial start immediately?"

"No," I said, putting my papers back in my bag and getting to my feet. "I'll ask for an extension in order to evaluate the possibility of adding new grounds to the appeal drawn up by Costamagna's people, and above all to have more time to submit evidence. The possibility of our succeeding

77

in this depends on many factors. The main one is whatever information you have and can tell us."

I shook his hand and said goodbye.

It wasn't Smaldino who saw me out, back through corridors, bays, gates and bolts – he must have finished his shift. It was a tough-looking young officer with bulging muscles and a shark tattooed on his neck, just under his high tapered hair.

Lorenza

Verio came to pick me up with a friend of his I didn't know, a guy named Antonello, who succeeded in the not very easy enterprise of immediately striking me as irredeemably unpleasant.

The party was in a large apartment in an old block in the Corso Sonnino area. The host was a professor of theoretical philosophy, not especially well known for his contribution to the history of thought, but rather famous in the city for his affairs with female students with unquestionable physical virtues.

As Verio had promised, there were indeed a lot of people. They were all talking at the same time, producing a kind of low-level din. I knew almost nobody.

The apartment was full of books; they were everywhere, even in the bathroom and the kitchen. Our host was sitting in an armchair in a corner of the living room. On his knees was a girl equipped with a decidedly competitive chest; they were exchanging a joint of remarkable proportions. He was about fifty at the time – not much younger than my father.

In a room at the end of the corridor somebody was singing, somebody playing the guitar.

Verio and Antonello had immediately abandoned me, so I decided to grab something to eat and go and listen to the music. If I didn't find anyone – male or female – to make friends with within half an hour, I would leave. And I doubt anyone would have noticed.

The boy who was playing the guitar and the girl who was singing were on a sofa; around them, amid all the books, people were sitting on a rug on the ground or on chairs and stools. It was not the classic situation of an intimate party. It was more like a show, with two performers and an audience.

When I walked in they were doing Neil Young's "Harvest". The girl had a steady, slightly raucous voice; she came across as professional. She was looking at her hands and didn't get a single word wrong. She had long, elegant black eyelashes, very thick wavy hair and a face that had something old-fashioned about it, with a look in her eyes that was halfway between melancholy and arrogance.

I sat down on a stool at the back. When they finished, everyone clapped and the girl – not a young girl, she was older than me – thanked them with a couple of small bows. It was then that our eyes met. I thought – it's one of the things I remember most clearly – that I would like to get to know her and spend my life with her. Immediately afterwards it struck me that neither of these two things would happen, certainly not the latter, and that upset me.

Unaware, or maybe aware, of my torment, she whispered something to the guitarist. He nodded, retuned his guitar and started whistling – a structured, melodious whistle – the intro to "Heart of Gold". The girl sang and every now and again raised her eyes to me, cutting the air between us.

When they finished that, too, we clapped again; she again whispered something to the guitarist, he put down his guitar, and it was clear that the show was over.

Even before I could grasp what was happening, I saw her coming towards me.

"And who are you?"

"I sometimes wonder that myself," I replied, hoping I hadn't mistaken the tone. But there wasn't much choice. I could hardly state my particulars: I'm Guido Guerrieri, twenty-four years old (but almost twenty-five), a law graduate, a trainee prosecutor, I don't know what I'll do when I'm grown up and I don't even know if I want to grow up.

"Ah, a philosopher. Very good. Are you a student of our host?"

"You mean where girls are concerned?"

She laughed. "Why don't you go and get me a glass of wine?"

I stood up too quickly, went to get the wine (a whole bottle, just opened, so as not to be forced to interrupt the conversation again), and when I returned I found her on the sofa. She patted her hand on the cushion next to her, as you do with children or animals. I poured the wine and sat down obediently.

"I don't yet know your name."

"Guido."

"I had a boyfriend named Guido. He was quite forgettable. But maybe I shouldn't let that prejudice me."

"Guido's a cover name. I can't tell you my real name, it's classified."

"So you're witty too, *Guido.*"

I'd have liked to ask her what that "too" meant, but she didn't give me time.

"What do you do in life? Please don't tell me you're about to graduate with a thesis on the relationship between Kierkegaard and the philosophy of Jaspers, or something like that. I don't think I could bear it."

"I already graduated, with a thesis on criminal neglect. I think that's even less bearable. If you like, I can leave right now."

"Oh my God, are you a lawyer? How did you end up here?"

We continued chatting and drinking and smoking. We finished the bottle and grabbed another. Which is why from a certain point onwards my memories become vague. I couldn't testify with any reliability as to what I said and what she said. Partly because I was distracted by her proximity, her barely perceptible perfume, the contact established every now and again, apparently casually, between our bodies.

I do remember, though, that she laughed a lot and that I thought it was a laugh that spelled trouble, and that I *wanted* to get in trouble, as soon as possible.

After a while she looked at her watch, said she was late, that it was possible she was expected somewhere else.

Before I could reply she stood up, gave me a kiss on the lips, actually a lingering one, and left.

I didn't know what to do. I was already drunk and thought seriously that I should continue drinking. The party ended and somebody scooped me up from the sofa and took me home. Maybe Verio and Antonello, but I couldn't swear to it.

I spent a disturbed night, about which I'd rather not go into details. The following morning, I couldn't stand on my feet. I called the office and said I was ill and would have to stay home that day.

8

Judge Marinelli was not known as a great jurist, let alone a tireless worker.

He smoked a pipe. That was one of the few things that could be said about him with any certainty. He always had one in his hand as he wandered the corridors of the courthouse, and there was a rack full of them in his office, as if to avoid the risk of not being able to choose a different pipe for every smoke.

Pipe smoking and its rituals have never attracted me, but I must admit there was a pleasant smell of tobacco in the room. You just needed to be careful not to get too close to Marinelli, to avoid his breath.

When I put my head round his door he was sitting at his desk. Obviously with a pipe in his hand. He told me to come in. The way he acted, the way he spoke, the way he conducted hearings displayed all the superciliousness of someone who's convinced he is the legitimate holder of an absolute power but likes to show a magnanimous, almost sympathetic face. In all that he said, did and wrote – including his rulings – there was a hint of condescension. And so it was in a condescending tone that he motioned me to sit down in one of the two fake leather armchairs facing him.

As a start, I pretended to be interested in his pipes.

"There are always more of them," I said, just to say something.

"Have you seen the new one?" he said enthusiastically, as if talking about a newly born grandchild. He pointed to one in the middle of the rack. To me there was nothing remarkable about it, but he told me he'd gone all the way to London to buy it from a specialist shop. I smiled without making any comment. I didn't want to run the risk of letting him see what I really thought of someone who could make a journey from Bari to London just to purchase a pipe.

"So, Avvocato Guerrieri, tell me, what's the reason for your visit?"

"Before anything else, thank you for finding the time to see me."

He made a gesture of magnanimous, regal casualness.

"I'm here to talk about the Cardace appeal. The Gaglione murder. The hearing is in ten days' time, and there's a problem."

"What is it?"

"The defence at the original trial was entrusted to Avvocato Costamagna." I'd thought of saying "the late lamented Avvocato Costamagna", but I just couldn't do it. "The trial took place at a time when he was already in bad health and the effects of the illness were having an effect on his professional activities. I don't know if you've had time to read the ruling and the trial transcripts." I was almost certain he'd never even looked at the case file. His degree of attachment to his work was expressed in visual terms by his very tidy, very clear desk, without a single sheet of paper on it.

"I did glance at it," he replied evasively, "but I still have to examine everything carefully." Precisely. He was waiting for the summary from his associate judge at the beginning of the appeal hearing. He probably wouldn't even open the case file. "Have you been appointed by the accused?"

"Yes, Your Honour. I took the case only a few days ago, when the date for presenting new grounds for appeal and for submitting new evidence was already due." I leaned a little more towards him, across the desk, assuming a conspiratorial air. "May I speak very frankly, Your Honour?"

He frowned and now, in an equal and opposite movement, leaned towards me and looked me in the eyes. I imagine that to anyone watching we'd have looked like two characters in a farce. "Of course," he replied, nodding.

"When you do take a look at the proceedings, you'll realize that the quality of the defence accorded the accused, Signor Cardace, at the original trial didn't live up to the standards to which poor Avvocato Costamagna had accustomed us. In his last couple of years, he wasn't as clear-headed as he had been, and it's possible that not everything that could and should have been done was done. On this basis, as you can well imagine, I need a few days to prepare and, above all, to evaluate the possibility of formulating requests."

I paused, in case he wanted to cut in. He didn't. Basically, he just wanted to avoid problems.

"Obviously, I'd prefer not to make explicit or official what I've just told you about Avvocato Costamagna's difficulties in the last years of his work, and unfortunately of his life, but what we're talking about here is the requirement to safeguard the right to a defence. I repeat, I'd rather not go into details, let alone make these doubts public, but the problem does exist."

"So what would you like to do?"

"I'll do whichever of the various possible options you suggest, Your Honour. I can present you with a written request to extend the time limit, before the hearing; I can ask you for a simple prior adjournment of the hearing, which should also extend the time limit as under article 585, final paragraph; or else, if we want to avoid problems of notification, we can proceed with the hearing and, in the preliminary phase, I can ask you for an extension. I've come to ask you which of these solutions you find preferable, and I'll act accordingly."

Marinelli cleared his throat and turned his pipe around in his hands, looking at it pensively. "Avvocato Costamagna was a friend of mine," he said, "as well as a cousin of my wife's. I wouldn't want his professional memory to be tarnished by the revelation of any difficulties he may have had in the final part of his career and his life."

"I completely agree."

"So I'd rather your demands were satisfied without a pointless *strepitus fori.*"

"I have only two requirements, one of a more formal character – for the extension to be granted – and the other more substantial: I need the court to be flexible about the requests I'm going to make. Reading the file, you'll see that at the original trial the defence produced hardly any evidence that might have helped the accused and didn't even cross-examine the witnesses for the prosecution. Not to beat about the bush: in the appeal, I need to be able to do both these things which were completely neglected at the trial."

Marinelli put his pipe down on the leather folder he had in front of him, then again cleared his throat to give authority to what he was about to say and to emphasize that this was a kindly concession.

"Very well, Avvocato, here's what we'll do. Don't present any written requests. We'll see each other at the hearing, and at that point you'll ask for an extension of the time limit. We'll grant you a month. That'll give you time to formulate any additional grounds and your requests for submitting evidence. Which will be evaluated leniently."

"Thank you, Your Honour."

"They'll be evaluated leniently," Marinelli went on, "as long as you don't exaggerate, of course. This is still an appeal, not the original trial."

"Of course."

9

That evening, Annapaola and Tancredi and I went out for dinner together. Consuelo never joins us for these meetings outside office hours. She has a husband and a daughter and after work stays strictly with them.

We chose a restaurant called Il piede di porco.

The owner is a man named Orazio, a former specialist in robbing bank vaults and armoured cars. Orazio learned to cook – quite well – in prison, where he spent a number of years.

After having – as they say – paid his debt to society, he worked as a chef in various places around Italy. Then he returned to Bari and opened a restaurant of his own. He cooks the vegetables he grows in his own kitchen garden and the fish brought to him by his fishermen friends – some of whom are former colleagues from the old days. In spite of the name, no meat is eaten at Il piede di porco – The Pig's Trotter – on principle.

Tancredi once told me that robbers are the category of criminal with the highest reoffending rate. No sooner do they leave prison, even after long periods of detention, than they start all over again. They need the adrenaline that comes from dangerous acts; they rob for the pleasure of the sporting gesture, more even than for the money. Orazio seems to be an exception to the rule; to satisfy his need for adrenaline, he's taken up free climbing. It isn't clear, says Tancredi, if he deliberately replaced one thing with another, but from every indicator it appears that he's stayed clean.

However, his past being known to everyone, nobody ever dreams of asking him for money by way of protection, insurance, help to prisoners' families or anything like that. Let's put it like this: he's found a legal way to make use of his far from spotless track record.

The restaurant is situated over in Via Amendola, near the Mungivacca district. By the time I arrived, after an hour's walk, Tancredi and Annapaola were already there.

"So, how did your interviews go?" Tancredi asked.

"With Marinelli, fine. We agreed that we'd go to the hearing, and in the preliminary phase I'll make a request for an extension. He's promised me a month. It was pretty much as I figured: he doesn't want it to come out how badly Costamagna defended Cardace at the trial. I discovered Costamagna was actually a cousin of his wife's."

"And what about with your client?" Annapaola asked.

When she doesn't like the clients, they're *my* clients. In other cases, they're *ours*. I didn't respond to the provocation.

"So-so. My first impression was very bad. Then we talked and it improved."

"Yes, when we first meet a person," she said, "we always get a clear, irrational but reliable intuition of how they are. And then we think it over and everything gets mixed up."

"Damn, this is high-level stuff, worthy of a psychology textbook. I must write it down. Anyway, just to satisfy you, I will say that in the final part of our interview he turned into an arsehole again."

Having exhausted our skirmishing, we ate the raw seafood antipasto, which was very good, and then got back to the subject in hand.

"So, did the kid tell you anything useful?" Tancredi asked.

"Yes, it seems Gaglione worked as a nightclub bouncer. A few weeks before the murder, he beat up the wrong person outside a place called Chilometro Zero and was apparently very worried about reprisals. That's why he didn't go out much and was even thinking of getting away from Bari for a while."

"This is a serious lead, if it's true. Who did he beat up?"

"Cardace says he doesn't know. I got the impression he was telling the truth."

"This didn't come out at the trial," Annapaola said.

"Costamagna advised him not to mention it. Too vague. It wouldn't have helped in court. And on the other hand it might have alarmed these dangerous individuals, or worse. People involved with organized crime, that's what Cardace understood from what Gaglione told him. The argument makes sense."

"Anyway, it'd be good to check it out," Annapaola said.

"Yes. We need to know if the fight really happened. And if it did, who was involved. Maybe somebody ended up in Emergency, which means there'd be a record. I don't think it'll be easy, but if we can prove that Gaglione got in a fight with somebody dangerous, there'd be a glimmer of hope we could suggest an alternative to the narrative that's in the ruling." I turned to Tancredi. "Have you talked to your former Flying Squad colleagues?"

He placed the shell of the last oyster on his plate and heaved a sigh before answering. As if it was a burden to go from that sublime taste to trivial matters of work.

"I went to Headquarters today. The boys in Homicide and Narcotics are totally convinced it was Cardace. Without knowing about the fight in the disco, I asked them if as far as they knew Gaglione had been having problems with any-body, but there was nothing like that. So, if this fight did happen, they never knew about it. They told me everyone knew Gaglione was dealing Ecstasy and cocaine. The inves-tigation that involved them tapping his phones was aimed specifically at him – they're weren't keeping an eye on him to get to anybody else. In fact, after the murder they stopped the intercepts and the case was closed."

"The fact that the Squad didn't know if Gaglione was having problems with anyone," Annapaola said, "doesn't mean he wasn't."

"No, of course," Carmelo said, "it doesn't mean he wasn't. Normally, if a member of an important family is involved in a fight and somebody actually takes the liberty of beating him up, the news gets around. But obviously that's not an absolute rule. So let's find out who provides, or provided, security at Chilometro Zero and have a chat with them. Although these guys aren't usually especially cooperative."

"Now that I come to think of it," Annapaola said, "I know a disc jockey from Chilometro Zero."

"Do they still put on discs?" I asked, foolishly. "Don't they just select tracks on a computer?"

"You're elderly, Guerrieri. You shouldn't say anything about these subjects. Vinyl evenings are going great guns, old-style DJs are making a comeback. Maybe you remem-ber – even you were a kid once. If they do an eighties night, or even a seventies night, I'll take you."

Orazio appeared with three portions of spaghetti in par-cels and told Annapaola he liked beautiful women who didn't make a fuss when confronted with a little pasta.

"I also like beautiful women who love to eat," she replied with a broad smile. "I like them a lot."

I assumed Orazio didn't grasp the full meaning of the words, or the smile (Annapaola isn't exclusively attracted to the male of the species). He put the plates down in front of us and walked away. We opened the parcels and waited for the three-thousand-degree heat inside to die down.

"All right," Tancredi said, picking up his fork. "I'll talk to someone in security, and you, Annapaola, question your DJ friend. Let's see if anyone mentions this supposed fight."

For a few minutes, we devoted ourselves to Orazio's special recipe. Spaghetti with seafood, cooked in the oven in parcels with the addition of coriander and a special chilli unsuitable for delicate palates.

"We also have to track down the guy Cardace had a coffee with," I said. "He said his name is Sabino, that he's more or less the same age as him and that he thinks he works in a garage."

"What's the point?" Annapaola said. "What's so special about the fact that they met? The police didn't even look for him."

"Yes, but if he could give us some indication of the time they met," I said, "and confirm what Cardace says, it might be useful to us to maintain that Cardace was in the cafe *after* seeing Gaglione. Not *before*, which is what's in the ruling."

"We'll see if we can find him, sure. But in my opinion you're overestimating how much you can use any testimony he might give. Let's suppose he testifies and confirms the meeting, what's to stop the court maintaining that Cardace went back to Gaglione's place after this meeting and killed him then?"

Annoyingly, she was right. I replied that we'd deal with that if and when we found Sabino, and if and when Sabino agreed to testify.

"Then I need to figure out the business of the shooting practice and the powder found on the jacket," I said, eliminating the final vestige of food from Orazio's parcel. "How long can it stay on? Do we need to talk to somebody in Forensics or with a pathologist?"

"There's no need," Carmelo replied. "I can tell you. The powder from a gunshot stays on leather for a few hours, but can stay on fabrics for several days. So in theory, things could actually be the way the kid says. But did he tell you who he went shooting with?"

"No. He keeps saying he doesn't want to get his friend into trouble."

"Or maybe he simply made him up to explain the residue on the jacket," Annapaola commented. "If he doesn't tell us who he went shooting with, we can't do anything with this information."

"Actually, the problems remain even if he does tell us. We'd have to ask this person, whoever he is, to accuse himself of unauthorized possession and carrying of a firearm. Do you think anyone would do that?"

"Anyway," Tancredi said, "Cardace has to tell us something more about this phantom guy in the quarry. Then we'll figure out how to use the information."

"Agreed. I'll go and see him again in the next few days."

"Let's go together," Annapaola said. "We can play good cop, bad cop. It may work."

Orazio approached the table and asked us if we wanted a nice *frittura mista*. It was ten in the evening and a *frittura mista* struck us as something that would finish us off, so all three of us declined.

"Not even a portion to share, just a taster?"

"We'll have it next time, when we come for lunch," Tancredi said. "This beautiful girl is young and might be able to indulge herself, but Avvocato Guerrieri and I are both elderly gentlemen, and our doctors advise moderation."

This didn't strike me as amusing. I had to repress the impulse to point out that he was almost ten years older than me. I was even tempted to take a nice dish of *frittura mista* away with me – I'd eat it all by myself, just to show that I could.

"Yes, Orazio," Annapaola cut in. "I brought my old uncles to dinner with me, but we mustn't overdo it. One evening I'll come with my young girlfriends and we'll have whatever you suggest. For now, bring us some wild fennel liqueur and we'll finish up."

Orazio did an elegant about-turn and went to fetch the bottle. The fact that he would serve us himself was a mark of great consideration. There were actually several waiters moving around the restaurant. At least some of them, to judge by their faces, looked like they'd been with Orazio in his previous life, too.

"Anyway," Annapaola resumed, "you may be interested to know that I went for a little stroll near Gaglione's apartment. Former apartment, I should say. Anyway, I went over there, asked a few questions in the vicinity, and even went inside the building, where I discovered something that doesn't appear in the case file."

"What's that?" I asked.

"He lived on the mezzanine. The apartment doesn't face the street but has a window and a balcony overlooking the courtyard, which you can gain access to through a little gate at the far end of the entrance hall. The gate was open when I was there. If someone had come in that way, it wouldn't have been too difficult to surprise Gaglione. The prosecution case was that the killer came in through the front door. And if he did, then the argument that the victim knew him would be correct. But what if the killer, or killers, had come in from behind, from the courtyard?"

"I have to reread the papers to see if anyone thought of that. If they didn't, that's another thing we can try to bring up in court. Are there any security cameras in the area?"

"I didn't see any. There might be some that I didn't notice. I don't think there are any in the block where Gaglione's apartment is, but, I repeat, I might have missed them."

"Anyway," Tancredi said, "the prosecutor at the original trial was good."

"Cotturri," I said. "I've never been in a major trial with him, but he strikes me as a sound person."

"He is. He arrived in Bari just as I was retiring, but my former colleagues are keen on him. He puts them at their ease, makes them feel their backs are covered. Not that he lets them do whatever they like. But he's someone who does his job properly."

I sighed. Another piece of news that wasn't positive for us. If the assistant prosecutor who had been all through the investigation and the trial was so good, that reduced the likelihood that there were any significant gaps in the prosecution case.

Soon afterwards, having finished the fennel liqueur, we said goodbye to Orazio and left the restaurant. The air was mild, already almost springlike.

"Anybody want a lift?" Tancredi said.

"I have my bike," Annapaola replied. "Guerrieri came on foot because he's keeping fit. I'll take him home."

Tancredi looked at us in turn. He nodded, said all right, goodnight, and set off for his car.

"Was I brazen, Avvocato?" Annapaola said, with her most dangerous of smiles, when we were alone.

"You couldn't be brazen even if you tried. You're beyond brazenness."

"Then will you invite me over to your place for a drink, Uncle?"

"I'm elderly, you said. Or so I thought."

"You are elderly, but you're in good shape. As far as I recall, you keep fit. Are we going to start arguing about it, or shall we go?"

"Let's go," I said, taking the helmet she handed me and thinking that she was still having the same effect on me after several years. A rare stroke of luck.

Lorenza

Two days went by. My hangover had been quite bothersome, but it had passed. I kept wondering how to track down the girl from the party, but couldn't think of a satisfactory way. The one possibility was to contact Verio, but I didn't have his telephone number and didn't even know where he lived. In any case, with all the people who'd been crammed into the professor's apartment, it was likely that even Verio didn't know her.

I have the distinct memory that my boss – the lawyer I was a trainee with – had given me the task that afternoon of writing an appeal against a sentence for repeated aggravated theft. The verdict struck me as indisputable. The defendant was definitely guilty of a series of raids on apartments in the centre of town and the magistrate had given him three years, which I actually thought was too lenient.

So I did the task I'd been instructed to do, I wrote the appeal, but I can honestly state, thirty years later, that I didn't believe a single word. By the time I left the office I was very dissatisfied, and quite unconvinced – even more than usual – that I'd made the right choice in becoming a lawyer, which meant I was very worried about what the future had in store with me.

I had gone a few yards when I heard a strangely familiar female voice call to me.

"Avvocato Guido!"

She crossed the street, came up to me and gave me a kiss, all in a totally natural way.

"I came to get you because I wanted to invite you to dinner."

"Dinner?"

"Yes. It's something people do around here in the evening. You get given food and you eat it, something like that."

"Did I tell you where I work the other night?"

"You have no idea how many things you said. But not where you work."

"So how did you find me?"

"I have my methods. Enough of that now, or I'll get bored. And if I get bored, I'll withdraw the invitation and leave you to spend a sad, lonely evening regretting what might have been."

"No, no regrets. Never. Where shall we go?"

"I fancy a pizza. With that one premise, I'll leave you to choose the place."

I suggested a pizzeria near the prison, where they were in the habit – impeccable from a fiscal point of view – of writing the bill by hand on the paper tablecloth; a printed receipt was an arcane concept as far as they were concerned. But the pizzas were good and very cheap. She knew the place and approved of my choice.

"I have a car. But what kind of lawyer are you, without even a briefcase?"

"Technically I'm not a lawyer, I'm a trainee prosecutor and, between ourselves, it's not at all certain that I'm going to become a lawyer. Anyway, I do have a briefcase, a rather nice one, that I was given when I graduated. I use it when I go to the courthouse in the morning."

We reached her car, a cream-coloured Alfasud somewhat past its prime, parked a hundred yards from my office.

As we set off I realized I didn't know what her name was. Maybe she'd told me and I'd been so drunk by then that it hadn't registered. To avoid making a gaffe, I decided to proceed with caution and guile.

"You know, I don't have a very clear memory of all the things I said to you the other night."

She gave a quick laugh. "I don't think you remember *anything* you said the other night."

"Was I … indiscreet?"

"That's what I find adorable about you. I mean, the way you express yourself. Obviously it's something to do with the circles you mix in, but there's a touch of irony I find irresistible."

"I'm pleased you find it irresistible, but just to put ourselves on an equal footing, could you give me a summary of the most … let's say, the most embarrassing things I told you?"

"What's my name?"

"I'm sorry?"

"My name. What's my name?"

There it was. She had me.

"Actually, I was just thinking… Yes, I know, I'm making a fool of myself, but I'm sorry, I can't remember…"

"I didn't tell you. And to tell the truth you didn't ask me. But it was an amusing chat, you made me laugh a lot. That's such an unusual thing that I thought: let's see if he makes me laugh even when he isn't drunk, this young lawyer Guido. Or if it's just down to the wine."

Before telling me her name and providing me with a bit more information about herself, she waited until we were sitting over the double-purpose (service and bill) paper tablecloth. Her name was Lorenza, she'd graduated in Letters with a thesis on classical philology, she was a substitute high-school teacher, gave private lessons in Latin and Greek, wrote short stories for literary magazines, and also worked as a freelance editor for a number of publishers.

"I'm a country boy, so I hope you'll excuse the question, but what does a freelance editor do?"

She ate a triangle of four seasons pizza and took a sip of her beer. "The publisher hands me the manuscript the author has sent. I read it and identify the inconsistencies, the repetitions, the faux pas, any actual errors. I mark everything in the margin, the manuscript is sent back to the author with my annotations, and he or she decides which to accept and which to reject. After which the book is put into proof form, the proofs are corrected and the book is finally printed."

We continued talking about what she did – there were points about which she was rather evasive and I didn't insist – and about lots of other things. It occurred to me that I'd never met a girl – a woman, actually – who was simultaneously so beautiful, so fascinating and so funny. The fact that such an exceptional woman was here with me, having dinner and chatting away, and that she'd actually been the one who'd come looking for me, was a mystery I preferred not to delve too deeply into.

When we left the pizzeria she asked me if I fancied another beer, at her place. I searched for an answer that was brilliant but not too brilliant, and couldn't think of one. So I just said yes, of course, I'd love a beer.

She parked on Corso Italia, almost on the corner of Via Sagarriga Visconti. It wasn't, at the time, the ideal area for a woman alone.

"Where do you live?" I asked, getting out of the car.

"Via Eritrea."

I didn't know Via Eritrea, even though we weren't far from where I lived. I discovered it was the name of the little street going from Corso Italia to Via Crisanzio. One of those places that, as a child, I thought was inhabited only by dangerous people.

"I live near the Casa delle Rose."

"The Casa delle Rose?" I had no idea what that was.

"The Casa delle Rose was the most luxurious brothel in Bari until 1958. Then they passed the Merlin Law and the brothels were closed."

"How do you know? I mean that it was the most luxurious brothel in Bari."

"I was choosing where to live and I had a couple of options, both in the area. I told my parents. My father said it was best to avoid Via Eritrea. I asked why and he explained. At that point it became obvious I had to choose this apartment."

"But why didn't your father want you to?"

"He was afraid the reputation of the place might rub off on his daughter, even though it was more than thirty years ago and nobody remembers it."

We went in. It was a small but attractive apartment. She quickly showed me around. You went straight into a living room filled with shelves, lots of books and a table with a Lettera 32 typewriter in the middle; on either side of the typewriter, two reams of extra-strong paper: blank pages on one side, on the other, pages already written on and placed face down.

In the only other room, a bed with a brightly coloured Peruvian blanket.

The apartment was tidy, but not obsessively so, there was a nice smell in the air, and yet – I know I run the risk of applying to the memory a judgement I only formed later – there was something I couldn't quite put my finger on, something that produced a kind of dissonance. As if the place wasn't really inhabited. Used, but not inhabited. I don't know what it was, I'm not capable of saying what produced that feeling in me, nor can I say for sure that I actually had it at that moment. The fact remains that my memory of the episode is associated with a subtle but tangible unease. Almost a sense of latent danger.

"Do you mind if we don't waste time playing at being polite and have the beer and a cigarette later?"

"I've never been polite," was all I managed to say.

Later, she asked me if I wanted a lift home.

"Thank you, I'll walk, I don't live far."

"Then I'm going to sleep," she said, turning over in bed. "It's been a rough day, and I'm very tired."

She might already have been asleep by the time I closed the door behind me.

10

I went back to the prison, this time with Annapaola.

When they brought Cardace into the lawyers' room she was leaning against the window. She didn't move, either to say hello or to introduce herself. Cardace looked around, nodded at me and came and sat down opposite me. Only at that point did Annapaola take her place at the table, next to Cardace.

"Are you a lawyer too?" he asked, hesitantly. He wasn't sure who he was talking to.

"Do I look like a lawyer?" Annapaola replied before I could intervene.

"No."

"Actually I'm not a lawyer." It was an apparently neutral phrase, but it had been uttered in an obvious tone of menace. Cardace looked at me, ever more perplexed.

"Signorina Doria is a private investigator. She's going to help us find some new evidence we can present at the appeal hearing."

"Actually, our idea is that you help us find something to help you."

"What can I tell you? I —" Iacopo said. He was about to continue, but Annapaola interrupted him.

"There are two things you *have* to tell us. One: who you went shooting with in the quarry, if you really did go there. Two: when the fight at Chilometro Zero took place, provided that story isn't more bullshit, and who the people involved were. I'm not asking you for my own pleasure. If you want us to try and help you, this is information we need. So don't play games."

"I'm not playing games. All Gaglione told me was that he'd beaten up a guy who belonged to a powerful family. I asked him what family and he wouldn't tell me. When someone doesn't want to tell you a thing like that, you don't insist. And anyway, he didn't seem worried that somebody might want to kill him. He seemed worried that somebody wanted to harm him, beat him up, not shoot him."

"How do you know that?"

"That he didn't think they wanted to kill him? I don't know. When we talked I didn't get the feeling he was afraid of being killed. He was nervous, not terrified, if you know what I mean. He half intended to leave Bari for a few days, to wait for things to calm down. Maybe he wanted to try and get in touch with these people to clear things up and apologize."

"Is that what he told you?"

"He said he was thinking of going away for a few days. That he was thinking of trying to explain things to these people. No, that's what I assumed, but only because of everything he said. I don't remember exactly what —"

"And you don't know who *these people* are?"

"No."

"When did the fight take place?"

"I don't know that either. A few weeks before the murder, maybe."

Again I had the feeling he was telling the truth about this. Annapaola must have had the same impression as me.

"All right. Let's assume things are the way you say. Gaglione tells you about this problem he's got with some dangerous people, he doesn't go into detail and you don't ask him. But the name of the guy you went shooting with in that quarry – that's something you have to tell us. Now."

"I can't tell you a fucking thing. It would be —"

He didn't finish the sentence. The blow, a very fast one that came from nowhere and was practically unstoppable, caught him on his left cheek. It produced a noise like a sink being unblocked – in a comic book, they would have put a balloon with SPLAT in bold type. In other words, it was a strong, sudden, loud slap. Cardace was stunned. The last thing he would have expected was being slapped in the lawyers' room of the prison, by a woman, in front of his own counsel. The only thought that went through my head was that if a prison officer had come in just then, we would have been in trouble. That didn't seem to bother Annapaola.

"Listen to me, arsehole, and listen good. I don't know if you killed your friend Gaglione. I don't know and I prefer not to know. If I still have a doubt, maybe I can continue to work on this case. But you need to get one thing clear: we're your only hope. Read my lips: we're your only hope. If the gentleman you have in front of you," she said, pointing at me with a gesture I would normally have considered somewhat theatrical but which now seemed perfectly appropriate to the situation, "shows up in court without anything to show, for you it'll be like going in front of a firing squad. Obviously, if you killed Gaglione, and don't have the guts to admit it but want to atone for your crime, well, then you've made the right choice: you'll have all the atonement you want. If you want to make an appointment outside this place, consider dates after 2030."

Cardace had turned serious. He looked alert now. It was as if the slap had aroused him from his lethargy. Maybe it really had.

"Smoking's not allowed in here," he said incongruously, after a sigh. His face was two different colours: pale on one side, bright red on the other.

"Do you have cigarettes?" she asked him.

"I quit."

"I roll them. If you like, I can make two and we'll stand by the window."

He nodded. Annapaola took out tobacco and papers and prepared the cigarettes with rapid gestures, like a conjuror. They stood up, went to the window, opened it and smoked together, in silence, for a couple of minutes. It was Cardace who spoke first.

"If I tell you who the person is, I'll get him in trouble. The gun even has the serial number rubbed away. Plus, we did … *things* together."

"We're not the police, we're not magistrates, we don't have to put anything in writing and we don't have to report to anyone. You tell us, and we'll decide, together with you, what to do with the information, in case it's useful to your defence."

He didn't raise any further objections. They came back and sat down again and Iacopo told us who the gun belonged to – a petty criminal like him, one Giovanni Cipriani – where they had gone shooting and what things they had done together, he and Cipriani. Armed robberies. Mostly of pharmacies and supermarkets.

God knows if Lorenza had imagined any of this, I wondered.

"When you and Cipriani went shooting at the quarry, did you leave the cartridges there?" I asked him.

"No. We collected them so there was no trace left and also because he took them to someone who has the equipment to recharge and reuse them."

"Was Cipriani ever arrested?"

"No. I don't think so. Not while I was still free. I don't know if since then … but no, I would have known. They would have brought him here."

"Were you ever stopped together?"

"How do you mean?"

"Did the police or the carabinieri ever stop the two of you when you were together? Even just to check your papers when you were in the car?"

He shook his head. "No. But what difference would that make?"

"If there was a police report in which you appeared together we could get hold of it and use it to pull in Cipriani without you being the one to tell us his name. Well, it was an idea. Were there others involved in the things you did together? The robberies, I mean."

"No."

"Or anybody who went shooting with you?"

"We always went alone."

"When did you last see Cipriani?"

"When we went shooting, a few days before Gaglione was murdered."

"What does Cipriani do for a living, apart from the robberies of course?"

"He's enrolled at the university, although he hasn't done any exams for ages."

A pleasant couple, I thought. Your parents' pride and joy.

"You haven't forgotten anything that might be useful to us?" Annapaola asked.

"No. I don't think so…" He hesitated a few seconds, then added: "Maybe one thing. I don't know if it's important, but when I had coffee with Sabino I gave him a couple of the pills I'd been given by Gaglione."

"Did you tell this to the other lawyer?"

"No."

"Why not?"

"Apart from the fact that it only just occurred to me, he kept saying that I had to keep quiet, talk as little as possible. That the more defendants say, the worse they make things for themselves."

"All right," Annapaola said, putting her cigarette end in a piece of paper which she then carefully screwed up and threw in the waste basket.

"What are you going to do now?" Iacopo asked, again looking at me.

"I don't know. We have to think about what you've told us. Of course, we won't make any use of it without first agreeing it with you." I became aware that my tone was a lot friendlier now. "In any case, what's for sure is that at the appeal hearing you'll have to go on the stand and be examined, not just make statements. In other words, I'll question you and then the prosecution will cross-examine you. We'll have to prepare for that. We'll decide together what to say and what not to say."

Ten minutes later we were outside the prison.

"Will you ride in front?" Annapaola said, almost chirpily, when we got to the motorbike.

"The next time you decide to beat up one of my clients," I replied, "I'd appreciate it if you let me know in advance."

"Come on, don't be so serious. We played good cop, bad cop. Nobody got hurt and now we know more than we did. You should be pleased."

"It'd be interesting to hear Cardace's opinion of the statement 'nobody got hurt'. In any case, *you* played both the good cop and the bad cop. You kindly allowed me to watch your little number. By the way: thank you."

"It was just a slap, it saved us a lot of time."

I looked for something biting to say in reply, but couldn't think of anything.

"What do we do now, boss?" she said, with the most fake air of submissiveness I'd ever seen in my life.

"I thought you'd taken command of operations. I assume you'd also like to decide on the defence strategy. Maybe you can go to court instead of me and, if the need arises, give the assistant prosecutor a slap, too. Or maybe the judge."

"Yes, that'd be fun, wouldn't it?"

"Anyway, I don't know what we're doing. Let's see if we can track down this Cipriani, though, frankly, I don't see how we'd be able to persuade him to come to court and testify. He'd have to accuse himself at the very least of the unauthorized possession and carrying of a gun with its serial number rubbed away. Even supposing – which is completely unrealistic – that he agrees to talk to us, owns up to what he did and comes to tell all in court, after he'd said just a couple of words the court would have to cut the testimony short, according to article 63 of the code."

"Sorry, boss, remind me of article 63."

"If before a legal authority a person other than the accused or a suspect makes statements which indicate criminality on his part, the aforesaid authority interrupts the examination, informs him that as a result of such statements he himself may be investigated and encourages him to appoint a defence counsel."

"Oh, that rule."

"Yes, that rule."

"Okay. Let's face one problem at a time. In the meantime, let's see if we can find out who he is, what's become of him, etc. Who knows? If we're lucky, he might even have been arrested for possession of that gun. That would simplify things a bit."

"Yes, it'd be a real stroke of luck. So it's bound not to happen. I've never had a stroke of luck like that. And anyway, no."

"No, what?"

"I don't want to ride in front. The bike makes me nervous in town. And sometimes not just the bike."

11

I had been asked to give a talk to young trainee magistrates. Their official title is "ordinary magistrates in apprenticeship". When I was young, they were known by a term that's rather archaic but that I liked: "legal auditors". Obviously, this nostalgic observation is an unmistakable symptom of galloping senility.

The title of the lecture was "Verification of the facts and function of the defence in criminal proceedings". The morning they called me from the offices of the appeal court to tell me about it and ask if I was available, I was surprised and even quite flattered: it was some kind of recognition, I thought. Immediately afterwards, though, the thought hit me that they were calling me because, having passed the age of fifty, I was classified as a *senior lawyer*, and it's the seniors who usually get assigned such tasks. At this point, I stopped thinking, which is often a good idea.

In my odd moments of free time, though, I had pondered how to transform a vague title into the starting point for a talk of an hour or slightly more about something worthwhile.

I arrived a few minutes early and, outside the lecture hall where the talk was due to take place, I discovered that one of the magistrates in charge of coordinating the traineeships of these young people, and the person who would introduce me, was Cotturri. That is, the assistant prosecutor who had supervised the Cardace investigation and handled the prosecution in his original trial. He was a man of about forty – I find it a little disturbing that these days courtroom prosecutors are all younger than me – intelligent-looking, slightly overweight, smartly dressed. We had met a few times in court, but always for minor cases.

Once we'd greeted each other, it was he, to my surprise, who brought up the subject.

"I hear you've taken on the Cardace appeal."

I was about to ask him how he knew, until it struck me as a really stupid question to ask an assistant prosecutor.

"He wasn't very well defended at his trial," he went on.

"I'm afraid he wasn't," I agreed cautiously. "Costamagna wasn't well, he didn't have the clarity and edge he used to have."

"I have to tell you, I kept wondering about that all through the trial. Nobody doing my job feels very comfortable when the defence, for one reason or another, is inadequate. I always feel better if the accused has a good lawyer who's doing their job well." Then he thought for a moment about what he'd just said and gave a slight smile. "Okay, not everyone who does my job thinks like that. Some of us – how can I put this? – some of us like an easy victory."

"You'll think I'm asking a stupid question if I ask you your opinion on Cardace's guilt."

"No. There are times when you obtain a guilty verdict because the evidence against the accused is sufficient, in some cases technically unassailable, and yet have doubts yourself. Moral doubts, I mean. Not technical doubts. Those are the most unpleasant situations, but it wasn't the case with the Cardace trial."

"So you're totally convinced of his guilt?"

"Yes, but all the same it bothered me that he was so badly defended. Actually, I'm pleased you've agreed to handle his appeal. I don't envy you, though. If he wasn't guilty of the murder, and I can't imagine how that could even be possible, it'd be such an unfortunate combination of circumstances, it gives me the shivers."

I sighed. It had been kind of him to discuss the subject with me. But after those words, there wasn't much else to add.

The young magistrates I was supposed to be giving the talk to had arrived, so we went in. Cotturri gave a brief introduction, and while he was speaking I had a look at my audience.

They were all about thirty. The men in jackets and ties, the women dressed more freely, some of them pretty. Seen individually, they would have looked like what they were, that is, young adults. Seen all together, they looked like people suspended between being students, almost still adolescents in a way, and what they would soon become as magistrates. Judges and prosecutors, holders of the greatest (legal) power there is. I've sometimes asked myself what I would have been like if instead of becoming a defence lawyer I had chosen the magistrature. I've never come up with an answer. Some magistrates are like Cotturri, they have an awareness – and are able to preserve it through all the daily grind of their profession – of how inconceivable, even shocking, it is that a man can decide on the freedom and the destiny of another man. They treat this power with the necessary circumspection and a healthy dose of scepticism, especially towards themselves. Others don't. Everything becomes routine, people become files and papers, and in all this there's an element of terrible brutality, even if it's involuntary. I don't want to be moralistic about it. Of course, it's much easier to have an awareness of the people who are behind or beneath the paperwork if you're in defence. If you're a magistrate, though, and every day you're submerged by cases, arrests, trials to be handled and deadlines to be met, it's possible – and it's almost a question of psychological survival – that you forget the fragility of the material you're dealing with.

I was so absorbed in these ruminations that I almost gave a start when Cotturri handed over to me. I took a last glance at my notes, took a deep breath and began.

"The title of our talk may suggest a discussion of the investigations carried out by the defence. Let me clarify immediately that I won't be saying a word about investigations carried out by the defence. I'm going to talk about things that at first may strike you as off-topic. I'll ask you to suspend judgement until the end of this hour, or a little more, that we'll be spending together, when you'll be able to give an overall assessment.

"The law, the legal process – the criminal process in particular – are instruments put in place to regulate conflicts, and as such have to deal with the complexity of reality. In the complex reality we're obliged to confront, there are multiple points of view and reasons are almost always distributed, even if unequally, among the various protagonists of a relationship or a disagreement.

"A great mathematician, Stefan Banach, once said that good mathematicians are capable of grasping analogies. The same goes for jurists. A good jurist, too, is capable of grasping analogies, and to do so, naturally, it's vital in the first place that they possess the technical know-how.

"But that's not enough. To become aware of analogies a jurist cannot be content with the rules of the discipline within which they work. It's necessary to learn to observe these rules from the outside, in such a way as to grasp their nature and their limitations with the right degree of detachment.

"A jurist must – I emphasize *must* – devote a sizeable part of their time to things that to all appearances have nothing to do with the law: reading good novels, watching good films, even good television. In short, they must take nourishment from good stories.

"Why *must?* you could legitimately ask. Because it's the art of the storyteller that reminds us that there is not just one single answer to human dilemmas. These dilemmas are inevitably ambiguous. The characters in good novels and good films represent various points of view about reality. Think of a brilliant work like *Rashomon*, where a story that might appear very simple becomes, in the accounts of the four protagonists, a plurality of stories that are actually incompatible with one another. Or think of that passage from *The Brothers Karamazov* where Ivan asks his brother Alyosha if he would be willing to torture a little girl to guarantee the happiness of the whole human race."

I paused, to try to read in their faces the effect – if there was one – of what I was saying. They seemed attentive, although with different shades. Some looked sceptical – young magistrates often have very little sympathy for defence lawyers – and others curious. One young woman, more than all of them, attracted my attention for a few moments. She wasn't beautiful, but had intense, slightly stern grey eyes.

"Now I want to propose a dilemma in the form of a hypothetical story. Imagine the undercarriage of a train engine that's come loose and is hurtling out of control along a railway track to which five people have been tied. If the undercarriage reaches them they'll all be killed. Imagine you're on the spot and you can pull a lever that'll divert the undercarriage onto another track where just one person is tied. What would you do?"

They hadn't been expecting a question. After some hesitation, two or three replied that they would pull the lever.

"You're in good company. The vast majority of those who are asked the question answer that way. It's better for one person to die rather than five. Correct?"

Some nodded, others were puzzled, almost suspicious of falling into a trap. Decidedly, though, I now had their attention.

"Now imagine another situation. You find yourselves on a bridge beneath which the track with the out-of-control undercarriage passes. The five people are still tied to the track. With you on the bridge is a very fat man. If you throw him over, his body will bring the undercarriage to a halt. So, as in the first example, one will die and five will be saved. What do you do this time? Do you send the fat man to his death?"

For a few moments there was silence. Then the young woman with grey eyes spoke up. She had a low, slightly nasal voice, with a light but pleasant touch of accent. Undeniably, she was from Bari.

"Conceptually, it appears the same. But instinctively, I feel like saying no. There's something not right about this second example."

"You're right, conceptually it's the same thing: from a utilitarian point of view, it's a lesser evil if only one person dies and five are saved. In your opinion, why is there something not right in this example?"

"You would have to physically push the fat man."

"Of course, and that's unpleasant. But from the point of

view of ethical algebra it doesn't change anything. Okay, let's introduce a variant that eliminates this factor of psychological disturbance, that is, the idea of entering into physical contact with the person who will have to die. Imagine that there's a trapdoor and you can activate it with a lever, so that the man will fall onto the track without your having to touch him. What do you do? Do you activate the trapdoor?"

The young woman slowly shook her head. "No, I don't think so."

"Why not?"

She took a deep breath and half closed her eyes, like a short-sighted person trying to focus on an object in the distance. "Maybe the two cases aren't as similar as it seems. There's a subjective element, an element of intent. In the first example, we don't want the death of the single man on the track. In the second we actually want to kill the fat man, even though it's for a good cause. In both examples there would be a feeling of necessity, I think. But the second one produces what we could call a moral unease."

"Very good, yes. We could add that in the first example the death of the single man isn't even necessary to save the other five; he'll probably die, that's true, but in theory he could manage to get loose and run away, and in that case all six would be saved. In the second example, the fat man's death is necessary to our purpose. If after falling, after we'd made him fall, he managed to roll away, the five we wanted to save would die.

"So to save the others we have to want to kill an innocent man. That's the reason the majority of people who are asked the question, though they can't explain why, as you did, say they feel instinctively that this would be a bad act."

*

117

The young woman pursed her lips and made the kind of face made by someone who's pleased with a success or a compliment but doesn't want to show it.

I looked away from her and let my gaze wander over the faces of those young people. For many of them, I thought, becoming a magistrate was the culmination of a process – and a dream – that had begun on the first day of university and ended with their exams. I remembered my old friend and classmate Andrea Colaianni. He had studied law with passion and determination. His aim was to become a magistrate and change the world. You could say he got halfway to achieving it: he had graduated with flying colours, but had soon discovered that changing the world is, in the best of cases, an unintended consequence of our actions.

I had never had that passion. I hadn't had a dream which had reached its culmination. I had become a lawyer by chance, or at least so I've always told myself. Though some people say there's no such thing as chance and that we use the word to indicate something else we can't identify or don't want to understand.

Be that as it may, I had never had the privilege of imagining that my future lay in this profession. In fact, I had always thought of it as temporary. Sooner or later, I would find something I really identified with.

Somebody once told me that the most beautiful things to remember are the dreams you had as a child, especially if you've realized them, at least partly. They echo with the poignant note of the past and possess the indistinct excitement of the future.

The problem was that I hadn't allowed myself to cultivate the dreams I would have liked: to study the things I felt passionate about, to write, to produce ideas. Out of fear, I had decided that these were dangerous illusions. So I had forbidden myself to cultivate them. The adult world doesn't allow for enthusiasms: that had been my confused, childish thought as I faced life.

I resumed speaking.

"Legal conflicts often reflect moral dilemmas, the juxtaposition of different ways of seeing values and their hierarchy. And we mustn't forget that visions of the world change very quickly. Two centuries ago, or even less, the vast majority of people in the West (normal people, often decent, honest people) believed that inequality between blacks and whites, men and women was just and moral. They believed it was just that they should have different rights. They believed homosexuality was a disease or a crime. Obviously the list could be extended, to include for example the rights of children, the very awareness of children as human beings with rights of their own.

"Have you ever wondered which of our current moral beliefs will be rejected or even seem grotesque to future generations?

"Do rights come from nature? If they do, how can we know that a certain right exists and what its characteristics are? Thomas Hobbes defined natural laws as those that have been laws since time immemorial. Unfortunately, there are no laws of this kind.

"Nature is morally neutral. It consists of wonderful things and horrible things. It makes no distinction between right and wrong. In nature there are no rewards or punishments, only consequences.

"Think for example of the family, a category that's often invoked – often in bad faith – by some inept supporters of the existence of natural rights. Think of how the family was regulated in our system before the reform of 1975. It was a family founded on the subordination of the wife to her husband in personal relations, in property relations, in relations with the children. A family founded on the discrimination of children born out of wedlock from so-called legitimate children.

"If you had discussed the idea of the natural family in the 1950s, you would very likely have found people prepared to maintain firmly that such a family was in fact one based on the above-mentioned subordination and the above-mentioned discrimination. People no different from those who nowadays insist on denying rights to same-sex couples.

"All laws, says Jeremy Bentham, are imperfect and constantly changing human inventions. Even so-called natural law in all its variants is a human invention, disguised as a discovery or a revelation to give it greater authority.

"Abandoning this historical perspective, and looking at the present day, we must acknowledge the existence of different and opposing moral systems. The plurality of points of view about facts and values serves as an antidote to the danger of the absolute truths believed in by fanatics, about which the philosopher Norberto Bobbio spoke in a famous essay.

"The function of the defence counsel in a criminal trial is linked to this: the necessary awareness of the plurality of points of view about values, about rules, about facts. It consists, bringing it back to its theoretical nature, in systematically questioning absolute or pre-established truths in order to solicit judgements that are correct and that the largest number of people can agree on. In this perspective let us recall some basic principles of good judgement, taking our inspiration from Aristotle.

"We mustn't decide in haste: when decisions are made that involve important interests, we have to think slowly.

"We need to verify the information – in other words, take nothing for granted. Taking for granted things that can't be taken for granted produces flawed – that is, incorrect – arguments, because they're based on false premises.

"When we don't have sufficient instruments to evaluate a specific situation we need to consult independent experts.

"We need to observe the situation, examining the points of view of all the parties involved. If we say somebody is right, we also have to say that somebody else is wrong. We therefore need to be conscious of the fact that even the best judgement will be perceived in good faith by somebody as unjust.

"We need to consider the possible outcomes of a judgement, carefully weighing the pros and the cons. That is the case above all with protective custody, which basically involves a prognostic judgement. Article 274 clause c of the code of practice authorizes the limitation of personal freedom on the basis of a prognosis, a judgement of a predictive kind. A suspect is placed under arrest for a serious crime when it's predicted that, if they're let free, they will commit further serious crimes. Needless to say, this is a necessary rule, and helps to avoid dangerous individuals remaining at liberty while criminal proceedings are still under way.

"But in this case, as in others, we have to remember that man is an animal that's not very good at making predictions.

"In the second decade of the last century, a man named Charlie Chaplin asserted that the public weren't interested in seeing figures moving on a screen, only flesh-and-blood human beings on a stage. In 1932 Albert Einstein declared that it would never be possible to produce atomic energy. In 1943 the head of IBM, Thomas Watson, maintained that in the future there would be at most five people in the world interested in buying a computer. In 1995 Robert Metcalfe, the inventor of Ethernet, pontificated that the Internet would soon become a supernova and would collapse by 1996. In 2007 Steve Ballmer, the former CEO of Microsoft, said there was no possibility that the iPhone would capture a significant share of the market.

"I could go on. A professor at Berkeley, Philip Tetlock, has looked at tens of thousands of predictions made by hundreds of experts over a period of ten years, and reached the conclusion that the accuracy of such predictions would have been the same if they'd been randomly generated by a computer.

"There are situations in which making predictions is unavoidable. The awareness of how unreliable they are should, however, lead us to be cautious – whatever our profession, because in every profession we make judgement calls and gamble, often unconsciously, on their outcome – in order to thwart the enemy number one of good judgement: fallacies, errors made in the formulation of an argument that render it invalid or incorrect."

I went on to say that fallacies prevent a discussion – whether public or private – from advancing logically and in fact make exchanges of opinion pointless and judgements invalid or incorrect. I covered this subject at some length, and after a while realized I had to get to the point if I wanted to keep to the time limit.

"There are many kinds of fallacies, and we don't have time today to linger over the various categories, which are something cognitive scientists and exponents of argumentation theory deal with. Anyone who wants to go into the subject in greater depth – which I would strongly recommend – will find some excellent works on the market, some of them educational.

"Right now I'd like to use as a springboard the observation that what we say is often invalidated by procedural errors in the examination of the facts. Strictly speaking, what we mean by incorrect procedures are those characterized by infractions of the rules regarding due dates, time limits, filing of suits. But procedures that lead to fallacious arguments, whether or not those who perpetrate them are aware of it, are also incorrect procedures, because they infringe the rules on valid discourse.

"The function of the defence counsel is to make sure that nobody is convicted on the basis of incorrect procedures, and this function can be summed up as what we might call 'the act of asking questions while doubting'. Asking questions, of others but above all of ourselves, doubting accepted truths and rules. In each sphere – rules and facts – as an exercise of our intellectual and ethical muscles. Taking nothing for granted.

"Was the killing of Osama bin Laden a premeditated murder or a significant act of justice, a form of pre-emptive self-defence, given that the man might be planning further criminal acts? The same could be asked of the killing of Palestinian terrorists by the Israeli secret service. And is it legitimate to torture a terrorist to make them reveal the whereabouts of a hostage whose life is in danger or the location of a deadly device that's about to blow up and kill innocent people?

"I don't have unequivocal answers and I'm suspicious of anyone who claims they do. Many questions that are presented to those who exercise our professions – defence counsel, prosecutor, judge – don't have unequivocal answers.

"I come at last to my conclusion. Our task is to find solutions to the cases with which we are presented. But we need to be aware that the ability to find answers and solutions to conflicts is based on our ability to live with uncertainty, with the opaqueness of reality.

"The English poet John Keats called this 'negative capability'. He thought this was the essential talent that man required to obtain genuine results, to really solve problems. Keats called this capability 'negative' in opposition to the attitude of those who tackle problems in search of immediate solutions, in an attempt to bend reality to their own need for certainties.

"Looking for an immediate unequivocal interpretation from which to derive an immediate and reassuring solution is, in most cases, an automatic reflex and ultimately a device to avoid having to think.

"For Keats, by accepting uncertainty, error and doubt, it's possible to look more deeply, to catch details and shades of meaning, to ask new, even paradoxical questions, and in this way to expand the borders of knowledge and awareness.

"My grandfather taught philosophy. When I was little he often said something – I don't know if it was his or a quotation, and I've never wanted to check – that I only really understood when he'd been dead for some time. It went more or less like this: in every activity, in every kind of work, it's useful from time to time to take a statement we've always taken for granted and turn it into a question."

I paused for a moment. Nobody seemed distracted, nobody was checking his or her phone. A slight shiver went through me. Maybe it was that memory of my grandfather, which hadn't been in my notes and which had come out without my realizing it, like a distant, glowing echo.

"Thank you for listening to me, and good luck."

Cotturri was the first to applaud, and the others followed. Some with enthusiasm, others out of politeness.

For some, the speech they had just heard was a defence lawyer's spiel, a way of dreaming up more or less sophisticated obstacles to the possibility – the mission – of going out into the world, righting wrongs and doing justice. At all costs. Needless to say, these missionaries are those who share with idiots the record for the largest amount of damage caused, some of it irreparable.

I was by the door, saying goodbye, when the young woman with grey eyes came up to me. Looking straight at me, she gave me her hand; her handshake was as I expected, serious and firm.

"Thank you, Avvocato, it was … stimulating," she said with a hint of a smile.

Cotturri walked me to the stairs.

"I wasn't expecting a talk like that," he said before we parted. "I wasn't expecting it to have … that kind of theoretical concern. It was very good, very instructive. Not just for the kids."

You sometimes feel happy when you think you've done something well, I thought as I walked to my office.

Definitely feeling happy.

12

I had kept Lorenza informed of developments by telephone. Since her visit to the office, I hadn't seen her again. Two days before the hearing she called me.

"I'm sorry, Guido, will I be disturbing you if I drop by this afternoon?"

"No, that's fine."

"If it's all the same to you I'd prefer to make it late, when you've finished with your other appointments. That way we can talk in peace, without worrying about keeping someone waiting."

I took a quick glance at my diary and told her to come at 8.30, when I would definitely have got through my other commitments. When everyone's gone, I also thought, as if I had something to hide. A rather absurd thought, I told myself, quickly dismissing it.

She arrived a few minutes early. Pasquale announced her and admitted her to my office. He asked me if I still needed him and I replied thank you, I didn't need anything, he could go. The others, Consuelo and the trainees, had already left.

"Thank you for seeing me today, I know you're very busy."

I simply nodded and smiled rather stiffly, then asked her if she'd like a coffee or a fruit juice or something else to drink. I don't know why, but I was sure she would say no, thanks.

So when she replied that she'd have a coffee I was surprised. It was a trifle, but it made me think how we speculate about things, and are extremely certain about them, only to see them just as easily proved wrong.

I went to make the coffee, grabbed a fruit juice for myself and returned to my office. Lorenza had stood up and was looking around.

"I didn't really take it in last time, but this doesn't look like a lawyer's office. Not that I have much experience of them, but it's different from how I would have imagined it, definitely very different from Costamagna's."

I had been in Costamagna's office. His office was all in walnut, with leather armchairs and shelves filled with law books. It really was hard to imagine decor that was more different.

"If you want to smoke, go ahead," I said, "it doesn't bother me. In fact, I like the smell of cigarette smoke in here. It makes me feel at least fifteen years younger."

"How did you know I still smoke?" she asked.

I know because your clothes smell of cigarettes, too many cigarettes, and the thumb and index finger of your left hand – I remember you're left-handed – are stained with nicotine.

I didn't say that.

"I don't know, you seem to me like someone who doesn't quit smoking," I said. "But I realize that doesn't make any sense."

She smiled a little. And the smile made her seem fragile.

"Actually, I never have quit," she replied, taking out a packet of soft MSs. "There's no specific reason I asked if I could see you, so please forgive me if I'm wasting your time. You explained to me on the phone what's supposed to happen the day after tomorrow – in other words, nothing. Nothing significant, I mean. But the anxiety's killing me, so I thought talking to you in person would help."

Clients often visit a defender's office for no particular legal reason. They do it to alleviate their anxiety, to have confirmation that there's somebody on their side who knows (or it's assumed knows) how to handle a grim, threatening, often incomprehensible situation.

"As I told you, the day after tomorrow I'll ask for an extension to give me time to make requests for the submission of new evidence. I've already talked to the judge, who's aware of the situation and has assured me there won't be any problems. I would have called you anyway to clarify a few things, after studying the papers, so it's good that you're here."

She puffed away at her cigarette with the brutal, distracted greed of a true nicotine addict. For a moment I was on the verge of asking her for one.

"What do you need to know?"

I needed to know the truth of the alibi she had tried to provide for her son, which the assistant prosecutor had demolished so effectively. And I needed to know all about that old charge of aiding and abetting and resisting an officer of the law – an episode that, as it happened, dated from the time when she and I had been together. But I omitted to mention this last point.

Lorenza listened to me carefully and replied with great clarity. She came across as convincing.

I wondered why she hadn't done so the day she had been cross-examined in court. A stupid question. When you're in the witness stand, it works differently. If there isn't anybody helping you to keep calm, especially when you're caught off guard by an unexpected question, the risk of amnesia, or at least aphasia, is strong. The memories come flooding back only after the examination is over, accompanied by inevitable frustration. The *esprit de l'escalier* is quite a common phenomenon among witnesses in criminal trials.

"You've told me some useful things. Obviously before you testify we'll prepare well, to avoid any surprises like the ones that were sprung on you at the original trial. Maybe we can manage to set the record straight, at least in part. It isn't an easy case, but there may be some glimmers of light."

"Have you dealt with many cases … of this kind?"

"You mean murder cases?"

"Yes."

I counted. There were eight in all. Not many, but not a small number either for a lawyer who doesn't usually take on clients involved in organized crime. It's those who do who are more likely to handle certain kinds of case.

"How did they go?"

"Four acquittals and three convictions."

"Four plus three makes seven."

"In one, the defendant died during the trial. He had a heart attack. The judge ruled that the case couldn't go ahead."

"Was he guilty or innocent?"

"Guilty, I think. Though he swore he was innocent."

"If he hadn't died, would he have been convicted?"

"Hard to say. The evidence was circumstantial, but maybe yes."

"And in the other cases? The cases where your clients were convicted?"

"Two convictions out of the three were where the accused confessed. Then it's all about getting the mildest sentence, not getting them acquitted. As for the third … if I'd been in the judges' place, I'd have delivered the same verdict."

"And what about those who were acquitted?"

"Do you want to know if they were guilty or innocent?"

"Yes."

"One was a case of self-defence. The others … I like to think they were all innocent, but let's say I'm only reasonably certain about one of the cases. With the other two, I don't know, but the investigations had been badly conducted and acquittal was the right decision."

At that moment my mind went in a direction I couldn't control. It had happened to me before, every time I had dealt with a murder: I wondered what the last minutes of the victim's life had been like. What activity had Gaglione, bouncer and drug dealer, been engaged in just before he was killed? What had his last normal thought been before he realized there was somebody in his apartment about to shoot him?

I told myself it wouldn't be a particularly good idea to share this stream of fantasies with Lorenza. So, to cut it off, I looked at my watch.

"It's already twenty to ten. Come on, I'll close the office and we'll go down together."

I switched off the lights, checked there were no windows open (a little neurosis I'd developed ever since I'd found a bat in the conference room) and we left.

"Do you have a car?" I asked her, remembering from the reading of the file that she didn't live nearby.

"No. I like walking."

"Me too. Home isn't far, but in general I go everywhere on foot or by bicycle."

For a moment neither of us spoke. It might have been my old fear of silence, my always feeling uneasy and slightly responsible for other people, worried about what they were thinking, that made me say something I didn't really want to.

"Would you like a drink, maybe a bite to eat?"

As with the coffee, I thought she would say no, thank you, I'm going home to sleep. Instead of which, she replied completely naturally:

"Okay, but you choose where to go, I don't go out much in the evening. To be honest, I almost never go out, and I'm not very familiar with restaurants."

I took her to a trattoria near the university, a place I rarely went. It seemed only natural to choose a place where I thought – I hoped – I wouldn't bump into anybody I knew. I realized I was embarrassed to be seen with her, and I also realized that the embarrassment was to do with vanity. And that made me feel ashamed.

As we sat at the table and she studied the menu, I kept thinking. I'd always had vague visions – rather than genuine memories – of the brief period when our paths had crossed. Visions marked by a deep sense of unreality, as if certain events hadn't really happened, as if we'd never really met. At least not the way I thought I remembered it.

We ordered starters, salted sea bass and a bottle of white wine. She ate methodically and took large, regular gulps of the wine, as if complying with a prescription. By halfway through dinner the bottle was finished, and I ordered another without her raising any objection.

"Twenty-seven years," she said suddenly after finishing her fish. "What month did we meet?"

She'd caught me unawares. "It's *almost* twenty-seven years."

"Almost? So you really do remember what month we met?"

"March. The end of March 1987. But I don't know the exact date."

So we started talking about what had happened in our respective lives in those almost twenty-seven years. I didn't have any great desire to talk and I muddled through by mentioning just a few things that were more or less general and more or less true. She, on the other hand, after a slight hesitation, a slight holding back maybe, relaxed and gave me a thorough and, I think, quite honest summary of what had happened to her.

She had lived in Bologna and for shorter periods in other cities. Then she had returned to Bari and now lived in the apartment she had inherited from her parents.

"You remember how I used to say I wanted to write?"

I nodded: I did remember. And it had never seemed as if she was feeding me a line. No, it was more a declaration of intent regarding an inevitable and almost heroic future. When I had occasionally thought about her, I had always been surprised that I hadn't one day come across a novel of hers in a bookshop.

"I did write a novel," she said.

I wanted to appear interested, and was trying to formulate a question that wouldn't hurt her feelings (I'm in the habit of browsing in bookshops two or three times a week: the fact that I hadn't noticed the publication of this book of hers suggested it hadn't exactly been a success), but she got in first.

"It was brought out by a small publisher."

She said the name of a publishing house that was indeed small, but of good quality; I hadn't seen any of their books around for a while.

"They went bust a few years ago," she went on. "They were good at choosing books, but a disaster from a commercial point of view. I had some good reviews, I travelled everywhere at my own expense presenting it. I even won a few prizes, but there wasn't much distribution, you couldn't even find the novel in a lot of bookshops. Basically, it wasn't a bestseller."

"When did it come out?"

"In 2002, in September."

"What was it called?"

"*The Catalogue of Absence.*"

I behaved like a well-brought-up person; I didn't tell her the title suggested the kind of novel I'm inclined to fling at the wall at some unspecified point in my reading, certainly never later than chapter three. Instead, I asked her what it was about. If it was possible to sum it up, I added.

She sighed and assumed the manner of someone preparing to explain something the person she's speaking to may not understand.

"It was an attempt, I don't know how successful, to come to terms with myself, and with what had happened to me in the years that might have been the most important of my life. For good or ill."

"Which were?"

She drank the last wine remaining in her glass and threw a rapid glance at the bottle in the ice bucket. Catching that glance, I poured her some more.

"Let's say the nineties. A lot of the nineties."

I felt a touch of narcissistic pique: the most important time of her life didn't include the period when she had known me. It was expected, but all the same it bothered me to hear it confirmed.

"I started writing the novel in 1998, when I realized that in order to understand the meaning of my existence, I needed to strip myself bare in front of other people. Potentially in front of the whole world, because you're speaking to the whole world when you write a book. The idea is to enter into communication with humanity, if you understand what I mean."

While I was making an effort to remember what I was doing in 1998, concluding almost immediately that now wasn't the right time (it had been a crazy and unwittingly sad period), Lorenza explained that her novel was a kind of *conte philosophique* (those were the words she used) that connected with the existentialist thought and, above all, the themes of Sartre's *Nausea.*

"My character, who's partly autobiographical, is halfway between Roquentin and the Autodidact. The kernel of the novel, the result of the protagonist's philosophical and personal search, is that the true revelation of being is the incursion and therefore the awareness of absence, which is a category not very dissimilar to Sartrian *ennui.* In order to convey the sense of otherness, of elsewhereness, in relation to ourselves that defines genuine awareness, I used the stylistic device of telling the story in the second person. The I that is other than oneself, that is absent to oneself, is seen and questioned from the outside. Let's say, from a place in the consciousness that's a non-place."

This has to be a joke, I thought. Now she's going to confess that she's pulling my leg. There are some things that nobody – well, almost nobody – can say seriously.

She didn't confess that she was pulling my leg. So she meant exactly what she had said. She specified that a famous left-wing critic had written these things in an equally famous literary magazine. And that she identified with these "exegetical considerations".

Then, helped by the wine and the fact that I was listening without interrupting her, she went on with her story.

The novel hadn't done well, she said, readers hadn't understood it, and only a thousand copies or a little more had been sold. As she had already told me, the publishing house had gone bust a few years later and the fact that this first novel hadn't been a commercial success – the only thing that really matters today in the book world is sales – made it hard to find a new publisher and get a new contract. That was probably why she hadn't managed to finish her second novel, which she had started soon after the first one had come out, on a wave of enthusiasm at being published and optimism for the future.

"When your dream is to write and you manage to find a publisher, a real publisher, not those vanity ones, for your first novel, you have the impression you've arrived, that from then on everything will be plain sailing. In fact, the hardest part has only just begun. Do you know the shelf life of a novel in bookshops if it isn't an immediate bestseller? Thirty, forty days. Then the booksellers remove it to make room for other new releases."

"How do you mean, remove it?"

"It's no longer displayed in a visible way. Nobody sees it and nobody buys it, unless you've gone into the shop specially. And after a few months the booksellers return the unsold copies to the publisher, who after a few more months sends everything to be pulped."

What felt wrong in this conversation? Basically, it was an interesting subject, it was about books, which are my great passion. And yet there was a discordant note in Lorenza's words, as if she were reciting a script she had repeated too many times. It was an artificial speech, devoid of truth, even if the events she was telling me about had really happened, more or less. She was acting, and it didn't matter that I was the one who was listening. I was an audience like any other for a threadbare, mediocre repeat performance. Then I realized something else, something I had never thought about and that appeared to me all at once, as clear as a revelation. When after a long time you meet again a person you shared part of your life with, a person you actually thought you were in love with, it's inevitable they should seem different. They've changed, as we all change, and this strikes you as normal. Then, sometimes, if you look carefully, if you don't look away, you realize to your dismay that the person *isn't* different.

They're the same, at least in their basic characteristics. It was in the past, when you met, that they *seemed* different. You projected your desires, aspirations and needs onto them. In a way, you invented them, you created them, you told yourself a complex, cogent lie that's difficult, very difficult to untangle.

Lorenza hadn't changed, except physically. She had aged, but she hadn't changed. She had the same attitude as when I had known her and spent time with her: a lack of interest in other people, a total focus on herself, a sense of resentment towards a world unable to recognize talent – hers, obviously.

Another characteristic that didn't seem to have changed was her tendency to express extreme, clear-cut opinions about everything. Definitive, trenchant judgements on any and every political, philosophical or literary subject. Even on personal matters, matters of the heart. Other people's opinions only mattered to the extent that they matched hers.

Years later I came across the perfect expression – coined by David Foster Wallace – to describe this attitude, this difficulty in recognizing a space for other people's interpretations and positions: *ambiguphobia*. Lorenza was a perfect specimen of an ambiguphobic person.

When you think about it, changes only happen when you *really* interact with another person. They may just be fleeting moments but they have a crucial importance in our autobiographies. We're almost never aware of them. Even if we remember these moments for their perfection, we don't understand how vital they are to the changes in us.

We think it is time, slowly and persistently, that changes us. But time in itself doesn't change anything – at most it ages us. People incapable of really interacting with other people, like Lorenza, don't change.

I wondered how much this might also apply to me. What am I now that I already was back then? Not a single cell in my body existed then; no cell from then exists now. But what about my identity? Was it the same or had it changed?

While I was thinking this, she was talking and drinking.

"I make my living from substitute teaching, I'm the classic temp teacher because I never wanted to take the exam. I thought teaching would be a temporary job, that it wasn't worth it. But now, it'd be convenient to be a permanent member of staff. In any case, I have to make ends meet, and the salary's not enough, especially now with Iacopo's trial and all the costs. So I give private lessons, and sometimes, when I can, I provide assistance to elderly people. Only if they're self-sufficient, though. But you already know this, it's in the file."

When I had known her, it struck me now, she was twenty-nine and had already been doing substitute teaching for a while, had already been an independent, adult working woman for a while. That was what had fascinated me about her back then in 1987, when for a short time, depending on her whims, she had let me into her life.

Now she was pushing sixty and was still a substitute teacher. It made me sad.

"What about Iacopo's father?"

"We lived together with the child for a year, or just over. In Bologna, in an old building with other people. Then he left."

He'd left from one day to the next, without giving any explanations, unconcerned about the insignificant detail that he had a son.

After a few years in which he hadn't felt the need to visit Iacopo, let alone contribute to his upbringing, and after various adventures (some of which had aroused the interest of the Carabinieri), he had ended up in Cancún in Mexico, running a bar on the beach. One evening, as he was on his way home, his car had been hit by a truck and that was the end of that. Iacopo, to all intents and purposes, had never known him: that first year was beyond the scope of his memories.

As she continued to tell her rather painful story in the tone of a police report, I suddenly remembered an evening we'd spent together on a beach, at sunset.

We were with two girlfriends of hers, we had wine and pot. We talked – actually, as usual, Lorenza was doing most of the talking – about books, films, ideas. I don't remember exactly what the specific subject was – maybe it wasn't clear to anybody or maybe my capacity for concentration was too compromised by the alcohol and the cannabis – but I do remember thinking how exciting this bohemian life, the life of a *poète maudit* (yes, at the time I was lacking in a sense of the ridiculous) that I found myself leading – how exciting it was, what with drugs, poetry, sex and great literary discussions.

I was a confused, directionless young man who liked stories, fascinated by the idea of having the kind of experiences you read about in novels. When as an adult, at the age of forty or fifty, I try to remember my adventurous youth – this was what I told myself – it's evenings like this I'll think about.

That hadn't happened. I'd soon forgotten all about Lorenza and that world of chipped cups, kitchens with unwashed dishes in the sink, fake anti-conformism, rooms that weren't very clean or tidy (because cleanliness and tidiness were bourgeois and philistine) and books read – maybe – without any pleasure and without any interest in what they contained, just to be able to show them off.

She continued talking and drinking, and the second bottle of wine was also polished off, although I hadn't contributed a great deal to the undertaking.

When we left the restaurant she suggested we walk a little, to chat some more. Her eyes were a little clouded and softened by the wine. She looked almost cheerful, but there was an undertone I'd have preferred not to catch.

"It's late, I have a hearing tomorrow," I lied. And before she could say anything else: "I'll call you a taxi."

As we said goodbye, she thanked me, smiled and gave me a kiss on the lips.

It was a clumsy kiss, and it seemed out of place. I walked home, thinking that dinner hadn't been such a good idea.

13

Two days later, at exactly 9.30, I walked into the courtroom of the appeal court. As usual, there was nobody there yet, not even the clerk of the court, even though the time indicated on the summons was in fact 9.30. I thought of walking out again and grabbing a coffee. Then I told myself that I didn't really want a coffee and that the idea of getting one was just a way of telling myself: I'm not here to wait on the pleasure of the judges, the prosecutor, the clerk of the court; if anything, they should be waiting for me. So, to free myself of these childish impulses, I decided to make my way to the defence bench and take out the book I'd brought with me in anticipation of slack moments.

It's something I've been in the habit of doing for a few years, having a book with me to read when I go to a courthouse for a hearing or some other commitment. I started in order to fill the breaks, but I soon discovered that having a book is also an excellent antidote against pains in the arse – of the human kind.

You're waiting for your case to be called, and next to you there's, let's say, Avvocato Canestrari (actually, I don't know if there is a lawyer of that name in Bari). He's also waiting for a case of his to be called, and in the meantime he'd like to chat with you. Not because he particularly likes you – a fairly questionable privilege, being liked by Canestrari – but because he's bored waiting. His favourite topics are Bari's soccer team (a subject that holds as much interest for me as the cultivation of organic corn in the central Ukrainian plain or the latest developments in phrenology) and the restaurants in Bari and its province where you can eat the best raw seafood, included banned varieties such as date mussels. The fact that serving date mussels happens to be a crime doesn't bother Canestrari – or many others like him, to be honest.

But since I started bringing a book with me to read – an object that arouses mistrust and suspicion in many of my colleagues – the risk posed by the Canestraris of all kinds has lessened considerably.

When the judges are late arriving, or when they've been deliberating longer than anticipated in the case preceding mine, or when they're about to deliberate on my case, I sit down at the end of the defence bench, open my book and, as they say, immerse myself. Some people, with amazing insight, ask me things like: What are you doing, reading? Or else: Lucky you, Guerrieri, having such a clear head you actually feel like reading. But mostly they leave me alone.

That day there were no individuals like Canestrari, no pests to get rid of, but I had with me a book I'd been wanting to read for ever, which I'd bought the week before from my bookseller friend Ottavio and which I found really fascinating: *The Life and Opinions of Tristram Shandy, Gentleman.*

One of the greatest novels ever written, according to Schopenhauer.

To be precise: a very great novel of digressions, according to me. Digressions are my passion, in every field, and reading that book was a giddy pleasure.

After a quarter of an hour the clerk of the court appeared, and a few minutes later the assistant prosecutor.

Having put *Tristram Shandy* aside, I approached the latter, greeted him and informed him that I would be requesting an extension. I was about to explain the reasons, but he relieved me of that task with the gesture of someone who has important things to think about and doesn't want to waste time on pointless words.

"Thank you, Avvocato Guerrieri. Judge Marinelli has already informed me and I won't make any objection. Apart from anything else, this isn't my case. I'm only here today to replace the colleague who'll be dealing with it. In fact, if we get it over with quickly I'm more than happy."

"Thank you. May I ask who will be dealing with the case?"

It was Assistant Prosecutor Gastoni. She had spent a long time in the Prosecutor's Department in Trani before joining the Public Prosecutor's Office. A lot of stories were told about her, none of them especially flattering – among them, that she'd once had the telephone number of her husband's supposed lover inserted in a list of numbers to be tapped in a police drug investigation. There had been a criminal investigation as well as a disciplinary one, but nothing had come of either. That hadn't put an end to the rumour.

Gastoni was a beautiful woman, with a certain compulsion to flaunt her charms – I don't know if with a particular aim in mind or just to boost her self-esteem. I'd never liked her, but professionally she was perfectly competent. All things considered, it could have been a worse choice.

The court entered.

"Good morning, everyone," Marinelli said, adjusting his robe, which was falling from one shoulder. So, today we have just the Cardace case. Is the accused in court?"

"Your Honour," I said, "the accused has forgone his

appearance, just for this hearing. There should have been a message from the prison."

Marinelli turned to the associate judge, Valentini, who nodded to confirm what I had said.

In two minutes they got through the preliminaries while I looked at the jurors, trying to get a few pointers. With their sashes in the colours of the Italian flag, they looked, as jurors always do, slightly out of place.

Three women and three men. Two of the women were unassuming ladies in their fifties, who were looking around with bewildered expressions on their faces; one resembled a catechism teacher of mine who'd been in the habit of searching us at the start of the lesson ever since a joker had let off a stink bomb in class (more than one, to be honest).

I wondered what they did and couldn't think of anything more original than: housewives.

The youngest of the women had a nondescript face but bright, penetrating eyes. The minimum age to be appointed a juror is thirty, but she looked much younger, and in any other context I would have taken her for a university student.

The men were very different from each other. One was a gentleman in his sixties, in a jacket and an unbuttoned shirt, sporting a seventies hairstyle. I could imagine him haunting dance halls back then. Another one looked like a sacristan and had a nervous tic: every two or three seconds he touched first his chin, then his chest, with his right hand. There was something morbidly hypnotic about it, and I had to force myself to look away. The third one was a tanned, friendly looking man in his forties; I pegged him for a sporty type, maybe a yachtsman. I decided it would be good to address my remarks mainly to the young woman, both during the testimonies and during my closing statement.

I made my requests, reducing my arguments to the minimum given that we were already in agreement, and the assistant prosecutor made no comments. Judge Marinelli, after quickly exchanging a few words in a low voice with his associate, dictated an order extending the time limit for adding grounds to the appeal and submitting new evidence. Then he adjourned until 7 April. Even longer than the month he'd promised.

I thanked Marinelli and Valentini, nodded to the jurors, looking at all of them, one by one, for a moment or two, shook hands with the assistant prosecutor and walked out.

Lorenza

By the time I got home, my head was all over the place – to put it euphemistically. I kept being hit by waves of narcissistic exhilaration: a beautiful, fascinating woman, older than me – *a grown-up* – had noticed me at a party, had approached me, had found my conversation amusing, had gone to the trouble of conducting an investigation to track me down, had come to fetch me – technically: to *pick me up* – at my place of work and had taken me first to dinner, then to her place, with all that had ensued.

The exhilaration, however, was mixed with a sense that I had totally lost control. An awareness that my part in what had happened had been completely passive, that my intentions – let alone whatever decisions I might have made – had been completely irrelevant.

And there was another aspect. One that was more substantial – I can't think of a better word. Being with Lorenza, that night, wasn't like being with the other girls I had known and dated up until then.

It's hard to explain the difference. I can only think of one example, which some will consider inappropriate. Once, a professional boxer, who had actually fought in the Italian middleweight championships, came to visit the gym where I trained. At the request of the coach, he changed and sparred a little with us boys. It was a game, totally relaxed (at least he was) and sportsmanlike. And yet for the two minutes I was in the ring with him, I felt I was dealing with a creature of a different species. Made of different *material*. With loose, almost casual movements, he'd land these blows on your helmet, your arms, your ribs, that felt like stones; you tried to hit him and he dodged your blows as I could have done with a child's; there was an uncommon truth in the way he moved, dodged, parried, punched. There was total mastery; there was harshness and truth. He gave you the impression that whatever we did, in our training and our fighting – training and fighting hard, we thought – was little more than a pillow fight.

Well, Lorenza, that night, conveyed a similar feeling to me. The idea that all my previous experiences had been child's play.

When I got home, I realized to my annoyance that I hadn't even asked her for her telephone number. True, I knew where she lived, but the idea of staking out her building in order to make contact and arrange another date didn't strike me as very practical. Although, now that I came to think of it, I didn't recall noticing a telephone in her apartment.

Mixed up as I was, I went to bed and fell asleep a few seconds after laying my head on the pillow.

That was how it worked in those days.

I don't care too much about the fact that I'd become an adult, a *real* adult. Many things about me at that age seem strange to me now; I don't feel particularly sympathetic to the young man I was then and I wouldn't be very interested in chatting with him and hearing his opinions, which were often marked by an arrogant scepticism. But I do envy him his sleep. The ability to yield in a few seconds to that total loss of consciousness that lasted, uninterruptedly, joyfully, until the following morning. A wonderful ability, lost for ever.

All right, I'm sorry, I've digressed.

The next morning I went to court to attend a couple of hearings, but found it hard to concentrate on legal matters and court procedure. All I could think about was how to meet her again without having to pathetically stake out the area around the Casa delle Rose in Via Eritrea, waiting for her to come out or go back in.

The one brilliant solution I managed to come up with was to go to her building and ring her bell. I did that early in the afternoon. When I got there, I realized I didn't know her surname. So I rang every bell in the building and asked if Lorenza was there. Those who answered – mostly old people, their heavily accented voices filled with hostility – told me there was no Lorenza there and that they didn't even know who she was. There remained two apartments from which I didn't receive an answer: Delle Foglie and Pontrelli. So now I had reduced her likely surname down to two, and the next time I would at least know which bells *not* to ring.

In the weeks that followed I would try again several times, always without success. She was never at home, or maybe didn't answer her bell. One piece, among many, in that mosaic of elusiveness I would never be able to put together.

14

Nothing memorable happened during those weeks. Or if it did, I didn't notice. The days passed, almost all the same, slow and fast at the same time – and a little scary for that very reason, if you stopped to think about it.

I went twice to the prison to talk to Iacopo. He was starting to trust me and, quite unexpectedly, I was getting to like him.

In the second of our interviews an interesting element emerged.

The previous time I'd asked him to think over the afternoon of the murder, to see if he recalled any useful details. And he had done just that.

"I thought about it, and one thing did come into my mind."

"Go on."

"I don't know if it's important."

"Anything might be important, as I told you."

"When they came to get me, outside the bar, I knew one of the cops. After they searched me and found the pills on me, they put me in the car and he sat in the back with me."

"Go on."

"On the ride to Headquarters we talked. He asked me if I'd seen my friend Cosimo that afternoon."

"And what did you say?"

"I asked him if he meant Gaglione – I told him I'd never called him Cosimo, always Mino. Then I said I'd been to his apartment for a coffee, though of course without telling him he'd given me the pills."

"Did this police officer inform you that Gaglione was dead?"

"No. I only found that out when we got to Headquarters."

"This isn't mentioned in the case file," I said out loud, though talking more to myself than to him.

"Could it help?"

"It might. Do you know the officer's name?"

He did, and he told me.

"How can this help us, if they didn't even write it down?" he asked.

"That's just it – the fact that they didn't write it down."

"I don't understand."

"The prosecution case is based, among other things, on the fact that they can place you in the vicinity of the crime scene, at about the right time, thanks to the testimony of the woman in the cafe. The implication is that, if they hadn't identified you by questioning this woman, they wouldn't have known."

"Of course! I told them I'd been at Mino's place of my own free will. Which means I had nothing to hide."

"Put that way, it's a little too neat, but it's true. Calmly admitting, even if informally, that you'd been at Gaglione's place that afternoon doesn't exactly tally with you being responsible for the murder. It would have been natural for you to deny it."

Iacopo straightened on his chair. I'd already thought I noticed a new liveliness in his eyes the time before, but now Cardace seemed the older, more mature brother of the arrogant, apathetic street punk I'd met the first time.

"You mean, if I were guilty, I wouldn't have come out and said I'd been with Gaglione just before he died?"

"Precisely."

"But if it isn't written anywhere, how do we bring it up?"

"You can mention it when you testify in court. But I'd also like to call the police officer and ask him. It isn't the done thing in terms of procedure, but we'll see."

But the most significant event of that period was some hours spent with my friend Ottavio at his Osteria del Caffellatte, which despite its name is a bookshop. With a somewhat rare feature: it's only open at night.

It happens for no particular reason. Or at least for no reason I can pin down. It seems an evening like any other, I do more or less the usual things: I leave the office, go home, maybe exercise a little, then go back out for dinner or make myself something, watch a series on television, read a book. All normal. And yet just as I'm about to go to bed I realize – I know for a fact – that I won't be able to sleep that night. It's like a small electric shock that goes through my skin and into the spaces between my thoughts. Like an entity – an alien but very familiar entity – that usually goes about its own business, but which sometimes takes up a position next to me and decides we have to stay awake together.

Each time, I try to pretend it's nothing: I go to bed and tell myself it's only the power of suggestion, that in twenty minutes I'll be asleep, as happened in similar situations when I was twenty-five years younger.

It never happens.

After an hour spent tossing and turning in the dark between the blankets, sheets and pillows, forcing myself to "think of nothing, concentrate on your breathing" as I'd learned from an indispensable manual on the cure for insomnia, I finally decide to switch the light back on. If the next day I have any commitment that requires a modicum of clear-headedness and is therefore incompatible with a sleepless night, I knock back about fifteen drops and soon afterwards sink into an artificial sleep. Otherwise, I start reading, watch television and, if the electric shock is more intense than usual, and the anxiety less bearable, I go to the Osteria del Caffellatte.

That's what happened this time. I got dressed, grabbed an umbrella – it had been raining intermittently, wearyingly, for a couple of days – and set off through the shiny, spectral 2 a.m. streets.

There was only one customer in the bookshop: a sturdy, vigorous-looking old gentleman with a very short white beard and a red face typical of someone who spends a lot of time in the open air. He looked like a friendly old boatswain straight out of a children's book illustration. He was sitting in a small armchair, leafing through a volume, with other books on a little table next to him. Our eyes met and, although we had never seen each other before, we exchanged a smile and a nod.

As usual, Ottavio was behind the counter, also reading, and as usual, there was a very slight, almost imperceptible smell of caramel in the air.

"Hi, Guido, haven't seen you lately at this hour."

"I've been sleeping well for a while now. It couldn't possibly last."

"What'll you have?"

"I'll have a rum," I said, sitting down on one of the stools, "that very good rum from the Philippines whose name I can never remember."

Ottavio poured me the very good rum whose name I could never remember. "Any particular reason you can't sleep tonight?"

151

"I'm sure there are reasons, but I long ago stopped trying to identify them. I suspect I might not like what I found."

Ottavio nodded his approval, like someone familiar with the subject.

"When you were still teaching and didn't have the shop, did you stay awake every night?" I asked him.

"Every night. I'd start to feel sleepy at about five in the morning."

"But did you stay in bed or did you get up?"

"Sometimes I'd get up, read, then go back to bed about half past four. At other times, I was so tired I couldn't get up, so I'd just lie there and force myself to relax. Those were the worst nights. I'd lie in the dark wondering what I'd done wrong in my life. And the answer, basically and with few variations, was that I'd done everything wrong and there was no way out of my situation. Or maybe there was a way out – there almost always is – but I didn't have the courage to take it, which was even worse."

He poured another small glass of rum for himself and took a little sip.

"Then the inheritance came along," I said.

"Then the inheritance came along. And thanks to the inheritance, for the first time I decided to really do something with my life. I gave up teaching, opened this place ... well, you already know the story."

After just a few minutes chatting in that almost abstract yet familiar space, my anxiety passed.

"Something happened to me this afternoon," Ottavio said suddenly. "I was shopping in the supermarket when I passed a guy who looked familiar. I realized he was a classmate of mine from middle school who I hadn't seen since then – in other words, practically forty years. They used to call him

Giovanni the Fart. I don't suppose I need to go into detail about the nickname or why nobody wanted to sit next to him."

"No, I don't think you do."

"I think he actually had a physical problem with controlling himself. He was a kid with all kinds of hang-ups, so many that if a teacher even talked to him, let alone asked him a question, he'd get into a terrible state. He'd wring his hands so hard it was almost like he was trying to break them."

Ottavio's eyes wandered into the distance, as if to recapture the memory of those long-ago scenes. I kept quiet, waiting for him to continue his story.

"One day somebody decided we had to make it clear to him that the farting had to stop, or maybe he just decided to have a bit of fun at Giovanni's expense. So, during the break, we pushed him into the toilets and pulled down his trousers. He tried to defend himself – I can still remember how his skinny arm felt in my hands, like a thin rope stretched tight, while we held him still. Then one of us, maybe the person who thought up this stunt, wet him all over with the pump that was used to wash the toilet, saying maybe that way he'd stop stinking. He started crying desperately, almost choking. We let him go; what happened next I don't remember so well. The thing that's remained most imprinted in my memory was how humiliated the kid was and how ashamed I was. It all came back to me when I saw him in the supermarket."

"How come you recognized him?"

"He hasn't changed. I know that sounds absurd, but as soon as I saw him, I knew it was him."

"What about him? Did he recognize you?"

"I don't think so. I kept my eye on him while he was doing his shopping and for a moment I had the mad idea of introducing myself and apologizing for that stupid prank."

"But you didn't."

"Obviously. I never do such decent things when I have the opportunity."

"He wouldn't have understood. He probably doesn't even remember the episode," I commented unconvincingly.

He shrugged and refilled our glasses. A few minutes passed in silence. There was no hurry, no impatience.

"What is it you like most about this work?" I asked after a while.

"The weird characters I meet almost every night and sometimes talk to."

"Weird like me."

"Sorry to disappoint you, but you're not weird. Or rather, yes, you are, but in moderation. You wouldn't be in first or second place. There are some really strange people who come through here."

"I feel a bit bad about that. Who'd be in first or second place?"

"My favourite is the gay policeman, Arturo, who's often on night shift. He loves reading, he buys a couple of books a week, he's been writing a novel for years and has practically adopted his niece, the daughter of a cousin of his. The girl, Alice, has Down's syndrome, is very nice and has an incredible voice. Arturo once showed me a video of her singing 'Memory': it took my breath away. I have to introduce you to him some time."

"I think I met him a couple of times. Didn't he buy a book of poetry?"

"That was him. He buys all sorts, but poetry is his great passion. He's a real expert, apart from anything else. Then there's a Kurdish girl who escaped from Turkey. She's an engineering graduate, works in a bar and often, when she finishes her shift, she comes here before going home to bed, reads for free for half an hour and we chat. Every now and again she buys a book." Ottavio paused for a moment. "Even the professor sitting there isn't bad."

"Who is he?"

"He used to teach moral philosophy, but not in Bari. He was in some university in Central Italy, I can't remember which one. He came back here when he retired. When he was young, he was a wrestling champion. Now he's a philosophical consultant and at least once a week comes here about one, reads, makes notes; he always orders a cappuccino and a slice of cake. About four he leaves."

"What's a philosophical consultant?"

"It's not very easy to explain. If I've understood correctly, people with problems of an existential kind come to him and he helps them to find the system, the philosophical method that best suits their problem, so that they can overcome it."

"So it's a kind of psychotherapy?" I said, glancing over at the professor, who was still absorbed in his reading.

"Well, he'd say: absolutely not. They don't treat illnesses or mental disorders. They help their clients (who they carefully avoid calling patients) to think about their own lives in a new way. But if you want my opinion, it *is* a kind of psychotherapy. He's an interesting character. To give you an idea: he collects animal prints."

"What do you mean?"

"He goes walking outside the city, in the country, in the woods, on the beaches. He looks for animal prints and where possible makes a plaster cast of them, otherwise he photographs them. Would you like to meet him?"

"Why not?"

Ottavio invited him over to have a drink with us. The professor accepted willingly, and we introduced ourselves and started chatting. He explained what his work involved and insisted on one thing: if one of his clients presented a psychological or psychiatric problem rather than an existential one, he would direct him or her straight to a psychologist or a psychiatrist.

"How do you draw the line between an existential problem and an illness?"

"I admit it's not always easy. Not surprisingly, there's an area of overlap between the work of a psychologist – but not of a psychiatrist – and mine. There are types of personal suffering that aren't illnesses and that can be treated either with various forms of psychotherapy or with philosophical consultancy. Then there are actual mental illnesses, which absolutely aren't in my remit."

"So if I understand correctly, you talk to the client, get an idea of what their problem is and suggest a philosophical framework in which to fit it and rethink it."

"To be precise, I suggest different ways of redefining the problem and together we choose the one that seems preferable. When I say *different ways* I mean different philosophical systems. The basic question is to give a shape to the suffering, to put it into words."

"As Shakespeare says."

"There you've got me. What does Shakespeare say?"

"If I remember correctly: 'Give sorrow words; the grief that does not speak knits up the o'er-wrought heart and bids it break.' *Macbeth*, I don't remember where. Maybe Act Four."

"Yes, of course, that's exactly it."

Some customers had come in, and Ottavio had to see

to them. The professor and I continued our conversation, moving to the armchairs in the reading area.

"Are there philosophers you suggest most often to your clients?"

"Whenever I can, Montaigne. I also like Pyrrho and the other sceptics. That may seem strange, but it's an approach that can yield excellent results. I recently suggested Gorgias to a client who has problems with an excess of rationality. With the illusion of objectivity, let's put it that way."

"Why Gorgias?"

"For various reasons that can be summed up in the phrase: 'Tragedy is a deception that leaves the deceived wiser than the undeceived.' Letting ourselves be deceived allows us to discover hidden resources, ideas, strengths and gifts that we didn't know we had. That we didn't know existed."

"That's really very interesting."

The professor smiled.

"What about Aristotle?" I asked.

"Aristotle can be useful in many situations. A few months ago, I talked about him to a girl who's tormented by a sense of guilt; among other things she can't be faithful, and thinks – or thought – she was, so to speak, retarded from the ethical point of view. I tried to make her aware, using Aristotle, that our ethical qualities are like muscles: they atrophy if they're not regularly exercised, and they get stronger with practice. We become just by performing acts of justice, we become courageous by performing acts of courage, we become altruistic by performing acts of altruism."

We continued chatting about lots of things, some serious, some less so. When the customers had left Ottavio joined us again. It struck me that this was a night I would remember. That's a nice feeling when it happens.

"How's Annapaola?" Ottavio asked after a while. "I haven't seen the two of you together lately. Everything okay between you?"

"Yes, I think so."

"Don't let her go. She's in a special category. Someone who's incapable of cowardice – that's rare."

I simply nodded, avoiding stupid remarks. Annapaola is the kind of person you want close to you if you have to face serious danger. Ottavio was right: she was in a special category.

The professor left before five. We said goodbye, saying we would meet again there at the Osteria, one of these nights.

For breakfast, I had a coffee and a slice of chocolate and coconut cake made by Ottavio the previous afternoon. Then I returned home with an annotated edition of Montaigne's *Essays*. I was as wide awake and rested as if I'd had a full night's sleep.

15

Twenty days before the date set for the start of the appeal hearing, Consuelo, Tancredi, Annapaola and I met again to assess the situation.

Consuelo began.

"For me, there's no need to present additional grounds. The appeal is unremarkable, it sticks rigidly to the main points, but it doesn't stop us from bringing up others. It questions the undervaluation of the defendant's mother's testimony, as well as the reconstruction of Cardace's movements that afternoon. It could have been better, but it'll be material for the closing statement. On the other hand, I haven't found any procedural irregularities. In particular, the phone taps were properly authorized. Not flawless, as you said, Guido, but there are no grounds for suggesting they're unusable."

"Yes, we'd only make them nervous if we brought up the question of irregularities," I said. "They'd be convinced we don't have any real arguments."

"If you all agree," Consuelo resumed, "using what Annapaola and Carmelo have found out as a basis, I'd like to go over some aspects of the investigation to highlight what wasn't done, things we could bring up at the hearing." Nobody made any comment. "Everything revolves around the fact that, when Gaglione calls 118, the police are listening in and immediately link it to the quarrel he had with Cardace a few hours earlier. It was the most natural assumption to make. The problem, which we need to highlight at the hearing, is that from then on, as far they're concerned, the hypothesis that Cardace was responsible for the murder becomes the one possible truth. We can't even say they *stop* considering alternative hypotheses. They don't consider them in the first place. A few minutes after the murder, they're already sure about what happened and have no doubts as to who the guilty party is. They just have to find a bit of corroborating evidence. In my opinion, to introduce an element of reasonable doubt we have to emphasize the fact that potentially important checks weren't carried out, because they were basically convinced that the case was already solved."

"That's right," I said, "but we have to avoid this looking like an attack on the police. Apart from obvious cases of abuse, which we don't have here, judges don't like that. And some jurors even less. We have to treat the matter as objectively as we can."

"Of course. Anyway, here's the list of what wasn't done. Firstly, no footage from security cameras in the area was submitted in evidence – unless, which I doubt, they viewed the footage, thought it was irrelevant and didn't inform the Prosecutor's Department. In any event, we'll have to call the head of the Flying Squad or the head of Homicide and question them about that."

"Then there's the matter of the apartment being on the mezzanine," Tancredi said.

"Right," Consuelo said. "There's no mention of that in the documents relating to the investigation, apart from a few words in the transcript of the inspection, when they describe the apartment. It's obvious they didn't consider the possibility that the killer might have gained access from the inner courtyard. There's no mention of them checking the windows for signs of a break-in or anything like that. We'll have to point this out, too. It's quite a suggestive argument."

"All right, so which witnesses will we need to call, Carmelo?"

"The man who used to be head of Homicide. He was transferred somewhere else a while ago. He isn't a particularly pleasant guy and I don't think he was directly involved in drafting any of the reports. If you ask him why he didn't do this or that, it's likely you'll fluster him and he'll get on his high horse. So if you want to sow a few doubts, he's our man."

"Now listen, all of you: in my last interview with Cardace, something interesting came out. He remembered that, as he was being taken to Headquarters, one of the officers asked him informally if he'd seen Gaglione that afternoon, and he said yes. At this point nobody had yet said anything to him about the murder. It's unlikely that a guilty person would admit so calmly that he'd been in the victim's apartment. Maybe we can do something with that. 'I had nothing to hide, I didn't even know there'd been a murder.'"

"This doesn't appear anywhere," Consuelo said.

"Precisely. It's something new, and in my opinion it's quite significant."

"How are you planning to proceed?" Annapaola asked.

"Cardace will definitely mention it in his testimony – we've agreed he'll appear as a witness. And we'll also examine the officer concerned. Why would he deny it?"

"You want to ask a police officer to testify about a statement made by the accused?" Consuelo said. "That's forbidden."

Actually, this was a correct objection. Article 62 of the code of criminal procedure says that statements made by an accused person or a suspect in the course of police inquiries

161

cannot be used in evidence. The rule is there to prevent the police or anyone else, having obtained a confession without legal guarantees, from testifying as to its substance, which is completely unusable.

"I think article 62 only applies to statements that are self-incriminating or unfavourable to the accused. The aim of the rule is to safeguard the right to a defence. Interpreted in accordance with this spirit, it shouldn't prevent testimony about statements made by the accused that might be useful in his defence. Then there's also another argument."

"What's that?"

"In this case, we'd actually be eliciting testimony about a fact, not a statement. Let me explain: Cardace, at a specific and significant moment, said a certain thing. The substance of the statement doesn't matter as much as the fact that the statement was made."

They were all silent for about twenty seconds. My argument made sense, but it required a modicum of reflection. At last Consuelo nodded: she also thought it might work.

"Let's try."

I turned to Tancredi. "Carmelo, in your opinion, talking about the jacket and the gunshot residue, do we need to call an expert witness?"

"No, we just need the member of the forensics team. All we have to do is explain the procedure and draw attention to the fact that the residue was found on the jacket, but not on Cardace's hands or any other part of his body. That's an element in favour of the theory that the contamination occurred a few days earlier."

"So let's put whichever forensics person did the test on the list. If we need anything more, we'll have time during the hearings. Now the two most complicated points: the target practice in the quarry and the story of the fight at Chilometro Zero."

"I talked to an old informant of mine this morning and finally found out the name of the guy who was beaten up by Gaglione."

He told us it was the son of one Sebastiano Amendolagine, known as Pitbull. A provincial boss active between Cassano and Acquaviva with a group of his own, dealing in drugs and extortion, especially of farmers; those reluctant to pay often found themselves with their grape canopies cut. He was on excellent terms with a few families in Bari, especially with people in San Girolamo. When he found out that his son had been beaten up by a bouncer he'd gone crazy.

"How can we use this?"

"I don't know. As I told you, I got it from an old informant of mine. Obviously, I can't reveal his name, and anyway it doesn't mean he had direct knowledge of the event. He told me the rumour that was going around about the fight and how pissed off the father was. Just to be clear, nobody's said that what happened to Gaglione was the work of somebody sent by Amendolagine."

"Maybe we could check if Amendolagine Junior was hospitalized somewhere," I said.

"Already checked," Tancredi replied. "He wasn't in any local emergency department. But he may have been treated in Trani, Foggia or Brindisi. That, I don't know."

I took a deep breath. "If I could manage to bring it out that Gaglione beat someone up who then turned out to be close to some dangerous people, even without naming names, that might open it up a little."

"The one possibility is if Cardace mentions it in his testimony," Tancredi said. "But we should find somebody who can at least confirm the circumstances of the fight. Somebody who was in the disco, one of the bouncers maybe."

"We may have one," Annapaola cut in. "A guy who owned a gym with Gaglione. Let me check some things, and I'll let you know in the next few days."

"Then there's the guy Cardace went shooting with in the quarry," Consuelo said. "Cipriani, is that right?"

"He'll never testify," Tancredi said. "We already talked about that. He'd have to admit he owned and carried an unauthorized weapon. I can't see that happening. Apart from anything else, his apartment was searched a few months ago and nothing was found. If they'd discovered a gun then, we might have been able to use it as an excuse."

"And Cardace won't say his name in court," I said. "We'll never persuade him to do that. He doesn't want the other prisoners to think he's a snitch – you know what happens to snitches."

Tancredi continued. "Annapaola and I, though, have tracked down the guy Cardace had coffee with. We talked to him and, incredibly, he's willing to testify. He seems like a decent kid."

"Well, that's good news," I said.

"But do we just get a statement from him or actually call him as a witness?" Consuelo asked.

"Let's call him as a witness. If there's no statement, it'll be more genuine. It'll look like the witness is impartial. Of course, if he gets cold feet and denies everything we have a problem."

"In that case, put me up on the stand," Annapaola said. "I'll testify as to what he told me, and if necessary we'll confront him with it."

I passed my hand over my face, against the growth of beard. One of the gestures I make when I'm at a loss what to say. The idea of Annapaola testifying in court as to the substance of the witness's statements – in case the latter didn't say what we expected – was very risky. The kind of request that makes judges angry.

All right, I concluded, we'd think about that if the problem arose.

Lorenza

In my memories of those months there are sudden flashes, patches of light where everything is visible, everything is solid and real. And there are long interludes that I can barely make out, as if they're something vaguely dreamed about or seen through a pane of frosted glass.

There's no chronological order, no true connective tissue, in these memories.

I know only a few things.

I know that I always carried coins and tokens with me; that I kept only a small amount of paper money in my pocket, held together with a large paper clip; that I had a cigarette case I'd been given by a girlfriend, and a Walkman; that I used a scent called Drakkar; that I had quite long hair.

I saw Lorenza again a few days later. She came again to pick me up outside my office, without warning of course. From that point on, our relationship took on a rhythm of its own, neurotic but somehow regular. She didn't have a telephone and would decide when to meet at the last minute. As to her movements, her work at school, what she did on the evenings when we weren't together, they were shrouded in mystery.

Every now and again she'd call me at home, more often at the office. She'd ask for Avvocato Guerrieri, which annoyed me (she knew perfectly well I wasn't a qualified lawyer yet, just a mere trainee prosecutor, and the practice's secretary knew it too – whenever she put the call through to me, she couldn't conceal the irony in her tone) and flattered me, as you might flatter a little boy who's playing at being an adult.

Sometimes I thought of asking for her to be told that the *avvocato* was out of the office, just like that, to establish the principle that it couldn't always be her who decided the when, the where and the how. I never did it.

She always found a way to provoke me about something. I would try to respond by reasoning and she would retort, for example, that my excess of rationality was a clear symptom of a lack of conviction, or of insufficient mastery of the various subjects. She had a formidable ability to manipulate any discussion, to avoid the obligation to answer argument with argument. A natural talent for fallacies. She liked it when I became rattled, got angry, possibly lost control. Immediately afterwards we would make love.

Once, while we were in bed in Via Eritrea, she asked me:

"Would it be a problem for you if I was also seeing another man?"

I replied something I don't remember, putting on a show of nonchalance while a spasm of jealousy tore right through me. A little while later, I asked her if there really was someone else, and who it was. She changed the subject with her usual, unbearable vagueness, which she handled like a weapon.

One evening, she came to pick me up with a girlfriend of hers. We went to the Taverna del Maltese, had a few sandwiches, drank rum and various beers, and as the evening wore on the conversation became full of hints and insinuations. I became convinced that they'd decided to have a threesome, that this had been their aim from the beginning of the evening. But as soon as we left the place they walked me home.

They had another appointment, Lorenza told me almost chirpily as they waved goodbye and I stood there like an idiot.

One afternoon, I spotted her in a blue Audi with a man in his forties: they'd pulled up at a traffic light on Corso Vittorio Emanuele. He exuded wealth, power and virility. I felt stupid, inferior, humiliated, but when I saw her again, maybe two days later, I didn't have the guts to ask her any questions.

Only on a few occasions did she seem to forget about the character she was playing. When we chatted about books, for example. Then a fierce, genuine, even touching passion emerged. It was she who introduced me to Yasunari Kawabata, Sylvia Plath, Fernando Pessoa, Luciano Bianciardi, Anna Akhmatova and others.

She'd talk to me about a writer and I'd immediately go and buy one of their books because, even though I would never have admitted it, I wanted her to think well of me. But then I'd really read them, and my eyes would be opened to worlds and stories and ideas I hadn't even known existed before.

Of all our conversations about books there's one I've never forgotten. The subject was fairy tales.

"If you want to understand the dark side that's in each one of us," she said, "reread the classic fairy tales. Just under the surface you'll find things that'll leave you stunned. The ambiguity of love, for example, which is never pure but always mixed up with anger, resentment, even hate. Think of all the stories in which the mother isn't there any more and her place is taken by a wicked stepmother on whom the child can vent its anger without fear of destroying the object of its love. Think of the stories about abandoned children. 'Tom Thumb', or 'The Little Match Girl', which for me is the cruellest. They're all about poverty, illness, death. They're anything but kids' stories. Read fairy tales and you'll find the most powerful key to understanding the nature of the evil and fear enclosed in the human heart."

16

The seventh of April was a sharp, bright spring day. I woke early and decided to take a stroll before going to court.

The seafront was metaphysically beautiful. The air was limpid, at once weightless and tangible. The perspective of the cast-iron lampposts suggested an army of spirit guides placed there to defend the city. On a day like this, if I'd had more time and gone a few miles further south, I'd have been able to see, clear in the distance, the outline of the Gargano promontory.

At eight, after having breakfast in a little bar where they make you brioches with the filling of your choice, I returned home, had a cold shower, put on my regulation charcoal-grey suit, went out again and headed for the appeal court.

Consuelo was waiting for me outside the main entrance with my briefcase, the papers we couldn't do without, and my robe.

We walked into the courtroom at a few minutes to 9.30 and, to my surprise, I saw that the assistant prosecutor was already there. That meant that the judges were ready to come out, didn't want to waste any time and had asked the Prosecutor's Department to guarantee punctuality.

"Good morning, Dottoressa," I said to Gastoni, who was absorbed in reading the case file. She replied to the greeting without any warmth.

Looking her in the face I thought I noticed something different about her compared with the last time I'd seen her, though I couldn't remember when that had been.

"Strange, she looks ... younger. That is, not exactly younger. Different," I said under my breath to Consuelo, once we had taken our seats.

"She must have spent a couple of months' salary to 'look younger'," Consuelo whispered. Needless to say, she didn't particularly like Gastoni.

"What do you mean?"

"Sometimes I think you men are stupid. The plastic surgeon must have had a heavy hand. Can't you see she looks like a carnival mask?"

I didn't have time to reply. The bell rang and the court entered.

Judge Marinelli didn't look as if he was in a good mood. He told the clerk of the court to have the accused brought in.

Five minutes later, Cardace was behind the bars, in the space reserved for defendants who are in custody. He was dressed soberly, in a blue sweater and white shirt. More boyish and more adult at the same time.

Just as Marinelli was asking his associate judge to read out the charges, Lorenza arrived. She waved to us from the public benches. Consuelo went to her and told her she would have to wait outside: witnesses are not allowed in court until they have testified.

The associate judge, Valentini, had been an assistant prosecutor. A good magistrate, quiet, reserved and, in my experience, competent and honest. Not just in the sense that he wasn't a crook: he was someone capable of not taking advantage of his own position, not abusing his own power. Something which can easily be done even without committing crimes. Valentini was someone who didn't dig his heels in when he realized he had made a mistake.

It has long been a topic of debate whether, in a hearing such as the one about to start, a magistrate like that is better or worse than one who's less adequate. A magistrate who's mediocre, lazy and incompetent (just one of these unenviable qualities is sufficient, but they're usually found together in the same individuals) is easier to convince: you just have to suggest that any alternative solution to yours is very, very tiresome to account for.

A good defence lawyer (and one who's perhaps a little open-minded) is pleased to have a lazy judge in a complicated court hearing, the kind in which you have to use complex arguments to establish your version of events beyond a reasonable doubt. Let it be clear that writing a ruling justifying an acquittal, in these cases, is much easier than writing one that irrefutably justifies a guilty verdict.

Valentini gave his summary off the cuff. In twenty minutes he effectively summed up the ruling, without forgetting any important detail and without getting lost in the unimportant ones. He ended by saying that the defence had presented a number of cogent requests for the submission of new evidence.

Judge Marinelli asked if the assistant prosecutor wished to make any observations on the requests presented by the defence.

Gastoni stood up and in a severe tone said yes, she had a number of observations. Her voice was nasal and quite low. Not pleasant to listen to in general, and decidedly unpleasant in the context of a court hearing.

"Your Honours, ladies and gentlemen of the jury, I want to specify in the first place that the Prosecutor's Department objects strongly to every request of the defence that consists of a repeat of what was done at the original trial. In the absence of explicit, solidly based reasons for what seems a mere time-wasting repetition, all requests to submit new evidence, *in parte qua*, should be rejected. I refer in particular to the request to call Signora Delle Foglie, the defendant's mother, and the police officers already examined. It is hard to see what they could add to the substance of their original testimonies. I also object to the calling of police officers not examined at the original trial – I refer in particular to the then head of the Homicide section of the Flying Squad – since it is not clear as to what is the evidential *novum* that would require calling this person as a witness.

"Essentially, then, the only request to which I do not object is that of calling as witnesses Sabino Arcidiacono, who is I gather the person met by the accused in a cafe just before the murder, and Gaetano Rafaschieri, an acquaintance of the victim. I consider such requests basically irrelevant, but I have no objection to them. Nor do I have any observation to make regarding the request to call the accused to the stand, since at his first trial his testimony was limited to statements."

Judge Marinelli gave me the chance to speak, asking me to be concise. I was starting to feel nervous, but I forced myself not to adopt an adversarial tone towards Gastoni. I hoped Marinelli wasn't going to go back on the promises he'd made me – promises he might not have told Gastoni about, judging by what we'd just heard.

"Thank you, Your Honour. Without wishing to be argumentative, I would say in the first place that suggesting there is time-wasting involved in the defence of someone in detention, without considering the length of that detention and with respect to court proceedings that would require three or four hearings at most, seems to me misplaced. As for the other points: the requests to re-examine certain witnesses already examined at the original trial arise from the need to ask them questions not asked during that trial, questions connected to what we expect to emerge from the testimonies of the new witnesses. If you wish, Your Honour, I can go further into the specifics of each request."

"No, thank you. We're fine as we are. We shall now retire to decide, and meet again in half an hour."

When the judges disappeared behind the door of their chambers, Gastoni left, leaving the case file and her robe on her seat.

"Could they reject the request?" Lorenza asked me when we joined her in the corridor. "Didn't they tell you they agreed to reopen the case?"

"That's what Judge Marinelli told me."

"Why did the prosecutor object?"

"Because she's a bitch," Consuelo answered before I could. "She objects regardless – she thinks that's the right way to be a prosecutor."

I shrugged. Basically, Consuelo was right and there wasn't much to add.

I went back in and exchanged a few words with Iacopo.

"What happens now, Avvocato?"

"They should accept our requests and set a date to begin hearing witnesses. That said, the law is full of surprises, so let's wait until they come out with their decision."

Forty minutes later, Gastoni reappeared.

Another five minutes and the court returned. Marinelli read out the decree, agreeing to our requests, set the dates for the hearings, and adjourned until the following Friday, when the first three witnesses would be examined.

Gastoni stood up and left without saying goodbye to anyone.

"Nice, isn't she?" Consuelo said, putting the case file back in the briefcase.

"Yes, like a bad toothache," I replied.

17

For the first hearing we called the police officer Cardace had spoken to as he was being taken to Headquarters; the head of Homicide at the time of the Gaglione murder; and the forensics technician who had carried out the gunshot residue test.

We started with the witness who hadn't been examined at the original trial. His name was Nicola De Tullio, and he was a sergeant. Above all, he was an old street cop. Twenty years in the Flying Squad, moving from the street crimes unit to Narcotics and finally Homicide. A bit aggressive, according to Tancredi, who knew him, but a decent person and also a good officer.

He came into the courtroom with the determined manner of someone who is often called to testify in court and knows, or thinks he knows, all the possible tricks defence lawyers can pull – an excess of self-confidence into which experienced police officers frequently fall. He was wearing a leather biker jacket, had a thick grey moustache and looked like someone you'd rather not quarrel with if you could help it. He refused the card with the text of the oath when the bailiff held it out to him and recited the formula by heart.

"Conscious of the moral and legal responsibility I assume with my testimony, I swear to tell the whole truth and not to conceal anything of which I have knowledge."

"Please proceed, Avvocato Guerrieri," Marinelli said.

"Good morning, Sergeant, can you tell the court in which department you work?"

"Bari Headquarters, Flying Squad, Homicide section."

"Did you take part in the investigation into the murder of Cosimo Gaglione?"

"Yes."

"Can you describe to us what your role was in the immediate aftermath of the crime?"

"Yes, together with my chief —"

"Sorry to interrupt. When you say 'together with my chief', to whom are you referring? To the head of the Homicide section or the head of the whole Flying Squad?"

"The head of the Flying Squad."

"Wasn't the head of Homicide there?"

"I don't remember too well, but as far as I know he was on holiday. He came back the next day, I think."

"Thank you. Go on."

"Yes, anyway, together with the chief and other colleagues I went to Gaglione's apartment. Officers from the patrol cars were already there, and Forensics arrived soon afterwards. The chief gave us our instructions: question the neighbours and the local shopkeepers, locate the security cameras and get hold of the relevant footage…"

"In other words, the normal investigative procedure that's routine in such cases?"

"Definitely."

"Did you get hold of the security footage?"

"I don't know. Before we could head out, the chief received a call from the intercept room. Gaglione was under investigation by the Narcotics team and apparently he'd had an argument with an associate of his a few hours earlier."

"How do you know it was an associate?"

"Narcotics told us, I think. Or maybe it was a client. Anyway, somebody who did business with Gaglione."

"Was it the defendant in today's hearing?"

"That's right. Anyway, they told us that it was clear from the telephone calls between Gaglione and Cardace that there was some kind of … animosity between the two. The fact that the murder occurred so soon after his argument made us think right away that Cardace was involved in Gaglione's death."

"This happened when you'd just arrived on the crime scene? In other words, half an hour after the murder?"

"I can't really be that exact. Maybe a bit more than half an hour. But an hour maximum."

"And at this point, what did you do?"

"At that point, we dropped the other checks and went to Cardace's home."

"Did you find him?"

"No. His mother told us he'd gone out."

"When had he gone out?"

"I don't know."

"I mean: when had he gone out, according to what his mother told you?"

"If I'm not mistaken, she said he'd gone out not long before, but I didn't talk to her, the chief did."

"And the rest of you?"

"We went looking for him."

"How long afterwards did you find him, and where?"

"We found him almost immediately. We were told that Cardace was hanging around outside a bar in Poggiofranco, I don't remember the name. We went to check, and he was there."

"Did you already know Cardace?"

"Yes."

"How come?"

"For a while we used to go to the same gym. But I didn't know his surname, I only realized who he was when I saw him."

"Did you take him to Headquarters?"

"We found some pills on him, or maybe he handed them over when we asked him if he had anything on him. I don't remember exactly. Anyway, yes, we took him to Headquarters."

"Were you in the same car as Cardace?"

"Yes, I was."

"Did you talk during the ride?"

"Yes, of course."

"Did you ask him anything?"

At this point, predictably, Gastoni got to her feet.

"Objection, Your Honour. The question is in violation of article 62, which I quote from memory: 'Statements made by the accused in the course of police inquiries cannot be the object of testimony.'"

Marinelli turned to me. "What observation does the defence wish to make on this point?"

I stood up and arranged my gown, which as usual was tending to fall to one side. "Actually, Your Honour, sorry if I'm splitting hairs, my question was about what the witness asked the defendant, not the substance of the answer. But this, I agree, is indeed splitting hairs, because in fact I really am interested in knowing what Cardace said on that occasion and I don't think article 62 can be invoked to deny me this chance, for two reasons. Firstly, we have to ask ourselves what the *ratio* is for the rule. Its aim is to protect suspects and defendants from the possible use *against* them of statements made in the absence of legal guarantees. So it's not possible to make use of this rule for different purposes, purposes actually opposed to the principle of *favor rei*. Whenever testimony about statements made by the accused can offer evidence useful to the defence, evidence that may introduce an element of reasonable doubt, it must be admitted. The rule of article 62, which is there to safeguard the defence, cannot be transformed into a trap for the right of the accused to defend themselves with evidence. The second reason follows naturally. The things said on that occasion, in that police car on its way to Headquarters, are not important for their substance as a statement, their narrative significance. They do not prove the truth of what was said. Their importance is purely factual. Basically, we're interested to know if a certain fact, the fact that Cardace stated certain things, happened at a particular moment. What makes this event important to us, what makes it a declarative event, as we might so call it, is that it happened at that particular moment in time."

Gastoni tried to reply. "This argument is unacceptable. I don't think —"

Judge Marinelli interrupted her. "All right, Dottoressa Gastoni, you've already stated your objection. Let's not stretch this out."

He turned towards the associate judge, and they conferred for a few seconds. Then he turned to the stenographer and dictated.

"The court, having considered that article 62 of the code of practice should be interpreted in conformity with its *ratio* and therefore according to the principle of *favor rei*, and having heard and approved the arguments of the defence, overrules the objection and orders that the matter may be pursued further. You may answer, Sergeant De Tullio."

"I'm sorry, Your Honour, I've lost the thread."

"Did you ask Cardace something when you were both in the car on the way to Headquarters? And if you did, what was the question and what was the answer?"

"I asked him when he'd last seen Gaglione, and he told me he'd seen him that afternoon."

"Did he tell you where they'd met?" I asked.

"He said they'd had a coffee in the afternoon. I don't recall if he told me where."

"Did Cardace want to know why you were asking him that question?"

"I don't remember, Avvocato. Everyone was in a state. As far as we knew, Cardace was the prime suspect in a murder, and we were in a hurry to get to Headquarters to do tests. What he told me didn't really matter – unless he'd confessed to the murder."

"Did you ask him that?"

"What?"

"If he'd murdered Gaglione and if he wanted to confess?"

"No. Maybe I asked him if they'd quarrelled, if anything had happened. I kept things vague."

"Did you make a written note of this conversation anywhere? In a duty report, maybe."

"Avvocato, you know as well as I do that it's forbidden to write down this kind of conversation."

"You're right." I threw a glance at Consuelo, who gave me a sign as if to say: I also think that's as far as you can go.

"Thank you. I have no further questions, Your Honour."

Marinelli turned to Gastoni, who was sitting with her head down, ostentatiously making notes. She hadn't appreciated the hasty overruling of her objection.

"Does the prosecution wish to cross-examine?"

Barely raising her head, she made a gesture with her hand. "No questions."

"Then the defence may call its next witness."

18

The next witness was Montesano, the former head of Homicide. He hadn't been called to testify at the original trial, probably because he'd left Bari and because giving an account of the investigation had been entrusted to the head of the Flying Squad.

"Good morning, Signor Montesano, I'm Avvocato Guerrieri and I'm representing Signor Iacopo Cardace. Can you indicate to the court your job and your rank?"

"Assistant commissioner, working with the Flying Squad in Rome."

"Can you tell us what your job was at the time of the Gaglione murder?"

"I was working with the Flying Squad of Bari, I was head of the Homicide section."

"So you dealt with that particular murder, is that correct?"

"Yes. I drew up the final report."

"Don't worry, I'm not going to ask you to recap the whole of the investigation. I've only asked you here today to clarify a few details."

"All right."

"Were you on the scene soon after the murder?"

"No, I was on holiday outside Bari. I was immediately informed and brought forward my return from Rome. I got here the next day."

"And took charge of operations."

"Under the coordination of my chief, the head of the Flying Squad, and the examining magistrate. But the crucial checks had all been carefully carried out in the immediate aftermath of the crime."

"Did you conduct a search of the victim's apartment?"

"No."

"Why not?"

"There was no need. It had already been done by the forensics team."

"So – correct me if I've misunderstood – you were *never* at the scene of the crime."

"I think I've already answered that."

First sign of irritation. It's never a good idea to get irritated while on the witness stand. It isn't a good idea for the witness and it isn't a good idea for the defence or the prosecution. The next step is that you lose your cool and the final (and potentially lethal) step is that you lose your head. Sometimes it's necessary to get a witness rattled, even though as time passes it's a practice I like less and less. And when a witness gets rattled, the best way to get them even more rattled is to ignore their bursts of irritation.

So I ignored the resentful tone of his answer, thinking Tancredi was right: Montesano wasn't particularly pleasant and the court wouldn't like him.

"Did you reconstruct the way the murderer got in and the way he got out?"

"In what sense?"

"I'm not sure how to make it any clearer. I repeat: did you reconstruct the way the murderer got in and out?"

He heaved a sigh of frustration. "There was nothing to reconstruct. This wasn't a murder committed in an open space, where there could have been various ways of getting to the scene of the crime and leaving it."

"Do you know what floor the apartment then occupied by Gaglione is on?"

"No, I don't think —"

"You don't know the apartment is on a mezzanine?"

"It's not a detail I bothered with."

"So am I to assume you don't know there's a balcony looking out on the inner courtyard of the building?"

"No, I don't."

"And you don't know what height the balcony is in relation to the courtyard?"

"Avvocato," Marinelli cut in, "let's avoid superfluous or pointlessly provocative questions. The witness has already said he doesn't have direct knowledge of the place."

"The avenue I'm trying to pursue, Your Honour, is whether or not the witness was informed by his subordinates —"

"Avvocato, please don't debate my decisions. Go on to the next question."

I nodded. I hoped the implication was clear: I don't agree with this decision, but all I can do is respect it. I turned back to the witness. His face was as closed as a fist.

"Does the name Sabino Arcidiacono mean anything to you?"

His hostile expression turned to one of bewilderment. "To be honest, no." Then he asked the judge: "If I can consult my papers…"

Marinelli nodded and I intervened.

"In the spirit of not weighing proceedings down with pointless wastes of time, let me just say that the name Sabino Arcidiacono isn't in any of the documents relating to the investigation. Just as, for clarity's sake, there's no mention of the height of the inner balcony or the possibility of entering the apartment from the back."

Marinelli looked at me and his eyes told me he was starting to get annoyed. Montesano had his hand on the papers he had started leafing through.

"If it's not in the papers I don't know what to tell you."

"So maybe, before going on to the specific point that interests me, it'll be necessary for you to give us a brief recap of the investigation."

His face registering a mixture of impatience and resignation, Montesano started recounting things we all knew already. This would usually have been pointless, but in this case hearing the list of what had been done would help – at least I hoped it would – to give an idea of what *hadn't* been done.

It lasted about a quarter of an hour and I was surprised that neither Judge Marinelli nor Assistant Prosecutor Gastoni made any comments or asked where I was going with this. Maybe the simple reason was that they had understood. When the account of the first day of the investigation was over, I cut in again with a question.

"So, Assistant Commissioner Montesano, if I understand correctly, a significant element in the investigation conducted in the immediate aftermath of the murder, when you had not yet returned to your post, was the questioning of the woman named Antonia Sassanelli, who worked in the cafe. Is that correct?"

"Yes. The statement she made allowed us to place Cardace in the immediate vicinity of the victim's apartment at a time that matched our working hypothesis."

"What was your working hypothesis?"

Montesano sighed ostentatiously. "That Cardace had quarrelled with Gaglione over something to do with narcotics, that he had gone to Gaglione's apartment to get even for some unspecified slight and that he had shot him, probably just with the intention of kneecapping him."

"This was the working hypothesis."

"Precisely."

"Were there any others?"

"No, there was no reason for any others."

"Let's see if I've got this right. A few minutes after the murder had been committed, you formulated a hypothesis to explain what had happened, which then, after the initial stages of the investigation, remained the only one. Is that correct?"

"That's correct."

"Do you know what work Gaglione did? I mean legitimate work."

"If I remember correctly, he worked in security, I think he was a nightclub bouncer."

"I see. Why isn't this mentioned in the papers?"

"Right now I don't remember if it's in the papers or not."

"You can take my word for it: it isn't. If you want to check, you may do so, obviously."

He took another deep breath. As often happens, he had come to court thinking he would only have to confirm what was in his report. And now he found himself in a situation that was starting to become irksome.

"If it's not there, it must be because we considered it irrelevant to the investigation."

"From which I think I may infer that you didn't carry out any checks on possible motives for the murder linked to Gaglione's work as a bouncer."

"No. As I just said —"

"Yes, you did say. There was a very promising lead, so you didn't follow any other, or even speculate on an alternative.

Let's continue. You told us that Signora Antonia Sassanelli stated that Cardace had been in the cafe that afternoon together with another customer. Did you ask Signora Sassanelli who this customer was?"

"I wasn't the one who questioned her, but I think so, yes."

"I ask you this because it's nowhere in your report."

"Objection, Your Honour, that's quite enough," Gastoni intervened at last. "What does counsel for the defence think he's doing? Is he challenging the report? As far as I recall, it's possible to challenge the substance of a witness's previous statements, not the substance of a police report or other official documents."

"Avvocato, the assistant prosecutor is right. You can't challenge the substance of the report, let alone any possible hypothetical omissions from the writing of the report or the conduct of the investigation."

"Your Honour, I wasn't challenging anything, I was merely attempting to bring up elements missing from the investigation. This is relevant to our defence strategy. I'll rephrase the question." I turned back to the witness. "Let me ask you again: Do you recall if a certain Sabino Arcidiacono was identified in your investigation?"

"No."

"Sabino Arcidiacono is the person who was with Cardace in the cafe when Signora Sassanelli saw them. Did you not know that?"

"This is the first I've heard of it."

"Did you instruct your subordinates to identify the person with whom Cardace, according to Signora Sassanelli's testimony, had been talking in the cafe?"

"I don't remember now, it's been years. I assume I did."

"I see. Given that you assume you did, can you explain why this person is not identified in any of the documents relating to the investigation?"

The look he gave me was almost one of hate. I couldn't blame him: my tone was deliberately annoying and suggested that there had been some shortcomings in his work and that of his men. It was what I thought, and it was what I wanted the judges and jury to think.

Sometimes when you ask questions of a witness the real aim isn't to obtain a specific answer, which very often is already known. It isn't to obtain an element of knowledge, that is, the object and reason for the testimony. The aim is to send, through the question, a message to the judges and jury. I ask you something to communicate indirectly with those who are present at our dialogue and will then have to decide on the case. It's a technique that should be used sparingly: if you overdo it, it becomes pointless, if not damaging, because it may annoy the judges.

"Obviously we considered it unnecessary. We had a lot of significant evidence against Cardace, as a result of which he was placed in custody, a measure that was later upheld several times in court."

It was his way of evening the score. My questions had suggested that the investigation had been incomplete and, above all, inspired by a single hypothesis. This answer of his reminded the judges and jury that the investigation had been so thorough as to justify a custody order that had been confirmed at every stage. Not to mention the trial verdict.

Montesano continued, almost didactic now. "A statement from this individual had become irrelevant. Mind you, I don't remember anything concerning this specific matter, but if you ask me the reason we didn't identify this individual and

I think back to my memories of the case and our investigation, I can say that in all probability that must have been it."

Ignoring the hint of provocation in his tone, I smiled. "So, correct me if I've misunderstood, you didn't consider it relevant to hear what a witness who had spoken with the prime suspect, or rather, the *only* suspect, immediately before or immediately after the murder might have been able to tell you?"

As sometimes happens, he realized too late that he had said too much.

"I didn't say that. I was speculating. You asked me why this person wasn't identified, and remembering nothing of the matter, which as far as I can see was irrelevant anyway, I tried to give you a plausible explanation."

"To be honest, I didn't ask you to speculate. Anyway, I note that Sabino Arcidiacono, who, by the way, we will be calling as a witness, wasn't identified and questioned during the investigation."

Judge Marinelli intervened. "All right, Avvocato, it seems to me the witness has answered fully. If you have no further questions, which I hope not, we could move on to cross-examination – if, that is, the assistant prosecutor has any questions for the witness."

Once again, Gastoni said she had no questions.

Marinelli dismissed Montesano – who didn't deign to look at me as he passed me on the way out – and said we could call the final witness scheduled for this hearing.

19

The name of the inspector who had handled the analysis of the gunshot residue test was De Luigi. He was wearing a jacket and tie like someone who isn't used to wearing them and looked like a young boy who had just joined the police. He was actually forty-four, as I discovered when he gave his particulars.

"You work at the regional laboratory of the Police Forensics Department, is that correct?"

"Yes. I've been working there for ten years."

"What does the gunshot residue test consist of? I ask you to explain given that the jurors probably have no idea."

"Yes, of course. The test is carried out when there's a suspicion that somebody has fired a shot."

"Can you describe to us the operation from the start?"

"Swabs are applied to the suspect's hands, arms, face, neck and hair to collect particles deriving from a shot, if there are any, though they may only be identified during the next stage, when the specimen is examined under a scanning electron microscope."

"One moment, I'm sorry. The test is done only on hands, face, hair, arms and neck? Aren't specimens also taken from the nostrils?"

"Yes, also from the nostrils, that's correct."

"And from the clothes?"

"It depends. If they're the clothes the individual was wearing … or rather, if they're the clothes the individual is believed to have been wearing at the time of the offence for which they're being investigated, yes."

"How exactly do particles end up, not only on the hands and arms, but also on the face and hair and in the nostrils?"

"When a firearm is discharged, a kind of cloud is released which spreads in a radius that varies depending on the type and calibre of the weapon. This cloud of volatile material falls rather like talcum powder, and may also settle on the face and hair."

"How many hours after the event is it sensible to do the test?"

"It isn't possible to indicate an exact time. It depends on a number of factors. If the individual has washed themselves thoroughly, it's quite unlikely we'd find anything even ten minutes after the shot. If they were wearing surgical gloves and removed them in the correct way, we definitely wouldn't find anything on their hands. Alternatively, if someone doesn't wash themselves and hasn't taken any precautions to protect themselves from contamination, like overalls, hoods and gloves which they then removed, traces can be found as much as four hours later. If more time passes, it's very difficult: these particles are very volatile and tend to disperse, even if no washing takes place."

"I have a specific question. If someone has fired a shot, and a few minutes later they're given the test and nothing is found on their hands, arms or face, it's very likely, not to say certain, that they've washed themselves. Is that correct?"

"That's correct."

"Has it ever happened to you that you've done a test on an individual, not found anything on their hands or face, but have found something in their nostrils?"

"I should say that I'm not the one who finds the particles. I do the test – the samples are analysed by others. That said, yes, it has happened. Getting gunshot residue out of your nostrils is more complicated, and sometimes people don't even think about it."

"If someone fired a shot, let's say an hour ago, then you do the test and nothing is found on their hands, face or even in their nostrils, what might you deduce from that?"

The assistant prosecutor objected. "Your Honour, the defence is asking the witness for his opinion."

"Yes, Your Honour, that's true. I am asking an opinion of the witness, given that he's an expert witness. I refer in addition, I think correctly, to the conditions laid out in article 194 paragraph 3 of the code of practice, which hypothesizes the impossibility of separating the personal evaluation of an expert witness from a testimony on the facts."

Judge Marinelli made a gesture of annoyance, as if to dismiss a small object that was bothering him. "Objection overruled. You may answer, Inspector."

"If I'm certain that someone fired a shot an hour ago and we don't find any residue on them, I'd conclude that they washed and cleaned themselves thoroughly and blew their nose, maybe even rinsed their nostrils with a saline solution."

"So an individual who washed themselves so thoroughly would show a remarkable degree of caution and even a degree of knowledge of this test, is that correct?"

"Your Honour, this really is asking for inadmissible speculation," Gastoni cried.

"Avvocato Guerrieri, this is an observation we could even make ourselves, if necessary. I'd say we've gone beyond the provisions of article 194 paragraph 3. Ask another question."

"Very well, Your Honour. Inspector, was it you who carried out the test on the person and clothes of Iacopo Cardace within the context of the investigation into the murder of Cosimo Gaglione?"

"Yes, though not alone, with colleagues."

"But you participated in the whole operation, is that correct?"

"All the test operation. The analysis of the samples is carried out at the central laboratory because you need a scanning electron microscope."

"The clothes on which you carried out the test were those that Cardace was wearing when he was taken to police head-quarters, is that correct?"

"Yes."

"And how many hours after the estimated hour of the murder did this happen?"

"I don't remember exactly, I'd need to look in the records."

Judge Marinelli gave him permission to do so. He took a little longer than necessary. In the end he looked up and turned to me.

"You asked me how many hours after the murder the test was done?"

"Yes."

"About four hours."

"Are you sure? Having the records at your disposal, maybe you could be more precise."

He checked again.

"Yes, I'm sorry, I made a mistake, it was about three hours."

"So we're still within the time frame during which the residue remains on the body of the individual, if no washing has taken place?"

"Yes, basically."

"Yes or no?"

"Yes."

"You then saw the results of the analysis carried out at the central laboratory using a scanning electron microscope?"

"Yes, of course."

"Can you summarize these results?"

"There were various particles of lead, barium and antimony on Cardace's jacket."

"What does that mean?"

"It means that while wearing that jacket Cardace fired a shot or was very close to somebody who fired a shot. You have to remember that particles of lead, barium and antimony don't exist in nature, and that in our current state of knowledge, they're the results of a single physico-chemical process, which is the discharge of a firearm. I should specify that lead, antimony and barium are part of the chemical composition of the powders produced by firearms."

"Were there particles of lead, barium and antimony on Cardace's hands?"

"No."

"Were there particles of lead, barium and antimony on Cardace's arms?"

"No."

"Were there particles of lead, barium and antimony on Cardace's face?"

"No."

"Were there particles of lead, barium and antimony in Cardace's nostrils?"

"No."

"So the particles were only on the jacket, is that correct?"

"That's correct."

"You told us earlier that particles remain on the surface of the skin, in the absence of washing, for four hours. How long do they remain on clothes?"

"That depends on many factors. How they've been kept, if they're washed."

"What if they're not washed?"

"They can remain for a few days."

"I again call on your technical expertise. If Cardace had fired a shot that afternoon, how would you explain the complete absence of gunshot residue on his hands, arms and face, and in his nostrils?"

"He could have washed."

"Thoroughly, we could say, given that there wasn't even anything in his nostrils."

"Yes."

"So the explanation would be that Cardace had washed his hands, face and all the rest, this showing full awareness of the need to eliminate gunshot residue, and yet continued wearing the same jacket. Doesn't that strike you as odd?"

"Objection, Your Honour," Gastoni said. "This is a leading question, and certainly outside the provisions of article 194 paragraph 3."

"I withdraw the question," I said before Marinelli could intervene. This time Gastoni was right. It wasn't a question, it was an observation I wanted to plant in the minds of the judges and jury. I would return to it in my closing statement.

I said I had finished and Marinelli asked Gastoni if she wished to cross-examine. This time she said yes.

"Inspector, I call on your experience. Has it ever happened to you that you carried out a test on a suspect and obtained positive results on the clothes and negative ones on the body – hands, face, etc.?"

"Yes. I remember at least two other cases."

"When these individuals were put on trial, what was the outcome?"

At this point it was up to me to object. It was a clever question, and a dangerous one.

"Objection, Your Honour, it's not possible to introduce —"

Marinelli interrupted me. "Avvocato Guerrieri, this is a line of questioning you yourself initiated. The prosecution is entitled to take it further. Then we can each draw our own conclusions. Objection overruled. Please answer."

"In both cases the defendants were found guilty."

"Partly on the basis of the forensics evidence."

"Definitely."

"Thank you, I have no further questions."

For a moment I thought of asking him some questions about those two cases. Ask him for further details, explore the differences there probably were between those cases and ours. Then I decided against it. Firstly, I didn't know what territory I would be stepping into: I had no idea what those cases had been about, I'd be asking questions blindly and didn't know what might emerge. Secondly, I would be giving the impression that Gastoni's questions had upset me because they might weaken the theory I was constructing at this hearing.

Marinelli adjourned until the following Monday, when we would call our other witnesses. That is, Lorenza, the woman from the cafe, and Rafaschieri, who had run a gym with Gaglione.

On Wednesday the defendant would testify, then, unless anything new emerged that required further checks, no further witnesses would be called and we would adjourn until the following week, after Easter, for closing statements.

I put my papers in my briefcase together with my folded robe and turned to go. Consuelo had already rushed off to be present at a preliminary hearing we'd both forgotten about.

Lorenza was at the back of the courtroom; she must have just come in. She looked at me as if she was about to say something. But if she was, it went no further.

Lorenza

By now it was summer.

Once – it might actually have been the night of the solstice – we went to the villa of a friend of hers, just outside Polignano. There was a little gate from which you had direct access to the sea. The air was sharp, and a light wind was blowing that at times made you shiver and gave you a sense that this was an unrepeatable moment.

After eating – somebody had prepared a huge *tiella* of potatoes, rice and mussels – I'd gone and sat down a few paces from the water with a cigarette and a glass of wine.

Lorenza joined me, took my cigarette from me, put it out and passed me a joint she'd just rolled. For several minutes we shared the pot and the wine in silence.

"When I was a little girl I sometimes stopped and listened to my heart and thought the beating was the footsteps of the Lord of Time."

"The Lord of Time? Was that something you'd read about or seen in a cartoon?"

"I don't know. I don't remember. I'd listen to his footsteps – in other words, the beating of my heart – and expect they would stop at any moment and the Lord of Time would appear and say that I had to make three wishes. I absolutely had to be ready to make them immediately, because otherwise terrible things would happen – none of the wishes would ever come true, the Lord of Time would stop walking, I wouldn't hear his footsteps any more, and time and the world would disappear."

"Disappear?"

"Yes. The salvation of time and the world depended on my ability to make three wishes as quickly as possible. It seems strange, but it's not at all easy. You always have the impression they're the wrong ones. Either too big and impersonal, or too small and wretched."

"What wishes did you think of?"

"I wavered between all sorts of things. I want to always be with Elisabetta – my best friend at the time. I want Mum and Dad to stop always quarrelling and for Dad not to walk out – something that happened a lot when I was thirteen. I want to become a famous children's writer, with a big villa by the sea, right on the beach. I think that came from an American film I'd seen where there was a woman writer with a villa on the beach."

"Up until what age did you think about the Lord of Time?"

"I had a dream. He was there even though I couldn't see him. I felt his presence. I knew he was coming, and I knew he was something halfway between the Scarecrow and the Tin Man in the *Wizard of Oz*, the first book I remember reading. I had to make the three wishes."

"Did you succeed?"

"No."

"And what happened?"

"I woke up. Feeling very sad. Since then I haven't heard the footsteps of the Lord of Time. Less than a month later I became a young lady, as my grandmother put it."

She stopped speaking and gave me a kiss, with a tenderness that wasn't like her.

"Who knows how we'll end up?" she said. She let a few seconds go by, then continued without waiting for me to answer. "Anyway, all this" – she made a vague gesture that took in the sea, the night, but also the wine, the pot, the two of us, everything – "nobody will ever take it from us. It's ours for ever."

From the villa came the muffled strains of "Have You Ever Seen the Rain?" At that precise moment, the first time I'd heard her use the word "us" when talking about her and me, I knew – for no particular reason, therefore with absolute certainty – that she would soon vanish from my life.

Sometimes she'd mention the novel she was writing. When I asked her to tell me about it, though, she would change the subject, retreating as if realizing that she'd exposed herself, shown a vulnerability she couldn't bear.

One Saturday morning – it was July by now – she phoned me and told me to pack a small bag, and make sure I included swimming trunks. She would pick me up in her car in half an hour. Before I could ask her where we were going she hung up.

We went to Santa Maria di Leuca in her beat-up old Alfasud. We took a room in a *pensione* on the promenade, then hired a small boat and made love out at sea. We were still there, surrounded by the motionless, limpid water, with the sun going down, when she told me about the time she and a friend of hers had gone to Othonoi in a motorboat.

"Where's Othonoi?"

"It's the nearest Greek island, in the Strait of Otranto. It's only about fifty miles from here."

"And how long did it take you to get there?"

"Two hours, more or less. It was a fast motorboat. We got there in the afternoon, had dinner there, slept in a fisherman's house, and the next day came back to Santa Maria di Leuca."

"And what does your friend who rides fast motorboats do?"

She shrugged, became evasive again and changed the subject. I thought about her mysterious, adventurous life, full of real, concrete things, including real men. Men capable of taking a motorboat out into the open sea, maybe of facing a storm. The adult version of those fearless boys who'd obsessed me during my years as a shy, rather clumsy adolescent. Those who drove motorbikes along dirt tracks, who played soccer well, dribbling easily, who dived elegantly into the sea from the tops of rocks.

I had never been gifted at sports. I'd become quite good at boxing only because I'd really committed myself, almost as if my life depended on it. Maybe, in a way, it did.

I thought about these things while Lorenza was lying in the bow of the boat with her eyes closed, her head resting on a rolled-up towel. The boat swayed gently, the sun was setting, and little flying fish gave off silver flashes as they jumped.

20

She was dressed in jeans, a blue blazer and a man's white shirt. She looked scared and at the same time daring. For the first time since I'd seen her again, I thought I caught a glimpse of the way she'd been when she was young. I think it was due to the conflicting feelings shown in her face, her eyes, her posture, the way she displayed both incurable fear and defiant courage.

Judge Marinelli motioned to her to sit down. "You are the mother of the accused, signora, is that correct?"

"Yes."

"I assume you already know that according to article 199 of the code of criminal procedure you have the right to refrain from testifying. Should you decide not to avail yourself of this right, you will be under the obligation to tell the truth, just like any other witness, with all the legal consequences for any false or partial testimony. Is that clear?"

"Yes."

"Do you wish to avail yourself of the right to refrain from testifying?"

"No, I want to testify."

"All right, then. First of all you have to swear to tell the truth."

The bailiff approached her and gave her the card with the oath.

She read it in a firm voice and after the last words she raised her eyes from the card and looked at the judge.

"The witness is yours, Avvocato Guerrieri. Please proceed."

"Thank you, Your Honour. Good morning, signora, I'm going to ask you a few questions. Then, if she deems it necessary, the assistant prosecutor will do the same. Before we begin, let me just say that if something isn't clear, I'd simply ask you to say so. Don't force yourself to answer questions you haven't fully understood. Do you understand?"

"Yes," she said, accompanying the answer with a slight nod.

"I'd like to begin immediately with a question not directly relating to the events about which you will have to testify, but which is important for evaluating your reliability. Have you ever been subject to criminal proceedings?"

"Yes."

"Can you tell us for what crime?"

"I was accused by the Treasury Police of aiding and abetting and of resisting an officer of the law."

"When did the events over which you were accused take place?"

"It was July 1987."

"Can you tell us what happened?"

Gastoni leapt to her feet, spreading all around her a perfume I knew but couldn't identify.

"Your Honour, frankly I don't understand what we're talking about. The witness was called to testify about a particular circumstance, that is, the supposed presence of her son at home at the time of the murder of which he is accused and for which he was convicted. But now we have defence counsel questioning her about events that happened almost thirty years ago and that have no relevance to the object of this hearing."

Marinelli turned to me. "Avvocato Guerrieri, can you explain the relevance of this question to the *thema probandum?*"

"The witness testified at the original trial. Her testimony was undervalued, almost to the point of being declared false, basically for two reasons. The first was that she is the mother of the accused, and therefore her testimony would not be credible until proved otherwise. I won't linger for the moment on the weakness of this argument, I'll leave that for my closing statement. What interests us now is the second argument. It was the assistant prosecutor at the original trial who introduced the question of the witness's criminal record. It was partly because of that record that the court declared the witness unreliable. The argument, in very broad terms, was this: the witness was charged with obstructing justice and only escaped the charge thanks to the amnesty of 1990. This, according to the ruling, suggested an inclination to obstruct the course of justice and therefore the unreliability of her testimony. The witness was not asked to explain the events that led to these proceedings, and the ruling not to proceed, produced in court by the prosecution, mentions only the charges and the non-existence of grounds for acquittal. So today it's vital we understand what events these were if we want to evaluate the correctness of the judges' ruling."

Marinelli glanced through the papers in the case file, exchanged a few words in a low voice with the associate judge, then again addressed me.

"Very well, Avvocato Guerrieri, you may continue. But let's not hold a trial now on the charge of aiding and abetting."

"Of course, Your Honour, I just need to elicit the witness's version of events to ascertain how well that ruling holds up. So, Signora Delle Foglie, let's go back to the point where we were interrupted. Can you tell us what you remember of the events that gave rise to the charges of aiding and abetting and of resisting an officer of the law?"

"Yes. I was with a group of friends on a beach, near Torre Canne. We'd spent all day by the sea, it was hot and we'd decided to stay there until after the sun went down."

"What were you doing?"

"The usual things people did on a summer evening in those days. Eating, drinking. Smoking."

"What were you smoking?"

"Some cigarettes, some grass. Or maybe it was hashish."

"Did the composition of the group remain the same throughout, or were there people who left and people who arrived?"

"There were people who left and people who arrived."

And where had I been that evening? I knew I would never be able to remember, and for a moment my mind wandered, thinking of all the things in the past that had disappeared.

"How many of you were there, more or less?"

"I don't remember exactly. Ten or so, maybe."

"What happened while you were all there in a group on the beach?"

"After a while, about the time it was getting dark, I'd say, there was a sudden commotion. Lots of yelling, people running … I couldn't tell you the details because I'd gone for a walk and saw it all from a distance."

"And what did you do?"

"I went back to the group, that is, towards the fracas. A friend of ours was running away and two guys I'd never seen before were following him. It was a nasty scene and I thought they were fascists."

"Why did you think they were fascists?"

"Many of us, especially in the previous few years, had been politically active. And there had been attacks by fascists, various clashes with them. Although to tell the truth it hadn't happened for a while. But in that frantic situation it was the only thing I could think of. I had no idea what was happening. Don't forget, we're talking about seconds."

"Go on."

"One of the two reached our friend and started hitting him."

"How far away were you?"

"By now I was quite near. About ten yards, maybe."

"And what did you do?"

"I joined them and pulled the guy I didn't know by the shirt … or the T-shirt, I'm not sure. Anyway, I pulled him from behind, to make him stop. He lost his balance and our friend started running again."

"And then?"

"Then the other one arrived, stopped me and handcuffed me, while the one I'd caused to fall started following our friend again. To cut a long story short, he caught up with him and stopped him. They arrested him for possession of drugs and me for resisting an officer of the law."

"Were they carabinieri, State Police, Treasury Police?"

"They were Treasury Police."

"When did you find out they were Treasury Police?"

"When I was already handcuffed."

"You mean they hadn't identified themselves before that?"

"I don't know. Like I said, I was a long way away and all I heard was shouting. It was only after they handcuffed me that they told me they were Treasury Police and that I was in big trouble."

"Did they take you to their station?"

"Yes, I was there for a couple of hours and then I was released. Our friend, on the other hand, was transferred to prison."

"So first they handcuffed you, then they let you go. Do you know why?"

"They told me I was lucky, that they'd called the duty magistrate to tell him what had happened and he'd told them not to arrest me."

"Were you ever put on trial?"

"Years later I received a summons. I took it to a lawyer and he told me I had nothing to worry about because there was an amnesty and the whole thing would be dismissed, something like that. I replied that I hadn't done anything illegal, so I didn't understand why I should have an amnesty."

"Did the lawyer explain to you that you had the right to refuse the amnesty?"

"No, or at least I don't remember."

"In your son's original trial, you were asked by the prosecution if you had ever been subject to criminal proceedings. You answered no, even though there had been these charges. Why didn't you mention them?"

"When he said proceedings, I thought he meant a hearing like this, in court, with a judge. I never had that. Like I said, I didn't get that summons until years after the episode on the beach, and the lawyer assured me there was nothing to worry about, that the case would be dismissed without any need to do anything. I forgot all about it."

Up until this point, Marinelli had been quite patient, I have to admit. He asked me how much longer we would be discussing this matter, and if I thought I could now go on to the main subject of the testimony.

"I've finished, Your Honour. One final question and I'll go on to something else. Signora, all the things you've told us now, and which we can easily confirm, if the court so wishes, by obtaining the file on that old case – did you mention any of them at your son's trial?"

"No."

"For what reason?"

"I was surprised and confused. I hadn't expected them to bring up that old business. I answered the prosecutor's questions without really understanding what it had to do with the trial. Nobody asked me to explain and it wasn't until I heard the prosecutor's summing-up and read the ruling that I realized I was considered an unreliable witness because I had a criminal record."

There. Unreliable witness. I had suggested she use the word "unreliable" about herself. Giving ourselves a label that corresponds to the negative opinions other people have of us, or the fears we arouse in them, helps – or may help – to defuse their unfavourable implications. If I say I know you consider me a bad lawyer who's inclined to make misleading arguments, I reduce the negative, prejudicial force of this opinion. Bringing it to the surface, making it explicit, I make it debatable, lessen its ability to work beneath the surface of your awareness as an insurmountable precondition of your judgement. Stating that nobody had asked her for any explanation also suggested, without overdoing it, some form of negligence on the part of the original defence counsel. He hadn't dealt with a problem that actually should have been faced head-on, and in that way had left an unfavourable opinion of the witness to fester, an opinion that had then been translated into a judgement of unreliability in the ruling.

"I want to look further at that expression you yourself used: unreliable witness. The negative opinion of you contained in the ruling didn't derive only from this criminal record of yours, which we've now clarified. There were also inconsistencies in your account of that afternoon, are you aware of that?"

"Yes, of course."

"Then let's examine these inconsistencies. You said you went to see the elderly lady you used to keep company for a few hours every day. Is that correct?"

"Yes, it's correct."

"Do you still go to see this particular lady?"

"No, unfortunately she passed away."

"Until when did you go there?"

"Until about a year ago, which is when she died."

"Can you tell us the length of time you spent that afternoon, the afternoon of the murder, in this lady's apartment?"

"I was there from three o'clock to seven o'clock."

"How can you say this with such certainty and precision at this distance in time?"

"I'd like to clarify the misunderstanding —"

"I'm sorry, don't bother to clarify anything. Just answer my questions. How can you be so sure about the time after all these years?"

"Because in the days immediately after the murder, when it turned out that Iacopo was a suspect, I thought carefully about what I'd done and about the time when I'd seen my son come home. I assumed I'd be questioned by the police and I hoped I'd be able to provide him with an alibi."

"Is that what happened?"

"No, I was never called by the police."

"But when your son was arrested, didn't you think of going to the police or the prosecutor and making a statement that would clear him?"

"Yes, I talked about it with his previous defence counsel and he told me it was better to keep this option for the trial. He said they'd never believe me while the investigation was still ongoing, they'd think I was lying, wholly or partly, in order to provide Iacopo with an alibi."

"So the first time you made any statement about this was in court at the first trial?"

"Yes."

"But, as you told us a few moments ago, you'd already gone over in your mind your whereabouts on the afternoon of the murder in the days immediately following. Is that correct?"

"Yes, it is."

"Why didn't you say that when you testified at the trial?"

"Because I got confused. The prosecutor asked me how I could be so sure of the time and, for some absurd reason, I don't really know why, I said I was sure because that was the schedule I had with that lady at the time. Which was partly true, even though I was already occasionally doing different schedules. Basically, I didn't explain it well."

"To avoid any misunderstanding and to make sure your testimony today is completely transparent, I ask you now: have you ever discussed with anyone else the substance of this testimony, today's testimony, I mean?"

"I discussed it with you."

"Can you tell the court, in broad terms, what was the tenor of our conversation?"

"You showed me that my testimony at the trial was contradictory and that it was understandable that the judges had doubted it. You asked me to go over the whole story again

211

calmly and to explain why I remembered the time so precisely. And I told you what I've just repeated here in court."

"And what did I say?"

"You told me that if that was the truth, we should request that I be called again as a witness to clarify all these misunderstandings. Both about that old episode, and about the day of the murder."

"Thank you, signora. Your Honour, I have no further questions."

Marinelli nodded, half closing his eyes. I had the definite feeling that my examination of Lorenza had made an impression on him.

"Very well. Does the prosecution wish to cross-examine the witness?"

"Yes, Your Honour," Gastoni said.

"Please proceed."

"So, the accused is your son and naturally you want him to be acquitted, is that right?"

A flash of something I couldn't interpret passed through Lorenza's eyes. "Naturally," she said after a few seconds, as if she'd had to think carefully about her answer.

"You would be prepared to do anything to save your son, I imagine."

I stood up. "Objection, Your Honour. That's a speculative question, asking the witness for a hypothetical opinion, and it also includes an implicit threat. It is therefore forbidden for two reasons: because it violates the prohibition on asking opinions of the witnesses and because at root it impugns the honesty of the answers according to article 499 paragraph 2 of the code of practice."

"Assistant Prosecutor, ask questions about facts, not speculation," said Marinelli.

"You said you spoke with defence counsel and only after that conversation did you decide to change your version. Have I understood that correctly?"

"No, you haven't. I said that talking with counsel, and even before reading the judges' ruling and the transcript of my testimony, I realized I'd said some things that were unclear and that lent themselves to being misunderstood. That's why counsel and I decided that I should testify again."

"And you prepared the substance of your testimony together."

I thought of standing up and objecting again. It would have been a correct objection, because the question implied that we had sat round the table and prepared the substance of the testimony, twisting it to suit us – in other words, it implied that I had done something improper. Then I realized that the objection would be a kind of pre-emptive self-defence, a demonstration that I was oversensitive and vaguely guilty. So I decided not to react – hoping Lorenza would find an effective answer.

"I don't think it's right, putting it like that. We didn't *prepare* the substance of my testimony. I calmly told counsel why I remembered the time so clearly, he asked me if I was sure, I said yes and he said that then it would be necessary for him to request that I be called again to testify."

Gastoni made a gesture of annoyance. "The court will evaluate if what you say is the truth or if it's an attempt to fix a testimony that was rightly considered unreliable."

Now an objection was unavoidable.

"Your Honour, could we ask the assistant prosecutor not to argue with the witness and not to make observations at this point that she'll be able to develop, if she so wants, in her closing statement?"

Marinelli sighed briefly. "Assistant Prosecutor, do you have any further questions? Questions, not observations."

"I have no further questions," she said ungraciously.

21

We had decided that the last two witnesses would be examined by Consuelo. So I made room for her in the central part of the bench and sat down at the side.

Judge Marinelli asked the bailiff to bring in Sabino Arcidiacono, the young man Cardace had had coffee with near Gaglione's apartment.

He looked haggard, almost crestfallen, with something wary in the way he moved. He walked through the courtroom to the witness stand with his eyes down, as if finding himself here embarrassed him, as if it were something a little shameful.

Looking at him, I remembered an episode I had been told by a magistrate friend of mine about his time in Calabria. During an interrogation he had asked a guy if he had a criminal record, and the man had replied that he guessed he had a criminal record now, because this was the first time he had ever given testimony.

Marinelli informed Arcidiacono that he had to read the oath. He did so, slowly, reading some words syllable by syllable, but without getting anything wrong, which often happens.

Maybe it was because I didn't have to examine him and was watching the scene from a different perspective, but hearing him read in that way, awkwardly but full of dignity, moved me deeply for a reason I couldn't understand.

Consuelo stood up, let a few seconds go by, then addressed the witness.

"Good morning, Signor Arcidiacono, I'm one of the two lawyers representing Iacopo Cardace. I'm going to ask you some questions. Please answer only if everything is clear to you. If you have any doubts don't hesitate to say so. All right?"

The man nodded half-heartedly.

"Signor Arcidiacono, let me take the opportunity to make one thing clear. Everything here is recorded, but only in audio form. If you just nod without saying anything, nothing will appear in the transcript, and it might be difficult to understand exactly what you meant. So I ask you to always answer out loud. All right?"

"All right," he replied, just as half-heartedly.

"Then let's proceed. Do you have a job?"

"Yes, I've always worked."

"What do you do?"

"I'm a car mechanic."

"Do you have a garage of your own?"

"No, I work for someone."

"Do you know why you were called here today to testify?"

He nodded again, then remembered. "Yes, I do."

"Do you know the man sitting opposite you, behind the bars?"

"Yes."

"Have you known him for a long time?"

"Yes, but we've never really hung out together. Every now and again we have a coffee or a cigarette. I saw him at the disco a few times."

"Do you remember his name?"

"Iacopo."

"Do you remember his surname?"

"Cardascio, I think."

"Cardace. Tell me, Signor Arcidiacono, have you ever used narcotics?"

Arcidiacono looked round. Once again he gave the impression he was searching for a way out.

"Don't worry, nobody's accusing you of anything. You can answer quite safely."

"A joint every now and again. But I don't do it much these days. I got married."

"Did you ever purchase drugs – grass or anything else – from the accused? For your personal use, of course."

"A few times."

"How did that work? Did Cardace have a place where he sold the drugs?"

"No, no, he wasn't a dealer. We'd meet and I'd ask him if he had anything. If he had, he'd say yes and give it to me and I'd give him the money. But we're talking about nothing, just a few joints."

"Of course, small quantities. Apart from pot, did he have other narcotics?"

Another hesitation. A longer one. This time Consuelo waited.

"Sometimes he had pills," Arcidiacono said at last.

"By pills you mean Ecstasy?"

"Yes."

"Did you ever purchase any?"

"I think so, a few times. At the disco."

"When was the last time you met Iacopo?"

He sniffed, as if to summon up courage. "I saw him the day … the day the thing happened."

"Are you referring to the murder of Gaglione?"

He nodded.

"You need to speak out loud, for the transcript."

"Yes, yes, that day."

"Can you tell us what you remember?"

"Nothing really, I was outside the cafe and he passed and we said hello."

"Why were you there? Were you working in the area?"

"No. My boss had sent me there because I had to look at a car that had been in an accident, for an estimate."

"Was Iacopo in a hurry? How was he walking when you met? Quickly, slowly, normally?"

"Normally."

"It didn't strike you that he was in a hurry?"

It would have been natural for Gastoni to object to this question. Consuelo was asking him for an opinion, and opinions, in general, are forbidden. But Gastoni said nothing and the examination continued without interruption.

The witness shook his head. "No, he was walking normally."

"He was walking normally and you said hello. And then?"

"I asked him if he fancied a coffee and we went into the cafe."

"In the cafe, did you sit talking?"

"Yes."

"About what?"

"I don't remember … this and that."

"Is it possible you also talked about drugs?"

Arcidiacono stared at Consuelo, who returned his gaze and gave him an imperceptible nod of encouragement.

"Yes," he said at last.

"Did Iacopo have something?"

"Yes."

"What?"

"Pills."

"Did he have them with him?"

"Yes."

"Did he give them to you?"

"He asked me if I wanted to try them. They were new."

"And what did you reply?"

"That I didn't have any money. But he said he'd give me one, and if I liked it I could buy the others."

"Did you accept?"

"It was for free," he said as if apologizing.

"Of course. Had Iacopo ever given you anything for free before? Pills or anything else."

"A few times. He wanted to sell, so first he had to get the new stuff known about. It's normal to give away a taster."

"I'm sorry, I'm going to go over this for a moment to see if I've understood correctly."

This was a delicate moment. Recapitulative questions are only allowed if they really are recapitulative, that is, if they are used only to take stock of what has been said up until that moment. They make it easier for the judges and jury to follow and at the same time put the witness at his or her ease. A proper recapitulation sends the witness a specific message: what you've said was clear, we've understood and we ask you to continue in the same way.

Sometimes, though, the formula of the recapitulative question is used to conceal a degree of manipulation. You recapitulate up to a certain point, then slip into the recapitulation something the witness hasn't actually said, at least not in those terms. Maybe it's a logical or likely consequence of what was said, or maybe it's a totally arbitrary implication. The fact remains that these questions that are recapitulative only in appearance tend to suggest an answer or even to pass off as an established fact something that the witness hasn't actually said and maybe never would say.

In short, recapitulative questions, in theory harmless and even useful, are to be handled with caution. Many defence lawyers and many prosecutors object to them regardless, out of caution, to avoid any risk of the testimony being manipulated.

But once again Gastoni said nothing, which surprised me. Maybe the fact that the witness was talking about offences committed by the defendant – basically, he was accusing him of drug dealing – had distracted her from such procedural matters.

"So you said that you met Iacopo near the cafe; he was walking calmly and you invited him to have a coffee; you went into the cafe, you had your coffee, he told you he had something new, meaning a new kind of pill, and he offered to let you try it for free. You agreed, he took a pill from his pocket and gave it to you. Is that correct?"

"Yes."

"Did he give it to you in the cafe or had you gone out by then?"

"He passed it to me in the cafe, under the counter."

"Who paid for the coffee?"

"I don't remember."

"How long were you in the cafe?"

"I don't know, five minutes…"

"Did Iacopo tell you he was in a hurry?"

"No."

"Do you know who he'd got that pill from?"

"He said he'd gone to see someone who'd given it to him."

"Do you know who that was?"

"No."

"Do you know when he'd been to see this person?"

"He lived somewhere nearby."

"You mean Cardace had been to see Gaglione just before you met him outside the cafe?"

It was a leading question, there was no doubt about that.

"Objection, Your Honour, that's a question that's clearly trying to suggest the answer," Gastoni said, barely rising but placing her hands on her bench.

"Sustained. Ask another question, Avvocato Favia."

"What had Iacopo been doing just before you met?"

"I think he'd been to that other guy's apartment."

"You mean the apartment of the man who'd given him the pills?"

"Yes."

"When you said goodbye did Iacopo tell you where he was going?"

"No."

"Did he rush off or did he go away calmly?"

"Calmly."

Consuelo had finished. Marinelli asked Gastoni if she wished to cross-examine.

"Yes, Your Honour."

"Please proceed."

"So you don't know where Cardace went after you met him."

"No."

"For all you know, he might even have gone back to see the person he got the pills from."

"Objection, Your Honour," Consuelo said. "A conjectural question. In fact, it's not even a question. It's a conjecture the assistant prosecutor could make in her closing statement if she wants to."

"Ask questions, Assistant Prosecutor," Marinelli said.

"Have you been examined before today?"

"How do you mean?"

"Has anybody questioned you? The police, an examining magistrate?"

"No."

"Have you ever told anybody this story?"

"A man and a woman – they said they were private investigators. And then the lawyers," he added, turning and nodding in our direction.

"When was this?"

"A few days ago."

"What did they say to you?"

Marinelli glanced at us, expecting us to object. Gastoni's questions hinted that we had behaved improperly. Once again, theoretically, I could have objected. In practice I didn't do so, for the same reason as a little earlier: it would have suggested that we were worried, that we were trying to stop what had happened from emerging because it contained something reprehensible. I shook my head and remained silent: I had nothing to say and the assistant prosecutor's questions didn't bother me at all.

"Nothing really, they asked me about that time I met Iacopo. And then if I wanted to come here and give my testimony."

Gastoni seemed about to insist, then must have thought it was better not to.

"Why is it you never told the police any of the things you've told us today?"

"Because nobody called me."

"But you knew Cardace had been arrested and then tried for murder?"

"Everyone knew. It was even on television."

"And why didn't you come forward before to tell anyone what you've told us today?"

"Because nobody sent for me."

"But didn't you realize your testimony might be important?"

"How was I supposed to know that?"

Gastoni made a gesture of exasperation and sat down again. Marinelli asked us if we wished to re-examine. I replied that I just needed to clarify a few things.

"Signor Arcidiacono, let me go back to what you were just asked by the prosecution. You said nobody sent for you. No policeman, no carabiniere, no examining magistrate?"

"No, nobody."

"Can you tell the court what I said to you when we talked a few days ago?"

"Objection," Gastoni almost growled.

"Why?" Marinelli asked in a not very friendly tone.

"This is an irrelevant topic."

"It seems to me you were the one to introduce it during your cross-examination. I'm surprised that you now object to a question seeking to clarify it. Objection overruled. You may answer, Signor Arcidiacono."

As happens when there are these skirmishes, the witness was confused, he didn't know who to answer and wasn't even sure what the question was. So I helped him.

"I just want you to recall briefly what I said to you when we talked a few days ago. First of all, where did we meet?"

"In your office."

"What did I say to you?"

"That I had to come to court and testify."

"What else?"

"That I had to tell the truth and there was nothing to worry about."

22

Finally it was the turn of Gaetano Rafaschieri, Gaglione's former partner. A man of medium height with lots of muscles, the kind you see even when he's dressed, and an almost completely shaved head. Like most people who find themselves testifying in a court of law, he didn't seem happy to be there.

After the ritual formalities, Consuelo began her examination. "Good morning, Signor Rafaschieri. Do you own a gym?"

"I *did*. I sold it about a year ago."

"What do you do now?"

"I work in other gyms, or in people's homes as a personal trainer. Let's say I'm freelance."

"For how long did you have a gym of your own?"

"Four years, more or less."

"Why did you sell it?"

"It wasn't bringing in much money any more."

"Were you the sole owner?"

"At the end, yes. Before that I had a partner."

"Who was this partner?"

"Mino Gaglione, I mean Cosimo Gaglione."

"Were you equal partners?"

"Yes."

"How did you split the running?"

"It wasn't a big gym. I did mainly weightlifting, he did courses in kick-boxing and martial arts in general. But if it was needed, he helped me with the rest."

"Do you know the accused, the man who's behind the bars over there?"

"Yes."

"How do you know him?"

"He used to come to the gym, he was a pupil of Gaglione's: mixed martial arts, he was actually quite good."

"Obviously you know what this hearing is about?"

"Yes."

"What terms were Gaglione and Cardace on?"

"They were friends."

"Did they see each other outside the gym?"

"As far as I know, yes."

"When did your partnership with Gaglione come to an end?"

"About a year before the … the thing happened."

"Why did it end?"

"He was bringing in people I didn't like, there were drugs going around, I wanted a clean place."

"Did you quarrel?"

"No. It was a joint decision. I bought out his share and that was it. I didn't want to argue, I just wanted to find a way to get out of the situation. I was afraid there'd be problems and that my customers, who were normal people, women, kids, would be scared off. Some had already stopped coming."

"After the end of the partnership, did you maintain relations with Gaglione?"

"No."

"Did you ever see him again?"

"It happened. But only to say hi, good morning, good evening."

"Did you ever find out what he was doing? Did he have another gym?"

"I don't think so. I heard he sometimes worked as a nightclub bouncer."

"Did you ever hear of any specific episode connected with this work of Gaglione's? I'm referring to an episode that took place in the weeks before the murder."

The witness looked at Consuelo. His face expressed something like: Do I really have to talk about this stuff? He remained silent until Marinelli prompted him.

"You must answer. If you have something to say, of course. If you don't, just say no."

"There was a rumour going around that he'd quarrelled with some dangerous people in a club. That he'd beaten up a kid who'd got drunk and was causing trouble, and … well, they were people it was better not to go near."

"But did Gaglione know that? I mean that he'd beaten someone 'it was better not to go near'?"

"When it happened, no. Then he found out and started to get worried."

"Are you able to tell us how long before the murder this episode took place? Weeks, days?"

Gastoni stood up to object. She was perfectly right to do so. In fact, I was surprised she and Marinelli had allowed us to go ahead like this with inadmissible questions.

"Your Honour, the witness said 'there was a rumour going around', which should already have been enough to make us interrupt the examination, being an answer contrary to article 194 paragraph 3 and article 195 paragraph 7 of the code of practice, which prohibits testimony based on common rumour, and in the case of indirect testimony requires that the witness indicate the person or the source from which he or she learned the facts which are the object of the examination. As if that weren't enough, in his subsequent question counsel for the defence takes it for granted that an episode happened when there is no usable evidence pointing to the event having occurred at all."

"Objection sustained. Signor Rafaschieri, from whom did you hear about this quarrel in a disco?"

Rafaschieri opened his arms wide. "I can't say, Your Honour. The rumour was going around, even in the gym, it was common knowledge…"

"Precisely. Testimony cannot be based on rumour. Avvocato Favia, Avvocato Guerrieri, do you have any further questions? Admissible questions, I mean."

It was the most we could do. The story of the fight in the disco hadn't (yet) formally been allowed as part of the evidence that could be used to elicit further testimony later. But the thought had insinuated itself into the heads of the judges and jury. It would be a good starting point for suggesting an alternative narrative. Material I could work on in my closing statement.

"We have no other questions, Your Honour, thank you."

The hearing was adjourned until the following Wednesday, when the accused would testify.

"You did well," I said to Consuelo. "You couldn't have done more."

She shook her head. "Let's hope it helps."

23

On Tuesday afternoon I went to the prison to give Iacopo a full run-down on what would happen in court and how he should behave. I made him go over everything he had told us and advised him to talk about what he remembered, without making any effort to tinker with it or embellish it.

"How's it going to end, Avvocato Guerrieri?"

"It's very hard to make predictions in proceedings like this."

"But is there any hope?"

I looked at him for a moment, thinking that, since the time we had first met, his face actually seemed to have changed.

"We have a shot. We aren't the favourite team in this championship, but we have a shot."

When I got to the court – I was on my own: Consuelo had a trial in Trani that morning – Lorenza was at the door waiting for me.

"Hello, Guido."

"Hello, Lorenza."

"Today's when Iacopo testifies."

"Yes."

She was silent, as if she had a question she couldn't quite formulate.

"Everything all right?" I asked.

"Are we … sure?"

"Sure of what?"

"About him testifying. Is it the right thing to do? Iacopo's fragile. The prosecutor could confuse him. Isn't there a risk we'll only make the situation worse, maybe with something coming out that they could use against him?"

It took me a moment or two to realize. She didn't trust her son. She didn't think he was able to support the situation. As far as she was concerned, he was a child. This, I told myself, probably explained many other things. I had to control my irritation before answering, and what came out sounded so paternalistic that I hated myself for it later.

"I think it's not only the right thing to do, I think it's necessary. If we're going to introduce an element of reasonable doubt by proposing an alternative narrative to the one in the original ruling, then Iacopo's testimony is indispensable. If you want to talk about it with him again, then do. My professional opinion is that we should go ahead."

She stared at me for a few seconds, as if to catch a hidden meaning in my words. Then she said: all right, and went in and took her seat in the courtroom.

"Signor Cardace, you are charged with the murder of Cosimo Gaglione, known as Mino. Did you commit this murder?"

"No. I'm innocent. I've committed crimes in my life, but not murder."

"Was Gaglione your friend?"

"Yes."

"Did you have interests in common?"

"Yes. Drugs, and also sports."

"Can you be more specific? Can you tell us first of all how you met?"

"I was doing mixed martial arts, and so was Gaglione. In fact, he was an instructor, he had his own gym. He saw me in a competition, he said I was good and offered to train me."

"And you accepted?"

"Yes, and we quickly became friends. We saw each other outside, too."

"You mentioned drugs. Are you aware that in talking about certain things you could be incriminating yourself?"

"Yes."

"Then continue."

"What do you want to know?"

"About the drugs."

"Well, Gaglione supplied me … that is, he managed to get hold of banned substances that are used to increase muscular mass."

"Like anabolic steroids for bodybuilders?"

"Not just for bodybuilders. He got hold of them through doctors, I think, and I helped him to sell them in a few gyms."

"Just that kind of substance?"

"At first. Then we started working with other things, like Ecstasy."

"Were you partners?"

"Not really. He'd supply me and I'd sell the stuff to people I knew, in discos and clubs around the province."

"I'd like you to tell us now how you spent the day Gaglione was killed."

"All right. In the morning I woke up late. The first thing I did was phone Mino … Gaglione, but I couldn't reach him."

"Why did you call him?"

"There was a problem and I had to talk to him."

"Was it a problem with drugs?"

"Not really drugs. A few days before, he'd given me some

bodybuilding products and I'd sold them to a guy who had a gym. But he'd complained to me, because he'd had the pills analysed and he said they weren't … I mean, they didn't look like what he'd been promised. They'd got him into trouble and he asked me for his money back."

"Did you give him his money?"

"Yes, and he gave me back the pills. I was looking for Mino to talk to him about it, about this problem."

"You were angry."

"It's only natural. He'd supplied me with the stuff and he'd made me look bad."

"When did you manage to talk to him?"

"In the afternoon."

"How did the conversation go?"

"I told him what had happened and complained about the fact that I hadn't been able to reach him that morning."

"What did he say?"

"He said something like: 'And who are you, my mother, always checking if my phone is on or off?'"

"But what about the problem you'd had with the man from the gym?"

"I don't even know if he quite got what I was talking about. Anyway, he cut me off and said he'd call me right back."

"And did he?"

"No. After half an hour I called him again."

"Do you remember what the two of you said during that second call?"

"He wasn't very pleasant, he said I was pissing him off, he'd told me lots of times that I said too much on the phone. I replied that I was going straight round there, that way he couldn't use the phone as an excuse."

"How was your tone? Calm?"

"No, I was pissed off."

"And what about Gaglione?"

"He said: Come on then. Here I am."

"In a challenging voice?"

"I'd say so, yes. He was angry too."

"What happened then?"

"I went to his place."

"By car?"

"Yes, of course. We live near the Russian church, and Gaglione lived in Fesca."

"What time did you start out?"

"About half past five."

"What time did you get to his place?"

"About six, more or less."

"How did the conversation go? Was it heated?"

"At first a little, then we cleared things up. He said he'd check up on that consignment, and that if I was right he'd give me my money back. If not, we'd go and see the guy at the gym together."

"How long were you in Gaglione's apartment?"

"Half an hour."

"How did you part?"

"What do you mean?"

"On friendly or hostile terms?"

"Friendly – we'd sorted things out."

"Did Gaglione give you anything before you left?"

"Yes, he gave me some Ecstasy pills. He said they were very good, something special that had just arrived."

"Why did you meet at Gaglione's apartment and not in a bar, for example?"

"It was a time when Gaglione was going out as little as possible."

"Why?"

"He was working as a bouncer. Sometime before there'd been a fight in a disco."

"Can you tell us which one?"

"Chilometro Zero. Anyway, this fight had broken out, the security people had intervened and he'd hit one guy who'd been especially violent. But it turned out he was someone dangerous, I mean, someone who belonged to a dangerous group."

"Did he tell you about it himself?"

"Yes, he was worried, he was scared they might do something to him, as punishment. So he was avoiding going out if it wasn't necessary. He even thought of going to stay with a cousin of his in Milan for a while."

"Who was the person he'd had this fight with?"

"He didn't tell me. He just said ' dangerous people' and I didn't ask him any more questions."

"Did he mean people involved in organized crime?"

"Yes."

"Why didn't you mention any of this before? In your statements, for example?"

"My lawyer told me it was better not to mention the subject. If I couldn't say the names it'd be useless, because the judges wouldn't believe me and at the same time I'd be putting myself in danger."

"Let's go back to that afternoon. After saying goodbye to Gaglione, what did you do?"

"I was going back to my car when I met someone I knew."

"Sabino Arcidiacono?"

"Yes, I didn't know his surname. I knew him as Sabino."

"How did you know him?"

"He was a mechanic. A good kid. I'd sold him stuff a few times."

"You mean drugs?"

"A bit of grass, a few pills."

"And that afternoon?"

"I gave him one of the pills Mino had given me."

"I see. Now let's go back a bit. At what time did you go out that afternoon?"

"Maybe about five, or a little earlier."

"When you went out, was your mother at home?"

"No."

"Do you know where she was?"

"She was working. She used to keep this old lady company. I think she read to her. She was round at her place."

"Do you know how often she went there?"

"I'm not sure, but I think it was every afternoon."

"What time did you get home?"

"I don't know exactly. Between seven and eight."

"When you got back, was your mother at home?"

"Yes."

"Then you went out again, is that correct?"

"Yes."

"How long after getting back?"

"Less than an hour."

I paused for a long time. I pretended to look for something in the papers I had in front of me, but in reality I wanted to take a look at the faces of the jurors. They seemed attentive, the young woman especially; the tic of the man who looked like a sacristan was particularly frenetic.

"Have you ever fired a gun, Signor Cardace?"

"Yes."

"Once? Several times?"

"Several times."

"Why?"

"I used to go shooting with a friend in a quarry, we'd do target practice with bottles."

"With what kind of gun?"

"A 7.65 calibre pistol."

"Was it yours?"

"No."

"Whose was it?"

"A friend of mine's."

"Can you tell us his name?"

"I prefer not to, I don't want to accuse a friend of a crime."

"Why a crime? Was the pistol being kept illegally?"

"Yes."

"So this friend committed the crime of unauthorized possession and carrying?"

"Yes. Plus, the pistol had its serial number rubbed away."

"How many times did you go shooting?"

"Several times."

"You mean you went regularly?"

"Not really. But we did go quite a few times."

"Where is this quarry?"

"Between Molfetta and Trani. It's abandoned, so it's safe to shoot there, you're not likely to hit anyone or be seen by anyone."

"When was the last time you went shooting with your friend?"

"A few days before Gaglione's murder."

"What were you wearing on that occasion?"

"The jacket I had on when I was arrested."

"You were wearing it when you fired the pistol?"

"Yes."

"Thank you, Your Honour, I've finished."

Marinelli asked Gastoni if she wanted to cross-examine.

"Just a few questions, Your Honour."

"Proceed."

"Signor Cardace, you've just told us you were frequently involved in dealing drugs. Can you confirm that?"

"I dealt for a while, yes."

"Can you tell us when you started?"

"I don't know exactly."

"Did you deal every day? Did you have a lot of customers?"

"Not every day. I sold banned substances in gyms and sometimes pills in discos."

"Would you describe yourself as a professional drug dealer?"

At this point, an objection was inevitable.

"Your Honour, the question isn't —"

"I withdraw the question," Gastoni said before I could continue. She had wanted to be provocative and she'd succeeded perfectly. When she resumed she changed the subject.

"So you're familiar with firearms?"

"I know how to shoot."

"Have you ever committed any crimes using firearms?"

Cardace hesitated. I hoped he wouldn't look at me in search of help. That would be worse than an admission.

"You mean a robbery?"

"Have you committed robberies?"

"Once, when I was a minor. But I wasn't armed. I had a legal pardon."

"And so you went to practise regularly in a quarry, with a person whose name you don't want to tell us, but you've never committed any violent crimes using firearms. Is that what you want us to believe?"

"Objection," I said, getting to my feet.

Gastoni raised a hand; I thought I also caught an ironic smile. She said she had no further questions.

Lorenza

As I already said, there's no order to my memories of those months. The events overlap and I don't know what happened first and what later.

What's certain is that we went to the cinema a lot, Lorenza and I. Almost always to see films she chose, first in cinemas – there were lots of them in Bari in those days – then in arenas. Often we were alone, but sometimes friends of hers came with us.

Together we saw things like Eric Rohmer's *The Green Ray*, Andrei Tarkovsky's *The Sacrifice*, Margarethe von Trotta's *Rosa Luxemburg*, Liliana Cavani's *The Berlin Affair*. Enough said.

We even went to the cinema on our last evening together. Although I had no idea it would be the last. The film was *Runaway Train* by Andrei Konchalovsky. The story was actually by Akira Kurosawa. Konchalovsky was the director of *Uncle Vanya*, Lorenza told me, communicating the programme for the evening.

I was a little worried because of my prejudice against Soviet cinema. I was afraid it would be like *Solaris*, which I'd hated. Instead of which, in a half-deserted arena (I assume many of the usual customers had a similar prejudice to mine and had stayed away) we found ourselves unexpectedly watching an action movie, completely American in style and pace. The main actress was the beautiful Rebecca De Mornay; the only thing Russian about the film, in fact, was the name of the director.

It was the story of a prison break. A drama with a grand finale of the kind I liked a lot back them – and even now, to be honest.

By the time it was over I was surprised and satisfied; Lorenza surprised and less satisfied. It wasn't her kind of film, but she couldn't complain because the film was by the great Konchalovsky and, above all, it had been her choice.

It was set on a moving train, which, as far as I recall, was why Lorenza started telling me a story. I say "as far as I recall", because I don't remember how we got there. We were walking along the deserted streets of the city and all at once she came out with those words. In my memory, it's as if she said them without warning, without any connection to what we'd been talking about.

"I was at the station in Bologna on 2 August."

"You mean *that* 2 August?"

"Yes."

At 10.25 on the morning of 2 August 1980 a timed device had exploded in the second-class waiting room of the station in Bologna. Eighty-five people died, and two hundred were wounded. It was the worst terrorist attack in the history of the Italian Republic. The investigations and trials led to the conviction of the perpetrators: a group of right-wing terrorists. The instigators were never identified. I was eighteen when it happened, I was by the sea, bathing, and after that event many things changed for ever. For me and for lots of people.

"You were in the station when the bomb went off?" I said incredulously.

"I was in Bologna on the night of 1 to 2 August. I was travelling with a friend, we were supposed to catch a train early in the morning. We got to the station the night before and decided to sleep there. In the second-class waiting room. We had no money, that's how we travelled. Around dawn I felt bad – we'd been smoking and drinking the previous night – and my friend took me to Emergency. When they discharged me, we tried to get back to the station, but the streets were cordoned off – there were police cars everywhere and ambulances with sirens, and nobody knew what was going on. Some people said there'd been a gas leak that had caused an explosion and there were probably victims. It wasn't until a few hours later that it was clear what had really happened. I think the bomb was about six feet from where we'd lain down to sleep."

While Lorenza was telling this story, I was thinking something very distinctly, something I'd thought before but never with such clarity. This woman belonged to a dimension of existence that was different from mine. She had brushed against History, she led a life filled with experiences and mystery and fascinating prospects. A life about which, by the way, I knew almost nothing. She would become a famous writer, she would travel, she would live through all sorts of adventures. I had no part in any of that. I was just passing through. Sooner or later that little piece of road we'd walked along together would come to an end and she would zoom off, far away, like a meteor.

We didn't even go for a pizza. Lorenza said she was tired, and we went home to sleep.

The next day she didn't get in touch, nor the day after. That was quite normal, so I didn't pay too much attention. We'd see each other, then she'd disappear and then reappear. She always decided, but with a kind of regularity, a kind of rhythm in a way.

Five or six days went by with no word from her and I started to worry. I thought something had happened to her and went looking for her at her building. I went back there several times, ringing her bell afternoon, evening and night, even early in the morning. I never got an answer. I realized I had no idea how to track her down. I didn't really know her friends, I didn't know where her family lived, I had no number to call. I was seized with panic. I looked up all the Delle Foglies in the phone book and called them one after the other, asking for Lorenza. Those who answered told me, more or less kindly, that I had the wrong number and there was no Lorenza there. I even considered calling the police or the hospitals, in case she'd had an accident, or had fallen ill and been admitted. Immediately, the idea struck me as absurd. But I did go to the library and carefully read the local news in the *Gazzetta del Mezzogiorno*, starting from the day after we'd been to the cinema. I looked for news of accidents or other similar events, but didn't find anything.

I was in a state of genuine anxiety – the fear that something had happened to her was equal to the fear that she'd simply decided to leave me without even telling me – when one evening I saw someone I'd met during those months I'd gone out with her. I couldn't remember his name, but that didn't matter. I went up to him and without too much preamble – actually, without any preamble – asked him if he'd heard from Lorenza. The guy looked at me a little bewildered; I'm not sure he even knew who I was. Anyway he replied that as far as he knew she'd left for a Greek island. Also as far as he knew, she would be there for several weeks. And no, he didn't know which island, he concluded, looking me up and down and walking away.

There followed a period of great confusion.

I was relieved that nothing had happened to her, but hurt and sad about how she'd disappeared. I thought seriously of leaving for Othonoi, joining her there and making a terrible scene. Then I forced myself to think. It was only speculation on my part that she was on Othonoi, because of the story she'd told me in Santa Maria di Leuca.

Gradually, as the days passed, I regained a modicum of self-control. It was a help to me to think – to convince myself – that when she came back she would come looking for me. Then, with all the necessary firmness, I would tell her that she had behaved in an unacceptable way and that I didn't want to have anything more to do with her. On the basis of her apologies and her entreaties, I would evaluate whether or not to back down from that intention.

It wasn't the best August of my life.

24

Easter came and went, and now we were back in court for the closing statements. They had all come for this last act: Consuelo, Tancredi, Annapaola. And of course Lorenza, sitting with her bag in her lap, looking unusually composed.

Judge Marinelli indicated the documents that could be used in the ruling and handed over to the assistant prosecutor for her statement.

Gastoni got to her feet, wrapping herself in her robe. Once again her overpowering perfume filled the air. I didn't like her, so my thoughts weren't objective, but it seemed to me that putting on so much perfume in order to go into court and ask for somebody to be sentenced to many years in prison wasn't exactly in the best of taste.

"Your Honours, ladies and gentlemen of the jury, I shan't speak for too long because in legal proceedings where things are clear-cut the most important thing is to avoid the risk of complicating them. The job of the defence, on the other hand – and it's a perfectly legitimate one – is to make them complicated in order to conceal a truth that in some cases, like this one, is obvious and irrefutable.

"I'm reminded of a famous passage in Manzoni's *The Betrothed*, the one in which Azzecca-garbugli says to Renzo: 'You need to tell your lawyer clear things: it is then up to us to confuse them.' I don't quote this to cause any offence, only to point to a common defensive procedure. A legitimate one, I repeat, because a defence counsel has to do his job: to try to get his client acquitted even when that client's guilt is obvious. Even when, I'm sure, he himself is convinced of that guilt."

Here I felt the impulse to stand up and object. Gastoni, while simulating respect, was suggesting to the jurors that the defence was only a pedantic obstacle on the road to the punishment of criminals; and that defence lawyers, starting with yours truly, were all more or less acting in bad faith.

I decided to let it go. Where necessary I would be able to criticize the argument in my closing statement, but objecting – and the squabbling that would ensue – risked only adding emphasis to that improper move of hers.

"Is it conceivable that such an impressive amount of evidence is the result of a chain of incredible coincidences? Is it possible that it's all a question of chance conspiring against the accused? Of course, if one considers every single piece of evidence, every single outcome of the process separately, it is conceivable that there may be alternative explanations, in terms of probability. But the more the evidence mounts up, the more drastically is the probability of an alternative reduced.

"Let us examine the mountain of evidence produced first by the investigation and then by the trial. We observe that such a mountain wasn't even dented by the efforts exerted by the defence during this hearing.

"The first piece of evidence comprises the two telephone conversations intercepted on the morning of the crime. As you will all remember, Gaglione's telephone was being tapped within the context of an investigation into criminal association for the purpose of trafficking in narcotics, in particular synthetic drugs.

"On the afternoon of 13 October 2011, members of the Flying Squad involved in the telephone-tapping record two calls between the accused and the victim. The subject isn't clear, but the tone is animated and it's quite obvious that there is some bone of contention between the two men. It isn't irrelevant to underline that both calls come from the telephone of the accused. It is he, in other words, who has an incentive, a specific motive, a reason, let's say, a claim on Gaglione. The second telephone call quickly degenerates into a quarrel and concludes with the decision, laden with threat, to meet in order to resolve the dispute.

"The threatening tone is already commented upon in the police notes appended to the transcript of the intercept operations, although nothing led anyone to suppose that the harsh conclusion of the conversation was the premise, the portent, of a lethal outcome.

"Be that as it may, and here we come to the second point, the accused soon afterwards proceeds to the home of the victim. It's possible to say that on the basis of the testimony of Antonia Sassanelli, who was questioned by the police in the hours immediately following the murder. The accused himself has admitted his presence in the vicinity, although giving it a different explanation during his testimony. A testimony, it's hardly worth recalling, given only during this appeal hearing. Up until then Cardace had availed himself of the right to remain silent. A right granted him by the law, but the exercise of which should be evaluated within the overall framework of the evidence."

*

She continued by listing in a somewhat fussy way all the evidence against Iacopo as described and commented on in the ruling by the original judges.

This went on for at least an hour. The faces of the jurors showed the first signs of fatigue. The only one who seemed focused was the young woman with the penetrating eyes. I would have liked to know if she was listening with such visible attention because she agreed with the assistant prosecutor or, on the contrary, because she wanted to be prepared to refute her arguments.

At last my attention was reawakened by a passage that wasn't a mere recap.

"There are still a few things to say. Notably, I must comment on the attempt by the defence to impress the court with elements that have no relevance to the matter of this hearing. Elements presented in order to distract your attention from the substantial grounds on which you must base your deliberations and come to a decision.

"I refer in particular to two circumstances evoked in a suggestive way and devoid of any, I repeat *any*, basis in evidence.

"The first is the assertion that Cardace fired a gun, wearing that jacket as chance would have it, a few days before the murder. This circumstance took place in an unspecified quarry, with an unspecified and obviously unidentifiable individual. A suggestion constructed deliberately to prevent any attempt to check it procedurally."

She paused for quite a long time, a pause that was somewhat bombastic but put there at just the right moment to grab the court's attention.

*

"I think the defence needs to respect the intelligence of the judges and in general of all the participants in these proceedings. Do you know how much this imaginary evocation is worth from an evidential point of view? Nothing, in fact worse than nothing. It is a fairy story told simply to impress. A fairy story which you can't and mustn't take into account.

"The second circumstance is the vague reference to a hypothetical motive for the murder linked to a phantom fight in a disco and to the desire for revenge on the part of an even more phantom group of criminals; this is what they've tried to imply.

"I shouldn't even have to deal with this grotesque suggestion because the judges have very conveniently, very correctly, already cleared the field of any stretching of the rules. I refer to the prohibition on testimony based on common rumour. But I would like to devote a few words to it, in the eventuality – and I hope I'm wrong – that counsel for the defence chooses to pick up on this topic in his closing statement.

"Allow me therefore to remind the ladies and gentlemen of the jury what the judges know as well as I do. The burden is on the prosecution to prove the charges, and this is a principle in law. But once the burden of proof is fulfilled, as in this case, once such impressive material is presented, it isn't acceptable for the defence to question it with vague conjecture, allusions devoid of any connection with the substance of the investigation.

"Your Honours, ladies and gentlemen of the jury, I want to tell you something that I hope will remain imprinted in your memory, and above all in your conscience, when you retire to deliberate. If we admit the possibility of acquitting a defendant against whom there is so much unequivocal and corroborating evidence, we have to abandon the very idea of punishment for the guilty and justice for the victims. I've been doing this job for a long time, and I can assure you that in few murder cases have I seen such an abundance of evidence, evidence pointing so clearly to the guilt of the accused.

"What would you think if you were the mother, the fiancée, a friend of the victim and somebody suggested the possibility that at this hearing, with this evidence, the accused could be acquitted? Wouldn't you find that unacceptable? Remember these words when you deliberate and come to a decision. I'm sure your decision will keep justice as your sole guide and will not be influenced by sophistry, equivocation or rhetorical exercises."

She paused one last time. She threw me a look that struck me as halfway between admonition and defiance, then looked at the judges and jurors and nodded slowly in a somewhat theatrical way.

"I'm coming to my conclusion. The way in which the accused has defended himself, his criminal record and his subsequent conduct prior to the murder are all factors that make extenuating circumstances inapplicable. I ask therefore that you reject the appeal and confirm the contested ruling *in toto*.

"The accused having given self-incriminating testimony regarding the offence of continued dealing in narcotics, I ask in addition that the transcript be passed on to the Prosecutor's Department with a view to further action."

25

I was sitting in the deserted courtroom.

The moments that precede the closing statement in certain trials and appeals resemble those that precede a boxing match. There's a very similar sense of solitude, a very similar mixture of feelings: a desire to run away and an impatience to get up in the ring, start the fight and put an end to the fear.

After Gastoni's closing statement, Judge Marinelli had ordered half an hour's break.

A few more minutes and the wait would be over. The question I had managed to evade for more than two months crept into my thoughts. Did I really believe in my client's innocence? Did I believe what he and Lorenza had told me? I was almost about to start arguing with myself, hoping to solve the question before I opened my mouth. Then I told myself it was a bad idea.

A very bad idea, given the moment.

So, to dismiss any other doubts, I devoted myself to a dogged and pointless rereading of my notes until everyone came back in and the hearing resumed.

"How long do you think you'll need for your closing statement, Avvocato Guerrieri?" Marinelli asked me.

"I'll require more or less three hours, Your Honour."

He cleared his throat and exchanged a glance and a nod with Valentini. "Very well, Avvocato. Then let's do it this way: you start; when you're more or less halfway you decide when to break. We resume tomorrow, you conclude your statement, we see if there are any responses, after which the court retires to deliberate. Is that all right for everyone?" he asked, looking first at me, then at Gastoni. Nobody raised any objections.

"Your Honours, ladies and gentlemen of the jury, this will be a structured statement, so I shan't bother with an introduction. I'll start immediately by referring to the interpretative premise laid out by the assistant prosecutor in her closing statement.

"The prosecution has reminded us that the evidential method, correctly understood, involves a unitary evaluation of the evidence presented. And she's right. Chipping away at the evidence, examining and refuting each piece of evidence one by one rather than in their totality, is an old technique, or rather, an old *device* of the defence.

"I want to assure you from the start that this is not the one we will adopt in this case. We shall evaluate the whole picture, in other words, the evidence as considered in the original ruling and the new evidence, irrefutable evidence – and I'm sorry if the assistant prosecutor can't see that – that has emerged during this hearing. We shall verify if the only hypothesis that explains this evidence, considered as a whole, is the one acknowledged in the assistant prosecutor's closing statement. Or if, on the contrary, reasonable alternative explanations should be admitted. Which is another way of saying: we shall verify if space exists for reasonable doubts about the prosecution case.

"Let us proceed to a rapid summary of what happened immediately following the murder, then discuss the forensic evidence.

"After going to his home and not finding him, officers of the Flying Squad track down Cardace outside a pub and take him to police headquarters. During the car ride, the accused mentions to Sergeant De Tullio, quite calmly, without holding anything back, that he saw his friend Gaglione just a few hours earlier. There is no mention of this in the documents, but you learned it here, in this hearing, no more than a few days ago. Before continuing, I want to ask you a question I'd like you to keep in mind. Does this seem to you the behaviour of someone who has just committed a murder like the one we are dealing with? Keep that question in mind, use it as a general yardstick to interpret what has emerged from this hearing.

"So, Cardace admits quite calmly that he went to Gaglione's home, and does so before knowing that there was a witness placing him in that area during the afternoon.

"At Headquarters, Cardace is given a gunshot residue test. On this point, we heard the inspector from the forensics team, who proved to be very precise and competent. He explained to us that gunshot residue, in the absence of washing, persists on the surface of the skin and in the nostrils for about four hours. The test was carried out more or less three hours after the murder. So the accused should still have had gunshot residue on his body, unless he had carefully cleaned his hands, arms, face, hair and neck, and even his nostrils.

"We can therefore assert that if, on that tragic afternoon, Cardace fired a gun, he then made sure to clean himself with extreme care and, consequently, with extreme awareness of the risk that he might be subjected to a test."

I paused for a long time, another rather bombastic pause, and nodded in the direction of the court while I prepared the next stretch of my statement. During that pause a thought crossed my mind: I had no more desire to do this work, with all its rituals, its techniques, its dressing up. The fact that this feeling should hit me just when I had to use all my persuasive powers to save a client from dozens of years in prison wasn't reassuring. Not to me, and certainly not to Iacopo, if he'd known.

"But the same individual, so aware, so careful that he washes his hands, face and hair, and even his nostrils, in order not to risk being caught out by a forensics test, the same individual, I repeat, completely neglects his jacket. He doesn't get rid of it, he doesn't take it to the laundry, he doesn't even hang it up in a wardrobe. No, ladies and gentlemen. This shrewd, aware individual continues to wear it while expecting to be tested, which duly happens.

"I repeat the question I asked a few minutes ago. Does this strike you as the behaviour of someone who has just committed a murder like the one we are dealing with?"

I spoke some more about the forensic evidence, recalled what the technician had explained, and went on to examine Lorenza's testimony. She was behind me, in the public seats, and I was talking about her testimony, in other words, about her. I had the unreal feeling that she had only reappeared in my life that very morning; that behind me, listening to me, staring at me, was the beautiful, elusive woman I'd known twenty-seven years earlier.

"In the original ruling the testimony of Lorenza Delle Foglie was undervalued. The court at that trial used two arguments to assert the total non-credibility of the witness.

"The first argument, I hope you will concede, is somewhat trivial: the witness is the mother of the accused and so is fundamentally not credible. This is an argument that in its brevity borders on the unmotivated. Taking it to its logical conclusions we would have to state that the testimony of a close relative is *never* credible.

"In reality, where the close relative has decided not to avail himself or herself of the right to refrain from testifying, he or she is to all intents and purposes a witness like any other. Where the legislature has deemed it necessary to introduce a specific criterion of evaluation for a category of testimony, it has done so explicitly. I think for example of the rules on the testimony of those who have turned state's evidence. In such instances, there has to be corroboration, according to article 192 paragraph 3 of the code of practice.

"Such is not the case with the testimony of close relatives: their testimony is evaluated like that of other witnesses, without any special or lesser status.

"Am I trying to say that it's not necessary to exercise extreme caution in evaluating the testimony of close relatives? No, of course not. I'm simply saying that the automatic reflex we find in the original ruling – the witness is the mother of the accused, therefore she is not credible – is improper.

"We shall return to this point, but let me now analyse the second argument used against the testimony of which we speak.

"At the original trial the prosecution dusted off a very old case, one dating back to 1987. Do you remember what you were doing on 5 July 1987? Or even what you were doing in the summer of 1987? How many details would you be able to give about such long-ago events if you were asked a question about them out of the blue, especially in a context as highly stressful as that of being a witness in a court of law? Try to put yourself in the witness's shoes: that is a basic premise for a correct rather than theoretical evaluation of what happened at the original trial.

"The witness was caught completely unprepared, as was the defence. This is a procedural method that raises several doubts. Doubts that intensify when, as happened in front of you, here at this hearing, we see what that supposed criminal record consisted of, what really took place, regardless of the charges, which, I cannot emphasize too strongly, were never brought before a court.

"You heard the witness's account, which there is no reason to doubt. The act of resisting an officer of the law, and the concurrent one of aiding and abetting, came about when the witness was not even aware that the two men who had set off in pursuit of her friend were officers. Or rather, when one of them had set off in pursuit, had caught up with her friend and was hitting him, according to the perfectly plausible account given by the witness.

"Basically, the witness defended a friend, though without any particular display of violence, from what she believed to be a politically motivated attack. I need hardly recall that the duty magistrate, that long-ago evening in 1987, must have seen the situation for what it was, because he ordered that the officers not proceed with the arrest of Signora Delle Foglie."

I lingered some more on Lorenza's reliability, reading out passages from her testimony, underlining how coherent and credible her account was, how the explanation she had supplied during the appeal hearing clarified the contradictions she had fallen into under cross-examination at the original trial.

I probably spoke even longer than I needed to. When I had exhausted the subject, I suggested we stop. Judge Marinelli agreed, and the hearing was adjourned until the following morning at the usual time.

Lorenza

That was how it ended, without a real ending.

Whenever I look back, whenever I look at the bigger picture of my actions, my emotions (including, above all, those I wasn't aware of), my ambiguous victories and very obvious defeats, I recognize certain fault lines, the results of subterranean upheavals in my consciousness. One of these is situated in that period in 1987. I went in a boy and came out, without realizing it, a man.

The encounter between Lorenza and me changed my life. I'm sure it didn't change hers.

She had been my involuntary mentor, the woman who had distractedly accompanied me through a metaphorical wood for a few months. Having emerged from that wood, I found myself alone in the open, dangerous spaces of adulthood.

I saw her again in the street one morning, by chance, towards the end of the year. It might have been November. It might have been a Saturday. It was cold, and I remember – God knows why – that I was wearing a thick jacket and a scarf. She was with a shabby-looking man, and they were talking excitedly, maybe quarrelling. I thought frantically of what I could or should say, how I should behave, without finding anything appropriate. She noticed me when we were almost about to pass each other. She didn't show any surprise, let alone a flash of contentment, or maybe of contrition or embarrassment over what had happened. Over the fact that she had vanished, or the arrogant way she had treated me. She greeted me distractedly – the way you greet a person you see every day without there being any particular relationship – and moved on.

Just like that.

And yet the strange thing was that within a few days all the pain, all the sadness, all the excruciating disappointment I'd felt over what had happened vanished. It was almost as if that humiliating encounter had been a kind of therapy, the kind you get from a chiropractor when you have a strong, persistent pain. At the time you feel even worse, but immediately afterwards, if the chiropractor is good, the pain goes away as if by magic.

I can't say with any accuracy how long it took, but definitely by the start of the Christmas holidays the whole affair seemed to have been relegated to a very distant past. A lot further back in time than the summer of intoxication during which I had convinced myself that I was in love with Lorenza. I stopped thinking about her and got on with my life.

I got over that crazy period of childish unawareness, but also at times of elusive and therefore genuine, pure happiness.

26

That night I had to take drops. I'd spent a couple of hours tossing and turning in bed and ended up convinced that I wouldn't get to sleep. Nor could I afford to see in the morning at the Osteria del Caffellatte.

When, the next day, I started speaking, I was still slightly dazed from the benzodiazepine.

"I'm now going to examine the testimony of Sabino Arcidiacono. His account is a key element in an alternative reconstruction of events to the one proposed by the prosecution. It's a key element in asserting the existence of reasonable doubt which must lead to the acquittal of the accused.

"The original ruling states that, *before* going to see Gaglione, Cardace had coffee near the victim's apartment with an acquaintance of his.

"This individual, identified by the defence investigations, was Arcidiacono, and his testimony demolishes this assumption on which the whole of the ruling rests. The two men went for a coffee *after* Cardace had been to Gaglione's apartment. And at that moment Gaglione was surely still alive. The witness Sassanelli, testifying at the original trial, said she could not indicate the exact time at which the two men were in the cafe, but she could say with some certainty that it took place not long before 'all that kerfuffle', by which she meant the arrival of the ambulances and the police following the 118 call by the dying Gaglione. That the encounter in the cafe, a perfectly relaxed one, took place after Cardace had been to Gaglione's apartment is demonstrated, quite apart from anything else, by the fact that Cardace gave Arcidiacono one of the pills that Gaglione himself had supplied him with a little earlier.

"From this point of view, Arcidiacono's testimony, highly commendable for its spontaneity and sincerity, almost constitutes an alibi. And sticking with the concept of an alibi, I'd now like to dwell on a possible alternative interpretation of the evidence considered in its entirety.

"I base this delicate part of my closing statement above all on the testimony of the technician from the forensics team, with which we have already dealt, and therefore I refer to the observations I have already made; the testimony of the head of the Homicide section; the testimony of Signor Rafaschieri, Gaglione's former partner in running a gym; and the testimony of the accused, given right here in front of you at this hearing.

"The point of calling Assistant Commissioner Montesano as a witness was basically to demonstrate a shortcoming in the investigation. Thanks to his testimony we were able to see how the almost immediate identification of an excellent working hypothesis orientated the investigation in a single direction, making the team neglect any other lines of inquiry.

"You see, when we adopt a single hypothesis with respect to a reality to be interpreted, a hypothesis which from the start does not admit different possibilities, this produces a phenomenon that psychologists call 'cognitive tunnelling'. This means that the hypothesis becomes the yardstick not only for the interpretation of the data, but for the actual *perception* of reality. It means that we perceive only what corresponds to the hypothesis, and we quite literally *don't see* what contradicts it. More generally, we don't see the things that don't fit the interpretative grid fixed by the hypothesis or else by the task we have set ourselves or that someone else has assigned to us.

"We don't work to scrutinize the hypothesis. We work to *confirm* the hypothesis.

"That's what happened to the investigators in this case. From the start, the one conjecture to be confirmed was: Iacopo Cardace quarrelled with Gaglione, he went to his apartment to have it out with him, he shot him and left.

"At no point in the investigation, let alone in the most delicate phase of this, that of the initial inquiries, was any alternative taken into consideration.

"The questions asked of the witnesses Montesano and Rafaschieri served to give you a glimpse of different investigative possibilities that should have been examined and weren't.

"This explains the fact – although it remains somewhat disconcerting – that the ways in and out of the crime scene weren't checked. I ask you, without any polemical intent: Does it strike you as justifiable that the possibility of a different way into Gaglione's apartment wasn't taken into consideration? Does it strike you as justifiable that a thorough search was not made for possible prints in the courtyard? Does it strike you as justifiable that no attention was paid to the French windows leading to the balcony to see if they were open or closed?

"And again: Does it strike you as justifiable that no footage was obtained from the security cameras that must have existed in the area?

"These were checks that were very easy to carry out in the immediate aftermath of the crime. Routine checks in an investigation like this, but which today are impossible. Because today, obviously, any possible prints in the courtyard have disappeared; because today, obviously, the footage from the security cameras in the area has been recorded over, as usually happens.

"I don't want to victimize the investigators. I understand the mistake, brought about by the desire to solve an alarming case as quickly as possible. What I wanted to show is that the investigation is not devoid of flaws, of gaps, of avenues of enquiry not followed up and now lost for ever. And it's precisely in taking account of what *isn't* in the investigation that we must ask ourselves if it's possible to have a reasonable doubt as to the guilt of the accused. A reasonable doubt which means a possible alternative explanation of the evidence.

"It is therefore time to deal with the fight in the disco called Chilometro Zero. The accused mentions it in his testimony and so does the witness Rafaschieri. It has been said that Rafaschieri's testimony on this subject is unusable because it violates the prohibition on allowing common rumour as evidence. I don't think the matter is quite so straightforward. I think the sanction of unusability must be modified on the basis of the principles of *favor rei* and *favor libertatis*. Unusability, in my opinion, isn't an absolute category, but a criterion for protecting the citizen from possible abuses on the part of the investigating agencies.

"Let's suppose there was a tapped phone call in the course of which somebody, perhaps even the dangerous criminal with whom Gaglione apparently came to blows, explicitly claims responsibility for the murder. Let's imagine that this call is unusable for a variety of procedural reasons. If we considered the criterion of unusability to be absolute and completely unchallengeable, we would have to ignore that conversation, even if it proved Cardace's innocence, and confirm the original ruling.

"Does this strike you as an acceptable hypothesis or, on the contrary, do you see it in all its frightening absurdity?

"In reality, I believe that unusability is a sanction intended to protect suspects and defendants. Tapped phone calls that are unusable can't be used *against* somebody, but they can, and in my opinion *must*, be used whenever they contain elements that clear a suspect; this in accordance with the two principles I spoke about earlier, *favor rei* and *favor libertatis*, in other words the general rules of the whole system, in the light of which individual rules should be interpreted.

"If a testimony about a common rumour, in theory forbidden, offers the prospect of an alternative explanation of the facts of a case, if an indirect statement about a common rumour opens the way to reasonable doubt, which is the cornerstone of the system, the principle of unusability must be overruled and the judges allowed to decide for themselves."

I paused, hoping that I'd got my message across. Because I didn't even believe in this argument myself.

I'd made a leap in logic. There was a significant difference between my example of the tapped phone conversation clearing an innocent man and Rafaschieri's testimony about a rumour.

In a hypothetical case like the one I had formulated, any judge, although there might be different nuances in his ruling, would admit the tapped conversation and acquit the defendant. He would do so anyway, however objectively complex the case was to interpret. Any judge would find a way to acquit, because there would be no doubt about the veracity and validity of that conversation, even if the procedure by which it had been obtained was flawed.

The rules on the unusability of phone-tap evidence protects suspects from unlawful procedures. The rule that prohibits testimony about rumours protects against the introduction of information that's completely impossible to check and verify. It would be all too easy to weaken or demolish a prosecution case if you could call witnesses who, to give an example, claimed to provide an alibi by saying they had heard a rumour, that everyone was saying it, that it was common knowledge.

So I was aware that what I was saying had no legal foundation and that, put quite simply, Rafaschieri's testimony, at least where it touched on the fight in the disco, was worthless. I was presenting this argument to make the jurors reflect on the possibility that there really was an alternative hypothesis, and that not even considering it exposed them to the risk of a grave miscarriage of justice.

"And in any case," I resumed, "regardless of what Rafaschieri told us, it was the accused himself who introduced the subject of how worried Gaglione was. Gaglione, who preferred not to leave home because of a fight that had taken place at Chilometro Zero, fearing a reprisal from individuals connected with organized crime. This testimony is perfectly usable. And what it offers us is a possible scenario from which we may conclude that there is reasonable doubt.

"The Supreme Court has repeatedly stated that evidence must allow for the reconstruction of events in terms of such certainty as to rule out the possibility of any other reasonable solution. On the other hand, it must exclude more theoretical and remote possibilities.

"What does that mean? It means that in an evidential hearing, and this is an evidential hearing, there is no reasonable doubt if the alternative explanation to that of the prosecution is theoretical or remote. In other words, the validity of a reconstruction cannot be contested with alternatives that are purely conjectural and, ultimately, absurd. Outside such cases, the presentation of a possible alternative solution must lead to a verdict of acquittal.

"Basically, in evidential hearings, we take the evidence that has emerged from the hearing and construct a story in which everything fits together in a plausible way. We could say: a plausible reconstruction of events that happened in the past. When is a story that reconstructs the events of the past plausible? It's plausible when it explains all the evidence, without leaving anything out, and if it is constructed according to criteria of narrative consistency.

"Having established this theoretical and methodological premise, let us see which stories the evidence presented here allows us to construct.

"The first is that proposed by the assistant prosecutor in her closing statement, which basically follows the substance of the original ruling.

"In this story, Cardace quarrels with Gaglione over the phone. Soon afterwards he goes to Gaglione's apartment, armed with a high-calibre revolver – in other words, intending to carry out an act of violence. Before getting to Gaglione's building, Cardace, even though driven to that act of violence by such intense malice, stops to have coffee with an acquaintance. Having calmly drunk his coffee, Cardace arrives at Gaglione's apartment, fires several shots at him and walks out, leaving the victim to bleed to death. He returns home, carefully washes his hands, arms, face, hair and nostrils, clearly conscious of the need to remove all traces of gunshot residue in case he is stopped by the police. Then he leaves again, inexplicably – if we consider how cautious he's been – wearing the same jacket he had on at the time of the murder, goes out for a walk and soon afterwards is spotted and picked up by the police. He calmly admits to the officers that he has been to Gaglione's apartment. He is given the gunshot residue test and this cunning criminal, who's washed and cleaned his body with such care, is caught because of the gunshot residue left on his jacket, which he's continued to wear instead of getting rid of it, as would have been normal.

"Some serious questions as to the plausibility of this story are not only possible, but right and proper. And above all: is this the only possible story that fits the evidence? Or to put it another way: can the evidence we have at our disposal only be explained by this story? If you wish to confirm the original ruling and convict the accused, you will answer this question in the affirmative.

"What you must ask yourselves, however, is if there are other plausible stories able to encompass in an exhaustive, coherent and uncontradictory way all the evidence that has been presented in this hearing. Because if there are other plausible stories, not merely conjectural ones, you have to accept the fact that the evidential framework is not unequivocal, that there is no certainty in these proceedings, and you will have to acquit according to article 530 paragraph 2 of the code of criminal procedure, which provides for acquittal when the evidence that the accused committed the crime is insufficient or contradictory.

"Well, in this hearing it is possible to imagine at least two stories, that is, two reconstructions that explain that mountain of evidence. And it is this possibility that requires you to find in favour of acquittal.

"The second story can be told as follows. Cardace and Gaglione are connected by friendship and by illegal activities.

In the hours preceding the murder, the two men quarrel over the phone. The second call, which is very tense, ends with an agreement to meet, partly to avoid talking about certain subjects on the phone. Soon afterwards, Cardace goes to Gaglione's home and the two of them clear things up, to the extent that Gaglione, almost as a gesture of reconciliation, gives Cardace some specimens of a new kind of pills of a narcotic nature. Cardace leaves, meets Arcidiacono, stops to have coffee with him and gives him one of the new pills he himself received a short time earlier. Then Cardace returns home, where he sees his mother, and stays there for a while. Meanwhile, *someone else* gets into the victim's apartment and kills him, maybe having had the intention of merely kneecapping him. Then Cardace goes out, wearing the same jacket he had on in the afternoon, the same jacket he had been wearing a few days earlier when he had gone shooting with a friend of his in a quarry. Soon afterwards the police pick him up and take him to Headquarters. On the car ride there, chatting to an officer he knows, the accused admits quite openly that he has been at Gaglione's home. At Headquarters, he is subjected to a gunshot residue test, with all that ensues.

"Is this merely a conjectural story? No. It's a story that's possible and even quite likely to an extent. So now we have at least two possible reconstructions in which all the evidence presented during this hearing can be encompassed.

"I exhort you in this respect not to make a mistake, that of thinking that in order to select the best story it's necessary to refer to levels of probability: we have two stories, one's likelier than the other, I'll choose that one. It doesn't work that way. The burden of proof being on the prosecution means that it's not enough for the prosecution to propose a story that's likelier than the others to obtain a conviction. The prosecution has to propose the *only acceptable explanation* in order to overcome the hurdle of reasonable doubt.

"Conversely, for the defence to invoke reasonable doubt and ask for an acquittal of the accused, it's enough to put forward a possible explanation, an explanation that's not far-fetched and not merely conjectural.

"A court hearing aims to reconstruct the facts of the past and has to do so to a very high level of probability, as defined by the evidential paradigm of article 533 of the code of practice: 'The judge pronounces a verdict of conviction if the accused is found guilty of the crime beyond reasonable doubt.'

"We are beyond reasonable doubt when it's not possible to imagine any alternative explanation to that of the prosecution.

"We are within reasonable doubt when, as in this case, the evidence, all of it, with nothing left out, can be explained in a different way from that proposed by the prosecution.

"It is not scandalous, as the assistant prosecutor seems to suggest with an appeal to emotion rather than reason, it is the rule as laid down by a justice system worthy of a civilized country, that an accused person, even when there is substantial evidence against them – and nobody disputes that in this case there is – must be acquitted if such evidence does not have one single, unequivocal explanation.

"You are being asked to decide with your emotions, while it is your task, and your duty, to decide with reason and intelligence. If you really want to imagine a situation, imagine you are the parents, siblings, friends of somebody who finds themselves involved in a terrible case through an equally terrible misunderstanding thanks to an unfortunate combination of circumstances, thanks to shortcomings in the investigation resulting from too much self-confidence or from the hastily formed belief that the right solution has been found immediately. The only possible solution.

"I could ask you to consider some other things. I could tell you that whoever fired those shots didn't do so in order to kill. That's very clear. Whoever fired those shots did so in order to kneecap his victim; the severing of the femoral artery, and the death that followed as a consequence, were almost certainly not the shooter's intention. I could tell you that the legal definition of this act, whoever committed it, isn't voluntary murder but unpremeditated murder. An instance, that is, in which the perpetrator acts to cause personal harm and death results from the act as an unintended consequence. I could tell you these things, but I'm not going to. I'm not asking you to consider them. I don't think it's right.

"All I ask is that this appeal court discharges the contested ruling and acquits Iacopo Cardace of the charges of murder and the unauthorized possession and carrying of a firearm, according to article 530 paragraph 2."

27

Gastoni did not ask to respond.

Judge Marinelli turned to Cardace and asked him if he wanted to make a statement before the court retired to consider its verdict. Iacopo looked at me and I shook my head.

"Thank you, I don't have any other statements." Then, a moment later: "Except that I'm innocent." It seemed like an entreaty.

Marinelli gave a nod that was hard to interpret. "We don't know how long we shall be deliberating. You may all go. The clerk of the court will call you when we're ready to come out to pronounce the verdict."

I remained on my feet, in my robe, facing the now empty judges' bench. I was still there when Annapaola joined me.

"Very good. You almost convinced me."

I smiled weakly. "What do you think?" Defence lawyers who've just finished speaking in a difficult hearing are like writers who've just finished a novel and give it to somebody to read. Desperate for encouragement. Terribly desperate.

"You did a great job," she said. "I'd acquit him."

Consuelo and Tancredi told me more or less the same thing. I'd done a great job. They thought we had a good chance. Even the fact that the judges didn't know how long they would be deliberating was positive: they weren't sure, they had to think it over. It was all good.

So why did I feel so insecure? So scared?

I went over to Iacopo, who was waiting for me with his hands gripping the bars.

"Thank you." He hesitated. "What's going to happen?"

"I don't know."

"Fifty–fifty?"

"Fifty–fifty, yes."

Iacopo nodded.

"I have to go now," I said. "I'll see you later."

Lorenza was just outside the courtroom.

"What do we do now, just stay here and wait for the verdict?"

"Best not to. Go home, try to distract yourself. I'm going too. When the clerk of the court calls me I'll let you know."

"They can't convict him, can they?"

I felt like hugging her, but held back.

"We did what we could. It's pointless making predictions."

On my way out of the courthouse, I told everyone I was going for a walk, left Consuelo the briefcase with the papers, took off my tie and headed for the sea.

I walked for half an hour, unaware of my own thoughts. And I ended up walking barefoot on the long, deserted beach of San Francesco; I rolled up my trouser legs and went into the cold, very clear water, almost up to my knees. It's nice that there's water like this in a city, I told myself, maybe it means something. As I was looking at the slight ripples on the surface of the sea, I remembered a quotation by Elias Canetti that suggested you shouldn't believe in anybody who always told the truth: "The truth is a sea of grass bending in the wind, it needs to be felt as movement. It is a rock only for those who do not feel it and do not breathe it."

I got to the end of the beach, put my shoes back on and continued as far as the pine grove.

With the passing of time some places in the city – the pine grove is one of them – remind me ever more intensely of feelings and fantasies from the distant past. A time of awe. That's it: some places in the city make me nostalgic for that feeling of awe. That feeling of being stunned by the force of something. I'd like so much for it to happen again. Maybe awe – if I was capable of learning it – could actually be the antidote to the way time accelerates so unbearably. Time is much more extensive for the young because they're constantly experiencing new things. Their life is full of first times, of sudden realizations. Time runs faster as you grow older because things usually get repeated. The possibilities of choice are reduced, the ways that are barred increase, until everything appears to be limited to one single narrow path. You don't want to think about where that path leads, and this produces an anaesthesia in your consciousness. It helps to alleviate the fear of death, but makes the colours fade.

Some young boys were playing football in the pine grove. There was one who was younger than the others and looked like a real talent. He moved naturally, almost lazily, and nobody could stop him: the ball seemed glued to his feet. Like in that old song by Francesco De Gregori. I calculated that the twelve-year-old protagonist of the song – if he had ever existed – would now be pushing fifty.

At this point, I decided this might be long enough.

I returned home, walking fast, and greeted Mr Punchbag. He grasped that something wasn't right and didn't say anything. I put on my trunks, bandaged my hands, put on the gloves and started to box. Ten rounds, maybe. Maybe more. I only stopped when I was completely exhausted. My legs and arms were shaking, my heart was beating wildly, and my face was as red as if I was sunburned.

Think what a pathetic end that'd be if they find you here on the floor, struck down by a heart attack because you've been too stupid not to realize that some things are not done. They're never done, let alone at your age.

The call from the clerk of the court came when I'd just got out of the shower and was about to have something to eat.

"Avvocato Guerrieri?"

"Yes?"

"Moretti here. The judge says they'll be ready in three quarters of an hour."

"Thank you."

It was ten past five. They had been out for six hours.

28

I phoned Annapaola and told her that I was on my way to court and that the verdict would be announced soon. I asked her to inform the others, including the defendant's mother, and to please make sure my robe was brought to me.

I was silent for a moment, almost as if I'd been on the verge of saying something and had thought better of it at the last moment.

"All right," was all she said. "See you in court."

She sounded serious, which scared me, like a bad omen. It was stupid, of course. What other tone could she have just before a grave, uncertain event like the pronouncing of a verdict on a charge of murder? And yet it gave me the feeling – as absurd as it was persistent – that she knew something I didn't. Something she didn't have the guts to tell me.

I put on a new blue suit that I'd never worn before. I knotted my tie, telling myself that if I didn't have to repeat the operation, that is, if the knot came out well at the first attempt, it would be a good omen. So I concentrated, as if the outcome of the appeal, the destiny of Iacopo Cardace, really did depend on it.

The knot came out well. Symmetrical, snugly fitting the collar of the shirt. And I took heart. A little.

In the street I had to stop myself indulging in those obsessive practices of mine, those examples of magical thinking like not stepping on the kerbs, avoiding the gratings of cellars, touching the wing mirrors of red cars.

Things I used to do as a child and which every now and again re-emerge at times of tension, like the impulse to retch.

In court hearings – in all of them, but particularly the most difficult ones – it would be a healthy thing to lose interest in the result once everything possible has been done.

I knew that perfectly well. I know it perfectly well.

It would be a healthy thing to do, but it never happens.

As I entered the courthouse, I looked at my watch. Ten more minutes and the judges and jurors would be coming out, according to the clerk of the court, Moretti.

The building was half-deserted, like every afternoon. Now even those who had been doing overtime in the offices had left. The very few still there seemed out of place, alien to the building even though they worked there every day. There was an unpleasant sense of transience in the air.

As I climbed the stairs, my thoughts became clear and distinct for a few moments. I wanted Iacopo – strange, I always thought of him now by his first name, not his surname – to be acquitted, and I wanted to know he was innocent. Both these things. A dangerous desire because, at least when it came to the second of them, I might never be certain.

I entered the courtroom. There was nobody there. A few dozen seconds later, as if at a signal, as if they'd been waiting for me to arrive, they all appeared. The clerk of the court, Assistant Prosecutor Gastoni, Annapaola, Consuelo, Tancredi.

Lorenza.

I put on my robe and, in the ghostly silence, I thought I heard a buzzing, a kind of muted alarm signal.

The bell rang, and the court emerged. First the presiding judge, then the associate judge, then the jurors with their sashes and their inscrutable faces.

They walked to their places, moving in a way that struck me as awkward. A sign of embarrassment – that wasn't a good thing.

Marinelli put on his glasses and cleared his throat; either he was hoarse, or it was again a reflection of unease.

"In the name of the Italian people, the appeal court of Bari, having read articles 592 and 603 of the code of criminal procedure, confirms the ruling of the high court of Bari on 15 May 2013 in the case of Iacopo Cardace and orders that he remain in prison. It further orders that the new ruling be filed within sixty days and that a copy of the trial transcript be sent to the Prosecutor's Department. Court is dismissed."

Confirms the ruling.

As Marinelli uttered these words, I realized that up until a moment earlier I'd been convinced they would make the opposite decision. I'd been convinced that I would hear different words: *rejects the previous ruling and acquits Iacopo Cardace, etc.*

I'd been so convinced, I hadn't wanted to admit it, even to myself.

For fear of feeling the way I felt now.

The judges and jurors left quickly. Only the young woman lingered for a few moments, and our eyes met. I didn't know if she was trying to tell me something or if she was just curious to see a reaction on my face. I didn't know if she wanted to let me know that she was sorry, that she had voted against the verdict, or else the exact opposite.

Something like: Justice has been done, Avvocato.

29

I'd like to be able to say that after the verdict of the appeal court I took the case to the Supreme Court and won. That there was a new hearing, that Iacopo was acquitted and that he was free again, ready to put his life back together.

I'd like to, but it didn't go that way.

I did, of course, take the case to the Supreme Court. Although by that point, I didn't really hold out much hope.

The Supreme Court doesn't go into the substance of the verdict, it doesn't say if a witness is more or less credible, if a reconstruction is valid or questionable, if a particular piece of evidence has been evaluated with due thought, whether or not the investigations were carried out with the necessary care.

To obtain an annulment from the Supreme Court, there needs to have been a serious violation of procedural rules, and in this case there hadn't been any violations of that kind. Or else the verdict needs to be compromised by a total lack of grounds or by grounds that were manifestly illogical.

I did try this. It's the final attempt, when a hearing has been conducted in the normal way. You maintain that the grounds for the ruling are lacking at some fundamental points or are so wrong as to be manifestly illogical.

In reality, that rarely happens. You just have to be a decent servant of the law to write a ruling that may be shaky from a theoretical point of view, weak from a grammatical point of view, even very questionable as to its ability to do justice, and yet free of the defects of an absence of motivation or a manifestly contradictory motivation.

The appeal court's ruling, as written by Associate Judge Valentini, was more than decent, and certainly not characterized by "lack, contradictoriness or manifest illogicality of motivation", as article 606 of the code of criminal procedure puts it.

I made an effort to find something to cling to, exaggerating the flaws that definitely existed in the ruling, in order to try to obtain an annulment, along with a deferment that would allow me to take my chances in a new appeal hearing. But I was the first to admit that a favourable outcome was unlikely. If I'd been in the shoes of the judges in the Supreme Court, I would have rejected my appeal.

Lorenza came several times to the office to keep up with developments. First for the filing of the appeal court ruling. Then the writing of the appeal to the Supreme Court. Then the date set for the hearing. She was strangely calm. I think she kept telling herself she had done everything possible to help her son and that, at least from that point of view, she had nothing to reproach herself for.

She was calm, and almost old.

Ageing isn't a linear process. Just as time isn't a linear entity. It isn't a comprehensible entity. Nobody really understands it. Nobody can define it. Try to talk about time without using metaphors, says a famous linguist. You'll come away empty-handed. Would time still be time for us if we couldn't waste it or schedule it? All we can really say is that it basically goes in one direction and that the final destination is well known.

Lorenza had aged in the many years during which we hadn't seen each other and had aged even more in that year and a half that had passed between the moment she'd come into my office to ask me to defend her son and the moment I called her to tell her that the Supreme Court had rejected our appeal. She greeted even that news without visible upset. She'd expected it, she said.

A few days later, she came to the office with an envelope full of banknotes. She wanted to pay me for my work.

I told her I didn't want to be paid.

For once the words meant exactly what they said.

I didn't want to be paid.

I didn't want the money and I didn't want to argue about it. I was blunt, maybe even brusque, and she didn't insist.

She put the envelope back in her bag and left. Outside, it was raining hard.

It was raining again that afternoon two years later when Tancredi came to the office with the news. He arrived about seven. The days were getting longer, and it was still light outside. Light and rain.

He had a strange expression on his face.

"I have something to tell you."

"What's happened?" I pushed my chair back and stretched my legs.

"Maybe it's best we go out and walk a bit."

"Walk? It's raining."

"Let's go and have an aperitif or whatever you like."

There was a hint of impatience in his tone. Something that meant: Don't ask pointless questions.

"All right."

I grabbed my jacket and an umbrella and we walked down into the street. A few minutes later we slipped into the Laterza bookshop.

"Why all this mystery? Are you afraid our phones are being tapped?"

I said it as a joke, then realized I'd hit the nail on the head. He'd wanted to come outside in order not to run the risk, even if it was a remote one, that our conversation might be listened in on.

He shrugged. "Don't be alarmed. I don't think – I don't have any reason to think – that you have bugs in your office. But you never know."

"You're making me nervous, Carmelo."

"The Flying Squad is mounting a big operation tonight. I didn't get this information legally. I shouldn't know about it. And you definitely shouldn't."

"Why should we be so interested in this information?"

"Because basically they're arresting the whole Amendolagine clan."

It took me a few seconds to remember and to put things together. "Amendolagine... That Amendolagine?"

"That one."

I felt a shudder go through me, the kind you get when you have a high fever and you can't think any more, you can't read, you may even rant and rave a little. It happened to me sometimes as a child.

Within a few hours there would be thirty-six arrests. Thirty-six men would be remanded in custody for Mafia-style association, and association for the purpose of trafficking in narcotics and extortion.

And four homicides.

"Four homicides..."

"Three men have turned state's evidence. One of them is the man who carried out the Gaglione murder."

"Has he claimed responsibility?"

"Yes. They're arresting Amendolagine tomorrow, partly as the instigator of that murder."

We stood there like that, surrounded by books.

I should have been pleased, instead of which I had a sense of defeat and futility.

"We'll have to put in a request to reopen the case," I said slowly.

Tancredi looked at me in surprise. "Hey, this is good news. What's got into you?"

"It's true, it's very good news. I don't know what's got into me."

"Anyway, the request to reopen the case will be made by the prosecutor in the next few days. It'll be filed as soon as the custody orders have been notified. Along with a request to suspend the sentence. In a couple of weeks maximum, the kid will be out."

"Have you read the papers?"

"Some. You did a good job."

"Were we also right about the ways of getting into the building?"

"No. The killer, who did only plan to kneecap Gaglione, came in through the front door, even rang the bell. Obviously Gaglione wasn't as cautious as all that. Maybe he thought Cardace had come back."

"I have to call Lorenza."

"Not now. Wait till tomorrow morning, we don't want the information to get out. A few hours won't make any difference."

He was right. That evening or the next day, it was all the same.

"He did six years in prison," I said after a while, as if talking to myself.

"It's a nasty business, you're right. But he's still young, he has time to rebuild his life. Let's look on the bright side. Why don't we go and grab a nice bottle of wine? Let's call Annapaola and tell her to join us and then we can tell her all about it."

Grabbing a nice bottle of wine was the best plan possible, I said. I was starting to feel better already.

Without even opening the umbrella, we walked out into the rain. In the meantime it had dwindled to a drizzle and made you feel almost cheerful.

30

The next day, at eight in the morning, after checking that the first news had appeared about the Flying Squad operation, I phoned Lorenza.

"Guido?"

"Hi, are you busy?"

"I'm at home. I don't have a lesson until hour 3. What's happened?"

"Nothing. Well, that's not true, something has happened, but nothing negative. In fact, it's very positive."

"Is it about Iacopo?"

"Yes, there's good news. If it's all right with you, I'd like to tell you in person."

There was a long silence. So long that I thought we'd been cut off.

"Lorenza?"

"Yes, I'm sorry. I'll come to your office."

"No, I'll come to you."

Another pause. Then I remembered the exact address, near the Russian church. I took my bicycle and twenty minutes later I was there. She answered the bell almost immediately.

"Second floor," was all she said.

It was an early-sixties apartment block. Ordinary and a little sad. As I climbed the stairs I could smell home odours – food, coffee, washing machines, detergent – as well as dust and a sense of modest, slightly stale well-being. Lorenza was waiting in the doorway. She looked like a frightened little animal.

The apartment was her parents', and clearly hadn't changed much since their day: old furniture, old ornaments, old rugs. The place she had run away from when she was a girl and had come back to, the culmination of a sad orbit around her own dreams.

"We can go in the kitchen, if you don't mind. I'll make coffee."

The kitchen was the same as the rest. Old.

"What's happened?"

I told her. Anyone watching the scene without sound, just looking at her face, wouldn't have deduced that she was happy: she seemed terrified. She didn't ask me any questions. When I'd finished speaking she pulled the soft packet of MS Blondes from a pocket of her cardigan, took out a cigarette with a meticulous gesture and put it between her lips. Then she got up and went and threw the packet with all the remaining cigarettes in the rubbish bin. She came back, sat down again, lit the one she had in her mouth and breathed it in almost angrily.

"I'd promised I'd quit smoking as soon as I found out."

I nodded. It made sense. Maybe I was about to say something, but she didn't give me time.

"As soon as I found out Iacopo was innocent."

I took me a while to understand the significance of her words.

She hadn't said: As soon as I found out Iacopo had been acquitted, or something like that.

No.

She'd said: As soon as I found out Iacopo was innocent.

But she should *already* have known that Iacopo was innocent. She had been at home when her son had come in about 7.30, she'd testified to that. The murder had been committed less than twenty minutes later, so it couldn't have been him.

"I'm sorry, Guido. I'm so sorry," she said, drawing me from my thoughts.

"What time did Iacopo get home that evening?"

"I don't know. After eight for sure. Maybe 8.15, 8.20. A quarter of an hour later he went out again."

"So he would have had time to commit the murder."

"Yes."

"Did you decide by yourself?"

"With Costamagna. He said things were looking bad and we had to at least try something. But we needed an alibi. I had to say something that didn't fit the prosecution case, or it would be no use."

"Obviously Iacopo knew that."

"Yes."

So I had discovered that Iacopo was innocent, something I'd been convinced of for a while. And yet I had also defended him using a false testimony. A false alibi.

"I had no choice," Lorenza resumed. "I had no idea how you'd react and I couldn't take the risk that you might not take the case, or that you'd take it but stop me going on the stand and giving that testimony."

There are moments when everything turns upside down, when the coordinates all change abruptly and the brain takes paths that are hard to interpret. Just one question came to my lips. A rather incongruous one, to be honest.

"When did you vow to quit smoking?"

"Just before the appeal hearing. When I saw what you were all doing, the investigations and all the rest, and I thought maybe you'd succeed in getting Iacopo acquitted."

"So why didn't you tell yourself: I'll quit smoking if Iacopo is acquitted?"

A brief laugh escaped her. Actually not much more than a gasp. "I know it's an absurd argument, but which of these arguments isn't? I knew you'd get him acquitted. But I also wanted him to be innocent and I wanted to *know* he was innocent. I didn't want to waste a wish."

I thought of going to get a cigarette from the rubbish bin and lighting it. I didn't.

"You mentioned coffee."

She shook herself as if from a kind of torpor. "Of course. I'll make it right away."

She filled the pot and we waited in a suspended silence for the coffee to rise. Lorenza poured it into two brown cups, the kind that were used in cafes all those years ago and, still in silence, we drank it.

"I have to go now."

"Guido…"

"Iacopo will be out in a few weeks maximum. I'll let you know from the office when we have more specific news. I assume you'll go to the prison to give him the news, so I won't need to."

"Guido, listen…"

"I'm going. I'm glad your son's getting out. I'm really glad. Personal disappointment is just a detail, one of many. And details aren't important."

It isn't true; details *are* important. But I didn't say this.

She hugged me at the door of the apartment. She held me tight and I smelt her smell and felt her thin body up against mine. I responded to the hug, thinking that we had never had such intimate contact all those years before.

In the street, I realized the wind had swept away almost all the clouds of the past few days. I felt like smiling.

It was turning into a bright spring morning.